THE PARALIPOMENA OF SHERLOCK HOLMES

Airship 27 Productions

™

The Paralipomena of Sherlock Holmes
© 2025 I.A. Watson

Cover Illustration © 2025 John Waeltz
Interior illustrations © 2025 Rob Davis

Editor: Ron Fortier
Associate Editor: Jonathan Sweet
Production and design by Rob Davis
Promotion and marketing by Michael Vance

Published by Airship 27 Productions
www.airship27.com
www.airship27hangar.com

ISBN: 978-1-969285-01-1

Printed in the United States of America

10 9 8 7 6 5 4 3 2 1

THE PARALIPOMENA
OF
SHERLOCK HOLMES

BY I.A. WATSON

CONTENTS:

The Paralipomena of Sherlock Holmes

I.A. Watson

FOREWORD:
THE SUPPORTING TEXTS

"My dear child, you can give it a long name if you like, but I'm an old-fashioned woman and I call it mother-wit, and it's so rare for a man to have it that if he does you write a book about him and call him Sherlock Holmes."

The Dowager Duchess of Denver, Lord Peter Wimsey's mother, speaking to her son in Clouds of Witness (1926, by Dorothy L. Sayers)

ALL HOLMES AFICIONADOS owe a debt to Dorothy L. Sayers and her author peers in the Detection Club (est. 1930)[1] and to fellow fans in the Sherlock Holmes Society (est. London, 1934). It was they who first began the "modern" expansion of the life and world of Sherlock Holmes after Sir Arthur Conan Doyle had set aside his pen.

Sayers was already a scholar at Somerville College, Oxford, as well as the author of her Lord Peter Wimsey mystery novels, when she published the first of her "academic" papers on the Great Detective in 1928. Over the next two decades she penned the meticulously-researched and much-footnoted "The Dates of the Red-Headed League", "Holmes' College Career" (which revealed his college and courses of study at Cambridge, along with a possible misprint

---

1   This still-existing fraternity was founded in 1930 by British mystery writers, including Agatha Christie, Dorothy L. Sayers, Ronald Knox, Freeman Wills Crofts, Arthur Morrison, Hugh Walpole, John Rhode, Jessie Rickard, Baroness Emma Orczy, R. Austin Freeman, G. D. H. Cole, Margaret Cole, E. C. Bentley, Henry Wade, Constance Lindsay Taylor, and H. C. Bailey, with special involvement by Anthony Berkeley. G. K. Chesterton was its first President,. John Dickson Carr became the first American member, elected in 1936.

     The Club's tongue-in-cheek initiation ritual was written by Sayers, and required an oath of each member, who was asked, "Do you promise that your detectives shall well and truly detect the crimes presented to them using those wits which it may please you to bestow upon them and not placing reliance on nor making use of Divine Revelation, Feminine Intuition, Mumbo Jumbo, Jiggery-Pokery, Coincidence, or Act of God?"

     As well as regular London dinner meetings, Detective Club members offered practical help on technical issues of each others stories. Club members informally agreed to adhere to "Knox's Commandments", named after Ronald Knox's summary about "fair play" mysteries where the reader must be given the information to successfully solve the crime along with the detective in the tale. The Club also published anthologies of its members' works, including multi-author stories such as *The Floating Admiral* (1931) where each contributor penned a chapter of an ongoing whodunit.

of the detective's name in his Tripos Class List), "Dr. Watson's Christian Name" (it turned out to be John, although his wife preferred to call him James, anglicising his middle name Hamish), and "Dr. Watson, Widower" (which first proposed the possibility that Mary Morstan was not the only woman who had become Mrs Watson during the good doctor's lifetime).

Further, for BBC Radio's "A Tribute to Sherlock Holmes on the Occasion of His 100th Birthday," (1954), Sayers wrote "A Young Lord Peter Consults Sherlock Holmes", also known as "The Case of the Missing Kitten", in which a juvenile Lord Peter consults The Master in the last Wimsey story completed by his creator.[2]

Nor was Sayers the only writer or scholar to expand the Holmes corpus. The Game Was Afoot—and in part for a curious academic reason to drive home an important academic point.

In the early years of the 20th century, critical literary theory became a fashionable way of deconstructing ancient manuscripts. The technique was particularly seized upon by agnostic bible scholars to demonstrate flaws in the Church's doctrinal position about the unchanging and perfect nature of Holy Scripture. In response to these assertions, mischievous scholarly wags such as Sayers demonstrated that the exact same methodology and assumptions that were being used to discredit Biblical source material and question the historicity of Christ could be used to verify the actual existence of Sherlock Holmes.

Thus the Great Game, played po-faced with absolute solemnity, wherein Sherlockian scholars would publish well-researched arguments that uncovered the "real" Sherlock Holmes, that adduced evidence of his further life and exploits beyond "the Canon" of tales published by Dr Watson's literary agent Arthur Conan Doyle, and that pierced the discreet "Watsonian misdirection" which Holmes's principal chronicler had employed, uncovering the true circumstances and identities behind many famous cases.

By the 1950s there were a good number of Sherlock Holmes pastiches, circulated as further accounts drawn from Dr Watson's notes in his "travel-worn and battered tin dispatch box", or as otherwise-recovered case files. Thus evolved a literary industry that has probably spawned more published stories than for any other fictional character[3]—assuming, of course, that Holmes was

---

2   These essays and the transcribed play were collected in the hard-to-find *Sayers on Holmes: Essays & Fiction on Sherlock Holmes* (2001, ISBN-10: 188772608X). Various possibly-legal transcripts appear on the internet.

3   I.A. Watson has been unable to uncover any actual evidence for this assertion. *The Guinness Book of World Records* has acknowledged Holmes as being the fictional human to appear in the most film and TV productions (human, note; Count Dracula has actually managed a few more), but there do not seem to be any definitive statistics on featured fictional characters

not actually a real person.

In literary analysis, a *paralipomenon* is a variant of an accepted text, such as a later and altered version of a Biblical document that probably offers different copying errors or amendments, but may just contain an earlier version of the source material. Paralipomena are the meat and drink of critical research, utterly essential in uncovering the latest hardback's exposé of "the real Jesus" (or whomever).

In a wider application of the term, paralipomena are supplementary literary materials that offer insights into the main text. As befits the character who was first used to demonstrate the limits of early critical theory, Sherlock Holmes has accumulated more paralipomena than any other modern subject.

This volume adds to that body of work, collecting several tales contributed by I.A. Watson to Holmes anthologies and adding two new accounts that have not previously been set before the reading public. Each one offers a different aspect of the Great Detective to consider, hopefully furthering our analysis of his life and work.

"A Case of Forensics" is set in the second year of Holmes and Watson's time together, before any Canon story except for the partnership's origin in *A Study In Scarlet*. It illustrates Holmes's development of a new branch of criminological science, his place in the pioneering of techniques that are now common in any major police investigation—and on every TV police procedural.

"The Adventure of the Abducted Bard", previously presented in *The MX Book of New Sherlock Holmes Stories—Part XXIII: Some More Untold Cases 1884-1894* (2020), demonstrates another element of Holmes's expertise as he is called upon to authenticate an antique manuscript and to recover it after its disappearance.

"The Ransomed Miracle," originally from *The MX Book of New Sherlock Holmes Stories—Part XX: 2020 Annual (1891-1897)* (2020), shows Holmes dealing with a very human tragedy around the abduction of an infant. Readers who know Dr Watson's character will be unsurprised at his fervent response to the case.

"The Confectioners' Captives" from *The MX Book of New Sherlock Holmes Stories Part XXVI: 2021 Annual (1889-1897)* (2021) tangles Holmes and Watson in international intrigue based upon actual history, with the added complication (for them and the author) of our heroes being tied to posts for the majority of the tale.

"The Adventure of the Absconded Corpse", formerly included in *After the East Wind Blows; WWI and Roaring Twenties Adventures of Sherlock Holmes*, vol. 1 (2021), extends Holmes and Watson's Great War investigations beyond

---

in prose. To set the bar, Frank Richards' creation William George "Billy" Bunter of Greyfriars School appeared in 1,670 novella-length stories in *The Magnet* between 1908 and 1965.

the last of the Canon material, reuniting the friends to thwart a German plot on a British prototype submarine.

As a final addition, "The New York Crakster" chronicles the further adventures of Doyle's more obscure character Jemmy Wilson, 'the Nottingham Crakster' from his non-Holmes story "Selecting a Ghost" (also known as "The Secret of Goresthorpe Grange", 1883), and of Miss Catherine Cusack from his Holmes Christmas yarn "The Adventure of the Blue Carbuncle" in *The Adventures of Sherlock Holmes.* Wilson has previously appeared in my Holmes stories in the *Airship 27 Sherlock Holmes, Consulting Detective* volumes 12 and 17, with Miss Cusack joining him in the latter publication. I am rather fond of the couple and have therefore indulged myself by imagining more for them here.

Each of these tales offers some Canon-compliant variation of the material chosen by Dr Watson and edited by Doyle for publication in the later Victorian and early Edwardian period. All flesh out the already-quite-corporeal body of further adventures of Mr Sherlock Holmes.

The research continues…

I.A. Watson
May 2023,
Deducing the missing chapters

A Case of Forensics

AFTER AN EXCELLENT dinner of gammon and roast potatoes and a fresh rhubarb tart, Holmes and I sat back with our visitors and finished off a bottle of hock whilst we smoked. Our guests that evening were Lomax the librarian and Stamford of Barts; it was Stamford who had actually introduced Holmes and I, and he was quick to take credit for it with Lomax.

"Must have been over a year ago," he mentioned, sucking on his cigar. "Holmes was in our labs doing something arcane and secret as per usual. We housemen had standing orders not to get in his way and just let him potter on. But of course, we were curious to speak with him because of that trick he has of reading one's mind."

"It is not mind-reading," Holmes insisted. "Merely a discipline of observation and deduction. It is a technique that any might master given sufficient application."

"Well, we thought you a wizard, Holmes. Anyhow, I bumped into Watson soon after he'd been packaged home courtesy of that assegai bullet..."

"Jezail bullet," I corrected. "An assegai is an African native spear. A jezail is one of those hand-made engraved long guns favoured by the Pashtun tribesmen and their neighbours. They fire .50 or .75 bore, man-stoppers. They certainly stopped me."

"I encountered him, I say," Stamford persisted. "Upon learning that he was seeking digs in London I dragged him to Holmes, who was looking for a flatmate to share the costs of his lodgings—these lodgings."

"You are fortunate in your rooms," Lomax admitted. "And also with your landlady." The cutlets had been excellent.

I had another question. "You say that your methods can be taught, Holmes, can be learned. Am I then especially slow, having shadowed you on several investigations to still be failing to replicate your successes in mystery-solving?"

"Or is he merely mortal like the rest of us?" Stamford suggested.

Lomax set down his glass and became serious. "Wait, though. This 'whole art of detection' of which you speak, Holmes, and which you are eager to document, do you really imagine that it can be taught for general use? Applied by people who lack your extraordinary facility for spotting and connecting what seems obvious to you but remarkable to the rest of us?"

"Of course," Holmes replied. "Take for example the question of arsenious oxide, arsenic, which as you know I have recently been addressing. Death by that poison was for most of history undetectable and unprovable, save by the crude method of feeding the contaminated food to some unsuspecting animal or slave to confirm the toxin's presence. Then in 1773, Swedish chemist Carl Wilhelm Scheele discovered a test for the chemical's presence. In 1806 the German Valentin Ross learned how to detect the poison in a victim's stomach lining. But the 1832 poisoning trial of John Bodle, who was accused of giving his grandfather arsenic-laced coffee, collapsed because of the insufficiency of that test. The forensic chemist for the prosecution[4] was so irritated that he developed an entirely new technique to detect the poison, the Marsh test. It too is imprecise, but much better than previous methods. My own researches have discovered a superior bellwether."

"Which you demonstrated to Watson and I at your first meeting!" Stamford interjected triumphantly.

"I believe your point, Holmes, is that repeatable processes that were once innovative can be documented and taught to become everyday procedures replicated by those of lesser skills," I summarised.

Holmes raised up a long thin finger to indicate that I had understood. "The rise of forensic detection will follow that of forensic medicine."

"Then it will be a slow affair," Stamford snorted.

"It has been a slow process," Holmes agreed, "beginning perhaps with the Chinese Director of Justice, Jail and Supervision Sung Tz'u.[5] His *Collected Cases of Injustice Rectified or the Washing Away of Wrongs*,[6] written in 1247, was the first forensic textbook. That volume established regulations for autopsy reports to court, for protecting evidence, and for demonstrating professional standards of impartiality. I might wish that all the inspectors of Scotland Yard be forced to sit down and read it cover to cover."

"I have never heard of this book," Lomax admitted, and he a sublibrarian at the London Library.

"Sung Tz'u described how to wash and examine the dead body to ascertain the reason for death, used sunlight and vinegar under a red-oil umbrella to discover hidden injuries to dead bodies and bones, established methods for calculating the time of death allowing for weather and insect activity. He included a section on discerning faked suicides. If the fellow had been European and his work translated into Latin then he would now be lauded as one of the

---

4   Dr James Marsh, now known as the father of toxicology.

5   The preferred 21st century Western spelling is 'Song Ci'.

6   *Xi Luan Yu.*

great geniuses of history."[7]

"He solved crimes, then."

"Washing Away includes an investigation of murder by trauma insult," Holmes recounted. He sucked on his Meerschaum and then carried on, "By practical experiment on similar wounds he made on the carcass of animals, Sung Tz'u determined that the murder instrument was a sickle. He ordered all the peasants in the locality to report with their sickles and lay the blades in the hot sun. The flies were attracted to the one that had a bloody residue, thereby betraying the killer."

"Were his methods put into practice, though?" I wondered. Holmes often demonstrated his brilliance, but I had not perceived much difference amongst the policemen and private investigation agencies that consulted him.

"He had rather more authority to chastise clod-footed policemen than I do, Watson." Holmes tamped his pipe and told us, "The day is coming when the evidence shall speak as plainly as the witnesses—and more truthfully."

And our conversation moved on to other matters.

By coincidence, only two days after, Holmes was given the ideal opportunity to illustrate his argument.

It is a disturbing thing to stagger down for breakfast in the morning, seeking only the solace of poached eggs and devilled ham, still drowsy and clad in one's rather travel-worn dressing gown—and discover one's old tutor sitting at table sipping Turkish coffee.

"Watson," Sir Gabriel Kipps gruffed as I made my appearance. The years had not changed him since I had been his dresser.[8] His bushy side-whiskers, florid cheeks, and student-slaying gaze were all the same. I was suddenly transported back to my junior doctor days, before ever I took the Netley course to join the Army Medical Service,[9] and found myself standing straighter and attempting to cover my unshaved chin without appearing to do so.

"I heard you'd been invalided," Sir Gabriel observed nevertheless. "I see you injured your shaving hand."

7　　The book was not translated into English until Dr Harland's 1855 Hong Kong edition.

8　　That is a surgical houseman, what is nowadays called a Pre-registration House Officer, a newly qualified doctor working a six-month supervised probationary period prior to being fully registered with the General Medical Council. Stamford was later Dr Watson's dresser at St Bartholomew's Hospital, London.

9　　*A Study in Scarlet* establishes that Watson received his medical degree from the University of London in 1878, and then trained at Netley Hospital near Southampton as an Army surgeon.

"No sir. Just in the process of getting up, sir," I mumbled.

Holmes regarded the exchange with mild amusement. "As senior surgeon at St Bart's, Sir Gabriel was the consultant who kindly arranged for me to have access to their excellent laboratories," he explained.

"Some useful research there," Sir Gabriel assessed, which was fine praise indeed coming from him. Holmes would have been a prize pupil. "Oh, sit down, Watson. I am not going to quiz you on the duodenal papilla and the hepatic ducts. Not before breakfast."

"Yes, sir," I responded. "May I enquire as to the reason for your, um, your very welcome visit?"

"You are not the only former houseman upon whom I keep tabs, Watson. There's a fellow named Falwein, before your time. Weak on his mesenteric lymph nodes, but I trust he has improved with age since he is now in general practice at Swale in Kent and is called upon as an Assistant County Coroner from time to time."

"Dr Falwein was summoned last night to preside over an interesting case," Holmes explained to me. "Given its unique features and his relative inexperience in the post of appointed coroner, the good doctor appealed for advice from his old mentor. Upon hearing of the circumstances, and presently unable to leave his practice at Barts, Sir Gabriel was kind enough to recommend me to comment upon the investigation."

"I might hazard that you will be of more help than I might be, Holmes," my old teacher suggested. "For the purely medical material, Falwein will be more than adequate should he follow your instructions." He glanced at me. "Once Watson has found his chin, I expect that he will prove capable of offering assistance in any crisis that might occur. It is one of his redeeming features."

I was still parsing that last comment, and finally deciding that my old tutor had actually given me something of a sly compliment, as Sir Gabriel took his leave.

"Well," Holmes declared cheerfully, "Sir Gabriel has offered us a rather interesting corpse, doctor. May I hope that you would accompany me to the Isle of Sheppey to succour Dr Falwein in his investigations?"

"I shall," I agreed, "Only grant me some time to shave."

We took the train from Victoria, and I was glad that our first class tickets separated us from the crush of third class passengers crowding aboard the rear carriages to holiday-make at Herne Bay, Margate, and Ramsgate.[10] Our destination, Leysdown-on-Sea on the Isle of Sheppey, was separated from the popular

10   A curious feature of many railway routes at this time was the absence of second-class travel.

seaside resorts by the Swale channel which makes that part of our coast technically an island, so we disembarked the LCDR express[11] before Canterbury and
commissioned a pony and trap to take us the remaining distance.

On the journey we had time to study the appeal to Sir Gabriel that had
galvanised us towards our Estuary shore.[12]

At low tide yesterday, winkle-pickers working the shoreline near Leysdown-
on-Sea had discovered a large sealed leather sack, some five feet square, containing several bulky objects. It was clear from the position of the flotsam or
jetsam that it had been deposited by the receding tide. One of the beachcomb-
ers slit open some of the stitching on the side of the sodden covering and was
rewarded with a vile putrefying stench.

Further investigation discovered a murdered man, hooded and shod but
otherwise naked, bound and presumably drowned. With him in his sack were
the waterlogged remains of a dog, a rooster, a viper, and a monkey.

"A most classical death," Holmes remarked as he read the terse description
of the discovery.

I had looked up the relevant classical passage before leaving Baker Street. A
dictionary of Latin quotations included a passage from *Digesta seu Pandectae*,
known in English as the *Digest*, a compendium of fifty volumes of juristic
writings on Roman law compiled by order of the Byzantine emperor Justinian
I in 530–533 AD.[13] A fragment preserved therein from mid-3rd-century jurist
Modestinus gave us the key to the bizarre find on Sheppey:

"According to the custom of our ancestors, the punishment instituted
for parricide was this: a parricide is flogged with rods stained red with
his own blood, then sewn up in a sack with a dog, a dunghill cock, a viper, and a monkey; then the sack is thrown into the depths of the sea."[14]

---

11   The London, Chatham, and Dover Railway, established 1859, took over the "crab
and winkle line" from the Canterbury and Whitstable Railway until its merger with Southern
Railway in 1923. 'The Chatham' was often criticised for its "lamentable carriage stock and poor
punctuality".

12   The island, positioned south of the Thames outlet, covers 36 square miles, centred 42
miles from London, and is part of the local government district of Swale. It is only technically an
island, being separated from the mainland by no more than a river's width, long-since bridged
over. Older channels that divided the area into three separate islands clogged up in the Middle
Ages. Sheppey is low-lying; the southern part of the island is largely marshy grazing land criss-
crossed by inlets and drains. Its name is derived from the Old English *Sceapig*, meaning 'Sheep'.

13   The Digest was part of the *Corpus Juris Civilis* ('Body of Civil Law') which collected,
revised, and codified all Roman laws up to that time. The other two parts were the *Institutes*, an
introductory textbook, and the *Codex*, a collection of statutes. Elements of the *Digest* still form
underlying principles of admiralty law and maritime insurance.

14   Translation based upon J. B. Moyle, D.C.L. (1893); Watson clearly refreshed his
memory from this later source at the time that he ordered his notes, at least eleven years after the

Dr Falwein had sought advice from his old tutor because the murder victim on the shingle had been executed in a manner that has been seldom used since the fall of the Roman Empire.

Falwein had commandeered a lifeboat hut on the upper shore above the sea-strand. Sir Gabriel had wired him to expect us and the local doctor was extremely pleased to welcome us upon our arrival. "Mr Holmes, Dr Watson, your appearance is quite timely. This is a bizarre and baffling occurrence. I am feeling somewhat out of my experience."

"Few coroners can have been called upon to preside over an inquest such as this one," I admitted. "You may be assured that Holmes will do what he can to unravel this remarkable incident."

My detective friend had little time for social amenities. He swerved around our greetings and made straight for the rough plank table where the contents of the leather sack had now been laid out. Presented there were a dead man, a middle-sized mongrel bitch, a bedraggled and part-crushed cockerel, a two-foot adder, and a small monkey the size of a weasel.

"Splendid!" Holmes declared.

"You must excuse my colleague," I warned Falwein. "Holmes is keen to trial certain techniques which he is pioneering, and feels that this case may allow him to demonstrate a method that could be replicated elsewhere."

"An autopsy, of course," the coroner agreed. "I don't doubt death by drowning, despite the… the other wounds and contusions on the corpse. The signs are clear. This is not the first drowned man to be washed up on this stretch of coast. The tides and currents sweep out the Thames into the bay and wash up suicides and other drownings from time to time. I have assisted the county coroner with two such tragedies in the short period since I was appointed, but he is visiting relatives in Edinburgh and is unavailable at attend on this occasion."

He proffered a chart wherein he had scribbled notes regarding hypercapnia, aspirated fluid, and irreversible cerebral anoxia, medical descriptions of a submerged man choking in water, technically sufficient to satisfy Sir Gabriel Kipps himself, but it was a commonplace diagnosis.

"You have removed the hood that was on the corpse," Holmes accused Falwein. "I read it plain from the disturbance to the hair and the lack of scratching above the neck. The animals confined in the sack went into frenzy as they were immersed in water and began to claw and bite at each other and events of his account.

at the bound man, yet there is no significant damage to his face, which was covered."

"There was indeed a hood pulled over the head," the Coroner replied. "I had to remove it to examine the victim's lips and mouth. The bag is over there."

Holmes examined the sodden container. "The hood is wolfskin. Possibly dog, but more likely wolf. It is stitched with sailor's twine, neatly and competently, with a drawstring to fasten it about the neck. There are no eye-holes. The wearer would be entirely blind, partially deafened, and scarcely able to breathe even before being plunged into water."

I shuddered at the unpleasant end that our subject must have suffered. "Why would anyone select such a means to dispatch an enemy?"

"You know why, Watson. This is an extreme version of the Roman punishment for parricide, which crime they defined as the murder of a parent or other close relative. Given the Empire's emphasis on family life and virtues, they treated such crimes with especial horror, amongst the vilest sins that could be committed. The *poena cullei*, the 'penalty of the sack', was first recorded a hundred years before Christ.[15] Our murderer may suppose, rightly or not, that his victim is guilty of such a heinous crime. We shall not theorise ahead of our data."

"What are the data?" Falwein wondered, staring at the odd collection of carcasses arrayed on his workbench.

Holmes rubbed his hands together and began to innumerate the elements of his case. "Item the first: an examination of the deceased man. We must review his injuries, determining which came from what animal, peri- or postmortem, and whether any came from some other source—perhaps the mur-

---

15   *Lex Cornelia De Sicariis*, promulgated in the 80s B.C., and the *Lex Pompeia de Parricidiis* promulgated about 55 B.C., both reference the punishment, albeit without the inclusion of wild animals, as does renowned lawyer, orator and politician Marcus Tullius Cicero, who expounds upon the sentence by writing:

"They therefore stipulated that parricides should be sewn up in a sack while still alive and thrown into a river. What remarkable wisdom they showed, gentlemen! Do they not seem to have cut the parricide off and separated him from the whole realm of nature, depriving him at a stroke of sky, sun, water and earth—and thus ensuring that he who had killed the man who gave him life should himself be denied the elements from which, it is said, all life derives? They did not want his body to be exposed to wild animals, in case the animals should turn more savage after coming into contact with such a monstrosity. Nor did they want to throw him naked into a river, for fear that his body, carried down to the sea, might pollute that very element by which all other defilements are thought to be purified. In short, there is nothing so cheap, or so commonly available that they allowed parricides to share in it. For what is so free as air to the living, earth to the dead, the sea to those tossed by the waves, or the land to those cast to the shores? Yet these men live, while they can, without being able to draw breath from the open air; they die without earth touching their bones; they are tossed by the waves without ever being cleansed; and in the end they are cast ashore without being granted, even on the rocks, a resting-place in death." [Translation by Berry, 2000]

derer. We must have his lungs out and verify that he was drowned, and also whether it was saltwater or freshwater that killed him. We shall check that fluid for particulate matter which might give us some indication of where he entered the water. We must estimate a time of death, complicated by period immersed and variations in rate and type of decay in a freshwater or saltwater environment.

"Item the second: we must review the accoutrements on his body. A wolfskin hood is not a common item. Wild wolves are extinct in England, so where did the pelt come from? Likewise we should investigate the origins of the twine and take note of the stitching techniques, which at first glance suggest a tailor or seamstress with professional skills. But there are inexpert seaman's knots on the ropes binding the victim's limbs.

"Of special interest are the wooden clogs into which the dead man's feet have been confined. The crude carved footwear has been fashioned so that the inner sole is ridged and the outer gradiented, making it painful to walk upon and difficult to balance. A platen has been cleated over the throat of the clog to form a tongue, sealing the foot inside and making the shoes impossible to remove. Additional attention to this detail may be telling.

"Item the third: the animals. A multibreed bitch is easy to source, although forensic examination of the animal may offer us some indication of recent diet and habits. Nor is a Common European *Adder Vipera berus* difficult to find, although this one is a well-fed specimen that may have been kept domestically for some time. We are on slightly better ground with the rooster; I shall want to undertake an examination of breeds and feeds, with better reference to expert avian advice. The South and Central American Capuchin Monkey, so beloved of organ-grinders and travelling showmen, may be our best chance to track an origin. One seldom has such an animal conveniently to hand when one wishes to reconstruct a Roman punishment. Nor has this specimen had its claws clipped or teeth ground down to prevent it from savaging an audience.

"Item the fourth: the leathern sack in which the rest was encompassed. At first glance it is comprised of eighteen-inch strips of rawhide, seamed with catgut and waxed at the joints. Domestic horsehide I should say. We perceive the same meticulous stitching, made all the more impressive given that a man and four fierce creatures were being confined into the container. As for filling the sack, I would be interested to uncover the basic procedure for how *that* might be done. An analysis for some opiate or other drug would be in order."

Holmes paused to take stock of his project. Dr Falwein shook his head despairingly at the long list of checks that lay before him.

I braced myself to take down and then send off the long list of telegrams that Holmes would inevitably dispatch me with as soon as his inventory was complete.

It became clear that Holmes would not be budged from the lifeboat shed without the involvement of a team of horses. I was drafted as an auxiliary medical investigator, despite proclaiming my inexperience at post-mortem procedures. I was somewhat heartened to discover that Sir Gabriel Kipps's older alumnus had somewhat less experience of corpses than I had; six months in Afghanistan and over a year with Holmes had offered me a broader range of dead men than I might have expected possible.

We worked through Holmes's list of forensic tasks, whilst he involved himself in analysis of some of the artefacts of the crime, employing one of the new Zeiss microscopes out of Germany. As we cut and weighed, my friend enthusiastically supplied us with facts about his new science of detection.

"Forensics is an ancient practice," he mentioned. "The Latin term *forēnsis* means 'of or before the forum', referring to information laid before a legal public court. Even before that, Archimedes was using his scientific understanding of volume and mass to prove in a trial before King Heiro II of Syracuse that a certain supposedly-gold votive crown was fraudulently made partially of silver."[16]

We ascertained that the dead man had drowned in fresh water. Furthermore, particulate matter suggested he had died in water fed by a chalk stream, which precluded the River Thames. Holmes detected the residue of water-crowsfoot and water starwort, and the larvae of the caddis. "There may also be some evidence of molluscs in the fluid from the lungs," he announced to us, before offering us an additional lecture on the first legally ordered autopsy, performed in Bologna, Italy in 1302.[17]

It was hard to estimate how long the victim had been dead. The usual evidences were useless because of the cadaver's immersion in different kinds of water whilst being confined in a thick sack that had prevented the depredations of sealife. Our best estimate was three or four days since drowning, but there was simply no definitive guide for comparison. Holmes felt that this was

---

16   The story is from Vitruvius's *De architectura IX*, Preface, 9-12, which reports that research for the trial was the cause of Archimedes' famous "Eureka" moment in his bath.

17   Bartolomeo da Varignana (d. 1318) was variously physician to the Marchese Aldobrandino d'Este, Marquis of Ferrara and to Holy Roman Emperor Henry VII. Bartolomeo, with colleague Giacomo Rolandini and surgeons Giovanni da Brescia and Tommasino Ginci, performed a magistrate-ordered autopsy to determine cause of death of Azzolino del fu Onesto, determining that she had perished of internal bleeding, not by poison.

a significant omission in the world's body of knowledge.

We were on slightly surer ground with the wounds on the body. The water had washed the insults clean but there was little evidence of scabbing, suggesting that the majority of the damage had taken place as the sack had been submerged, when the animals sewn inside had gone wild with fear. However, elongated formed bruises and weals which had broken the skin suggested a pre-mortem beating with a thin stick, possibly a willow-wand. These marks appeared on back, chest, legs, arms, and buttocks, and there were several less-severe strikes to the face that suggested that the beaten man was already hooded at the time. His gory soles proved that he had been staggering from blows from several directions, already shod in his strange cruel footwear. From the angles of certain blows, Holmes was able to reconstruct that our subject had then been suspended from the wrists with ankles bound together for part of his beating.

Expert written testimony arrived in response to Holmes's wires, informing us of the various customs of *poena cullei*. These practices had varied through the latter Roman period. Scholars disagreed about how widespread the punishment had been; noting that several sources suggested that exposure to wild animals in the arena was also a penalty for patricide or matricide.

One of Holmes's correspondents solved the question of the nailed clogs. These were punishment shoes, fashioned in the pattern of the footwear our classical forebears had fastened to criminals to prevent their escape, hobbles that the condemned man wore on his route to execution. The use of "red rods" referred to the instruments of discipline used to thrash prisoners on the way to their deaths; there was academic debate over whether the rods were painted red or stained by blood.

"This is an extraordinarily specific method of murder," I commented to Holmes as we reviewed the history.

"And one that requires significant resources to carry out," my friend replied, "including the likely help of accomplices."

"Do you really think that you can find the murderer—or murderers?"

"We have a good number of pieces of evidence to begin with. It is an interesting problem."

There was also the question of identity of the drowned man. "There are no reports of the disappearance of a plump bearded male in his mid-forties anywhere in Britain," supervising Inspector Amett reported to Dr Falwein. "If this chap is three or four days dead then we would have expected to have heard from someone that he was gone. From a relative or friend, a neighbour, a milkman, a paper-boy...[18] someone."

---

18   Daily doorstop deliveries of milk and dairy products and of newspapers were very common in Great Britain during this period. If a regular milkman, who would know his route and its occupants, noticed that previously-delivered supplies had not been taken into the house by his next delivery, he might alert a local constable to a potential problem. This was a common way of detecting the deaths of solitary people.

"We have a good number of pieces of evidence to begin with. It is an interesting problem."

Holmes looked up from his microscope—he had previously waxed elegiac about the discovery of such instruments in 1590 and their subsequent utility in examining hairs and fibres, observing tiny wounds, and identifying teeth—and said, "You should concentrate your searches on men of that description who were expected to go on a journey, who left for the railway station or their port of embarkation, who might be expected to be absent for some time without comment. Circulate a sketch of his appearance and a written description."

"Make a drawing of the dead man?" Falwein wondered. "Yes, we might try that, but the water-bloating…"

"Has not so affected his hair, moustaches, or beard as to render them anonymous. Nor does water-logging prevent the determination of his shoe size, his hand-size, his hat size, his belt size; all measures of his appearance."

"That is… rather clever," Falwein conceded.

"You must circulate the information between police stations," Holmes instructed Amett. "You might recruit the assistance of the press. They are surely curious about the murder on the shore?"

"There have been enquiries," the Inspector admitted. "Word of the bizarre animal contents of the sack has not yet circulated. Fortunately, the tide has come in and covered the spot where the bag was washed up. There is nothing for sight-seers to gawp at."

"And no evidence on scene," Holmes grumbled.

"In fairness, Holmes, even you cannot stop the tide," I mentioned in mitigation.

"I need not stop the tide to observe the track-marks it has not yet covered. Were the wet imprints trodden only by the winkle-pickers who haunted the receding waves, or was there sign of others discovering the body beforehand? Was there any indication that the bundle had been manhandled into position, dropped off by a boat or positioned on shore by helping hands?"

"We cannot know," I understood. "Nobody made observations before the tide turned."

"And the initial discoverers had not the wit to look," Holmes complained "I questioned them earlier and found their testimony singularly limited." He turned back to the corpses on the table and the pile of other 'primary evidence'. "Fortunately, these witnesses can tell us a better story."

We had arrived in Leysdown-on-Sea a little after one in the afternoon. At nine that evening Holmes was still continuing with his work in his makeshift laboratory at the rear of the lifeboat hut. Falwein and I stepped out onto the promenade, which was in truth little more than a shallow sea-wall used for mooring fishing skiffs, and we watched the sunset while taking a smoke.

"Do you really think that your friend can get somewhere with this strange affair just by looking at those bodies and things?" the Assistant County Coroner asked at last.

"I have seen Sherlock Holmes undertake remarkable feats of deduction," I assured the worried official. "Indeed, in the very first case that I ever saw him undertake, he discovered the murderer on little else but a single word written in blood on a wall."[19]

"He seems competent. He rattles off those facts as if he can scarcely get them out of his head fast enough. But what does a 'consulting detective' do anyway, that Sir Gabriel would recommend him?"

"Holmes has created the role for himself, in a world where there was no such job to fit him. When investigation agents or policemen are baffled, or when members of the public find that the experts to whom they have applied are unable to help, Holmes will review their case and offer some insight. In the same way as a medical man might call upon Sir Gabriel Kipps to perform some delicate piece of surgery that is beyond their experience, so detectives refer to Holmes—discreetly, of course."

"He has suggested a fee for his services. It was quite modest."

"Holmes is more interested in developing his skills than in profiting from criminal investigation. He seeks to develop what he describes as the art of detection, a toolkit of knowledge and techniques that can benefit all forensic pathology."

"Such as the database of descriptions that he suggested," Falwein understood. "Some standard data-set of measurements for hands, head, facial features and so on."[20]

"Holmes publishes monographs upon such topics. He can tell apart more than a hundred types of tobacco ash by sight, touch, and smell. He can often discern a man's profession by the state of his hands and cuffs."

---

19   During "A Study in Scarlet", first published in *Beeton's Christmas Annual 1887* and then as a book in 1888.

20   Such a system would eventually be introduced by French police officer Alphonse Bertillon (1853-1914) at the start of the 20th century. His system to log sixteen key skull features, introduced in a lecture in 1912, is still used by law enforcement today. Bertillon also championed the use of galvanoplastic compounds to preserve footprints, the use of a dynamometer to determine the degree of force used in breaking and entering, and the science of ballistics. However, Bertillon's evidence regarding handwriting at the famous 'Dreyfus Affair' trial was utterly erroneous and was a significant contributor to the false five-year Devil's Island imprisonment of Captain Alfred Dreyfus for treason.

"Surely not."

"It is a matter of the callosities of the fingers and palms and suchlike. If Holmes can teach the crime-solvers of the future to do what he does, our nation will be a safer and more just place."

Our conversation was interrupted by Holmes bursting out of the boat hut and exclaiming, "The rope had been used previously. It has traces of its former employment!" And he vanished back inside.

Morning brought another thick wad of replies to Holmes's enquiries, a mixture of telegrams and letters and one bulky textbook on sea and river microorganisms. Holmes was still active, collarless in his shirtsleeves at the workbench where he had stacked many samples on the bench beside his microscope and chemical gear. I did not know whether he had slept at all; he had kept Falwein and I busy with autopsy problems until after eleven the night before, when we had retired.

Inspector Amett rejoined us too, pressured by his Chief Constable for progress in this bizarre crime. By the looks of it he was regretting his choice of taking breakfast before he came to the lifeboat hut.

"What progress can we claim?" Falwein asked Holmes. "I shall have to call a public inquest tomorrow or the day after at the latest. At that time I may well not be able to keep quiet the facts about the animals in the bag with the deceased. The jury have the right to ask questions, and they will naturally be interested in the circumstances in which we... er... unpacked the drowned man."

"The longer that can be delayed, the better," opined Amett. "We are fortunate that the government is in crisis again. The newspapers are diverted with parliamentary goings-on—the Egyptian situation.[21] I would prefer to avoid a circus of pressmen interfering with our enquiries."

"The circumstances of the case are rather newsworthy," I admitted. "What can you tell us, Holmes?"

---

21   This would presumably refer to the Egyptian army coup against Tewfik Pasha, the Khedive of Egypt and Sudan, to an anti-Christian riot in Alexandria on 11th June that killed fifty Europeans, to the fortification of the city by mutineer forces of 'Arabi Pasha' (Ahmed 'Urabi), and to a subsequent shelling by British warships for 10½ hours. Thus began the Anglo-Egyptian War, dragging 40,000 soldiers under Sir Garnet Wolsey into conflict with 11,000 Egyptian and Sudanese regulars and 50,000 reservists. Throughout August, Britain won a series of battles, taking few casualties but inflicting significant losses. By September, British troops had occupied Egypt, marginalised French influence on the territory, and secured control of the area until the Anglo-Egyptian Treaties of 1922 and 1936.

Holmes gestured along his collection of bell-jar samples. These included sections taken from the unfortunate animals, which were now preserved in ice buckets against the far wall, and such samples as Falwein and I had taken at his request from the dead man before he had been removed to a funeral parlour.

"Since time is precious, I shall summarise. The whole process of discovery will take a significantly longer period of time to describe and must be written up precisely to demonstrate chains of evidence. Watson, we must go to Cambridge."

"To Cambridge?" Amett blurted, baffled.

"The stomach and lung contents, gentlemen! The victim was not fed for at least twenty-four hours before he drowned, which suggests captivity, as do the abrasions on his wrists and ankles where ropes have rubbed over a lengthy period of time. The animals were all fed, possibly to quiet them, and I have some indication of the feed they received—horsemeat, field mice, barleycorn, and peanuts. The peanuts for the Capuchin were the most helpful, of course, being the most unusual foodstuff."

"Peanuts are not usually grown in Cambridge," Falwein ventured.

Holmes ignored him. "The small organisms in the lungs were telling. When respiration ceased, the water in the lungs remained trapped there. It is largely uncontaminated by the seawater that immersed the bodies afterwards. All river-water has telltale signatures based upon the ecology and geology of its environment. Chalky residue narrows things down significantly, as well as discounting the Thames Valley and Estuary entirely—that's London clay, like this Isle of Sheppey.

"There is also the matter of the hempen rope used to restrain the dead man. On this line are traces of its previous employment securing some river-launch— it was a boat-tether! It bears residue of long immersion in river water before its brief sea voyage, including green mould that I have referred to another specialist. Tiny particles of fish effluvia amongst its strands offer certain indications, but there is no definitive study of such evidence to help narrow things down sufficiently; another gap in our forensic library. Fortunately, botany has been a British pastime for many years so plant spores, particles of pollen and fungi, have been better mapped."

"You have identified the river where this man perished by the traces he breathed in as he drowned and by the rope that restrained him," I recognised.

"Somewhat, Watson. I am awaiting expert confirmation of the presence in the mongrel's lung contents of eggs of the banded demoiselle dragonfly *Calopteryx splendens*. The insect favours slow-flowing streams and therefore helps to narrow the location. And then there is this."

Holmes drew us over to where he had cut a section of the leather sacking that had shrouded the body. The skin was pegged out tight on a square. Some of the hide was dyed a dull orange from some kind of chemical residue. An odd mark like a T and a half-moon was scarcely visible as a discolouration on the stain.

"A brand," he announced triumphantly. "An owner's brand, placed upon the cart-horse that supplied this strip of leather. It was rendered invisible by the tanning process, but a chemical procedure of my own has brought out the traces."

"From this you deem that the animal came from Cambridge," I surmised.

"Yes. This is a breeder's mark, and I have the address. I have contacted the breeder and confirmed the sign, but of course he has no way of distinguishing one flayed nag from another. He sells twenty such carthorses every year, and this one would have been sold off a decade or more before it was consigned to the knackery[22] at the end of its useful work-life. But this fellow's business is with local tradesmen, and the River Cam matches ideally the evidence of the lungs and the tether."

"How did the body get from Cambridgeshire to our shore?" Amett puzzled. "The Cam flows into the Great Ouse, does it not, and then into the sea at Norfolk. That's a long way up the coast from here."

Holmes had the facts, of course. "The Ouse's outlet into the North Sea is at King's Lynn, forty-six miles away. The currents there are highly unlikely to deposit a body here; nor has there been remarkable weather activity to explain it. Furthermore, there are a number of locks on the Cam which would prevent a body from floating down it without notice."

"Not to mention the river being covered with students punting about on the Backs," I pointed out. This was just the weather to take out a barge and pole along the middle river.

"The plant traces I found suggest that the place of immolation was the quiet upper course, above Jesus Lock. I have sent an enquiry to the lock-keeper, whose cottage is beside the lock itself, to check that there was no unusual nocturnal activity, but it is far more likely that the—dare we venture to say execution?—happened in a secluded spot further upriver and the whole apparatus was then hauled out of the water once more to be dumped at sea. You will note the heavy eyelet let into the sacking at the top right corner of the leather bag, suitable for attaching a thick rope to tow the bodies."

"A murder and a concealment!" Amett cried.

"We are a long way from the actual crime scene," my friend noted. "Now we shall go and find it."

---

22   A knackery was a factory for the disposal of large animals, mostly horses, which were rendered down for glue, leather, and dogmeat. The modern British slang "knackered", meaning very fatigued, refers to being so exhausted and close to death as to be fit to send to the knackery.

"How can you possibly do that?" Dr Falwein protested.

"Peanuts!" Holmes called to him, and began to gather his things.

"We had an adult male carablanca—that is, a white-faced monkey of the kind you described," the Reader in South American Botany from one of Cambridge's prestigious colleges confirmed to us. "It was brought back from an expedition to the Caribbean coast of Costa Rica, from Callero Island, a little over two years since. The animal escaped two months ago. The keeper was evidently careless in closing its cage. He was docked a shilling's wage for it."

Holmes asked for more details of the creature's appearance and was referred to a series of photo-plates and drawings made of the Capuchin during its captivity, and then met the unfortunate keeper who was blamed for its loss. Still denying culpability, this fellow Staggett was able to confirm that the sad bedraggled corpse taken out of the sea at Sheppey was almost certainly the specimen that had become something of a pet to the School of Botany. He suspected that the beast had been stolen as an undergraduate prank.

"What did you feed the animal?" Holmes enquired.

"Those monkeys eat a varied diet in the wild: fruit, leaves, nectar, nuts, buds, bugs, eggs, frogs, lizards, small birds. We tended to feed him fresh fruit: apples, pears, and such. And monkey nuts, of course. He loved monkey nuts."

"Those are American peanuts," I clarified.

"Yes. We bought them in specially for him."

Holmes was brightened by this testimony. "I am not yet familiar with the varietals of *Arachis hypogaea*, but I gather there are several distinctive strains of the nut. The legume consists of a thick outer shell covering a papery seed-coat over two edible cotyledons. There is also a radicle, an embryonic root which can be snapped off, and a plumule, the embryonic shoot emerging from the top of the radicle. These are usually removed at harvesting but were present in the samples from our drowned simian, suggesting that the nuts were grown locally in some glass-house rather than imported wholesale."

"Yes," agreed Staggett, "There is a groundnut tree in the college's tropical garden."

"And our murderer had access to it!" I recognised.

That was helpful, though on further enquiry the garden would evidently be closing for the night and Holmes had another location That he desired to visit before closing.

"The Bursar's office?" I queried as we strode across Christ's Pieces.[23]

"Indeed, Watson. We shall turn from forensic science to forensic accounting. It is something of a shortcut, but perhaps our unmissed victim was an academic of these halls who is thought departed on leave? If so, who might know better than the keepers of college finances? Expeditions and research travel must be funded. Periods of absence, leave, sickness, are all recorded in the Bursar's accounts. The drowned man may not have anything to do with the University, but if he does…"

"Then the books will reveal him!"

Holmes nodded agreement. "Tomorrow we shall hunt for monkey-nuts," my friend informed me. "Later on we must spend some time fishing."

I might have observed that Holmes was eschewing his art of detection for trudging for answers, but I knew that Holmes was cleverer than that.

Dr Whatten Mortonthwaite was a Lecturer in Roman Jurisprudence, accorded honours as an expert on his subject, scholarly author of an impenetrable text on the *Leges Regiae, Rogatae, and Datae*,[24] stuffed with enough Classical behaviour to send me shuddering back to my schoolboy days and our grim lessons in declension. He was also, we discovered via Holmes's line of fiscal investigation, now absent on a sponsored journey to the Vatican, examining certain articles held in their comprehensive archive. He had departed his lodgings five days previously for the night-train to Felixstowe, to catch the steamer *Palmeri*.

Mortonthwaite was described to us as a plump bearded man in his forties, a fine match for the figure washed up on the Isle of Sheppey. His landlady recognised the sketch that Holmes produced as being of her erstwhile lodger.

"We have him!" Holmes enthused as we sat to supper that evening in the Old Bank Hotel on High Street. "Now we know the man we shall learn his associations: his family, his students, his colleagues, his old mentors, and whether he might be charged with parricide, figuratively or literally. We shall examine the funding of his trip to Italy that so conveniently sent him apart for murder."

Holmes dispatched a long expensive telegram to Inspector Amett and another to Dr Falwein, alerting them to their need to co-ordinate with counter-

---

23   That is, the green space behind Christ's College, Cambridge, bordered by King Street, Emmanuel Road, and the North Court of Emmanuel College.

24   That is, laws of the Roman kings, popular magistrates, and higher magistrates.

parts in an alien county some ninety miles distant.[25] Then, evidently recalling his after-dinner conversation at Baker Street, Holmes added a quick postal description of his case to Stamford and Lomax to prove a point. I submitted a pro-tem account to Sir Gabriel, taking special care in my grammar and penmanship.

Holmes saw us through coffee and tobacco by advising me on the 1784 murder of Edward Culshaw of Lancaster. Examination of the pistol wad[26] impacted in the dead man's head proved the screwed-up paper to exactly match with a torn newssheet found in the pocket of suspect John Toms. It was an 18th century murder mystery solved by forensic detection. In the same way, the 1816 assault and murder by drowning of a young farm girl in Warwickshire had been solved by observation of a knee imprint of patched corduroy trousers in damp earth at the murder site, along with grains of wheat and chaff. These signs were matched with the clothing of a farm labourer who had been threshing nearby and thereby proved him the murderer.

"We live in the very age of progress, Watson," my friend insisted. "The art and science of detection must develop with it!"

The art and science developed the following morning in the form of Holmes's thorough search of Mortonthwaite's lodgings, under the scrutiny of local police Inspector Sadler, and of Amett, who had caught the milk train up that morning. The Cambridge fellow was suspicious of Holmes's odd examination of the dead man's rooms, and kept up a prickly stilted professional conversation with Amett of Kent. My part was to keep the police officers out of Holmes's way as he undertook his researches.

Or, as Holmes had said it beforehand, "Just keep those official boots off my clues so that I stand some chance of finding things before they are ground away by herds of dancing policemen!"

I distracted the law by revealing the results from the new flock of telegrams that had come in overnight as a result of Holmes's previous round of enquiries. We knew that Dr Mortonthwaite was an only child, son of a country vicar; that he was not well-liked by his associates because he was given to academic rivalry and acrimonious dispute; that his planned Vatican jaunt was a result

---

25   Sixty-four miles as the crow flies but much further by road because of the Thames Estuary.

26   Crushed paper used to secure powder and balls in the muzzle of early pistols.

of sponsorship by some scholarly foundation that could not be traced; that he had intended to be gone from his Cambridge digs for six weeks in the long vacation.

We had a list of people who had been regular visitors and attendants at the botanical garden to potentially raid the monkey-nut tree. It was naturally a very long roster, but Dr Mortonthwaite's name had been prominent as a regular caller; evidently it had been his habit to sit under the warming glass by the climbing vines and mark his undergraduates' essays in bright red ink.

There were long technical letters from the experts in mould, spores, fish eggs, and other microscopic matter that Holmes had extracted from his physical evidence. Amett and Sadler could make nothing of these, filled as they were with long chains of letters and numbers of chemical formulae and Linnaean descriptions in Latin; I admit to glossing over those accounts myself, but Holmes had found them telling.

As I was exhausting my diversions, Holmes called us over to look at Whatten Mortonthwaite's bankbook. There were the deposits of his usual stipend and additional fees for lectures and tutorials, plus one large sum from the elusive Tarquin Trust. Expenditures were listed for regular domestic costs including his landlady housekeeper, and for supplies suitable for a man expecting an overseas journey. There were several withdrawals of cash of between £20 and £50 for which there were no explanations.

"We shall try to trace the bank-notes," Inspector Amett promised, without much hope.

Tucked into the rear of the bankbook were bank notifications of honouring cheques that Mortonthwaite had issued. These proved to be especially useful, since they included a local farm, a surgical supplies store, a chandler's, and an upholsterer.

"Holmes!" I called out. "Are these not the very shops where someone might acquire poultry and domestic animals, stitched leather goods, ropes... I see no reason for medical goods such as tape and bandages, but..."

"Surgical ether can stun a man if he is caught unawares," Holmes noted gravely. "It is not easy to apply but it can render someone unconscious; perhaps for long enough to bind and stitch him into a sack?"

"One can hardly expect a dog, snake, monkey, and rooster to remain quiet in the same bag, even if the human is drugged, unless they too were somehow sedated. Nor would it be easy work even for several men to accomplish. But—I say!"

Holmes read my face. "You have come to it?"

"What?" demanded Inspector Sadler. "Come to what?"

"The items that were required for the Punishment of the Sack," I unfolded. "It seems that it was *Whatten Mortonthwaite* who purchased them, who assembled them. How then, and why, did that same Doctor of Classics end up executed by Roman sentence?"

Holmes and I strolled along the bank of the Cam, walking upstream past the clutter of Cambridge, enjoying the shade of chestnut trees and leafy leaning elms. The reflections on the water and the flitting of little birds made it a very pleasant walk.

My companion was in effusive mood too, returning to his present obsession, the development of forensic disciplines. "It is an ineluctable consequence of the modern scientific method, Watson. One day the world will hold 17th century French army surgeon Ambroise Paré to be the father of modern forensics. He documented and published scientific research on causes of death. That opened the way up for the studies of Italian surgeons Fortunato Fidelis and Paolo Zacchia. By the latter part of last century there were books such as Fodéré's *A Treatise on Forensic Medicine and Public Health* and Frank's *Complete System of Police Medicine*."[27]

"But as regarding our own present investigation…" I attempted.

"Nor should we disregard our own home-grown innovators, doctor. I am often scathing of the Detective Branch of Scotland Yard but it was one of their earliest officers, Inspector Henry Goddard, who in 1835 noticed a flaw in a bullet that had supposedly been fired at the butler of Mrs Maxwell of Southampton by armed intruders. He discovered the mould wherein the bullet was manufactured, and proved thereby that the ammunition was actually owned by this butler fellow Randall, who had been seeking praise and reward for his apparent courage. Goddard pioneered the technique of ballistics."

"But Dr Mortonthwaite… We have so far questioned none of his students, his colleagues, the shopkeepers from whom he made purchases, any remaining relatives who might know about his father, perhaps his father's parishioners…?"

"I have dispatched enquiries on those topics, never fear. But this is a case of forensics, Watson. It is the evidence that will speak to us. Hence our present sojourn."

"Fishing without lines? It's a pleasant day out, Holmes, but I scarcely see

---

27   That is, *Les lois éclairées par les sciences physiques, ou Traité de médecine légale et d'hygiène publique* (1798/9, 1813, 6 vols.) by the French physician Francois Immanuele Fodéré (1764-1835), professor of medical jurisprudence at the University of Strasbourg, and System *einer vollständigen medicinischen Polizey* (1779-1827 post., 9 vols.) by the German medical expert and hygienist Johann Peter Frank (1745-1821).

its purpose. Unless… are you seeking the place where Mortonthwaite was drowned? You found his general location by deducing the river, and we are presently above the locks that would have prevented the body from reaching the sea."

"We are in exactly the right ecology to leave those freshwater traces. Now we are looking for the place where a heavy, heaving sack entered the river—and more importantly, was subsequently hauled out again."

"By the loop-hole for a hasp or hook," I recognised. "A man and those animals must have had significant weight. Dragging it out would leave a trace."

"Or else the marks of a pulley scaffold, which I judge more likely because of the lack of grass-stains embedded on the leather. The sea may have washed most traces away, but I doubt it could erase all. Where are we at present?"

I consulted my map. "The Trumpington Hall estate. This weir pool is called Byron's Pond, evidently after the poet, who bathed here whilst studying at Trinity College."[28]

We followed the perimeter of the attractive feature as best we could, scrambling between Wych Elm, Pendunculate Oak, and lesser flora that matched Holmes's forensic estimates. Dragonflies skated over the water.

Holmes spoke as he searched. "It is clear from Dr Mortonthwaite's bookcase and his preserved old correspondence that he had a mentor. Professor N. J. Nolley was his tutor back in the 50s, the academic who set Mortonthwaite on to his lifelong interests. The old man retired two years since and died soon afterwards."

"Could that be the parricide?" I speculated. "A spiritual rather than actual father?"

"They certainly enjoyed a critical correspondence. They disagreed on many topics; but it appears that they still appreciated their sparring. Nolley seems to have maintained contact with several of his alumni who are also prominent classicists. So did Mortonthwaite, if by contact we mean venomous and critical attacks on their conclusions, and vice versa."

"How did the old man die?"

"Mortonthwaite retained the notice of death. Professor Nolley apparently took his own life."

"Why?"

"The inquest made no comment on the topic. College speculation was that Nolley might have been suffering from tumorous growths in the bowel which in time would have left him a pain-wracked invalid, and that therefore he chose to make a quick end of it. He was certainly alone in his study when he

---

28   This site still remains a local beauty spot, classified since 2005 as a Local Nature Reserve maintained by Cambridge City Council; ref: https://lnr.cambridge.gov.uk/nature_reserve/byrons-pool/

fell upon an antique Roman gladius."

"What a way for a Classical scholar to go! It could not have been murder?"

"I am still receiving accounts, but unless his whole household was collaborate then I doubt that any hand but Nolley's held the blade."

I heard the unspoken "but" in Holmes's sentence.

"Whether any other nudged the Professor to his decision, whether some disagreement became too bitter, some rift too hard to bear... that I cannot yet say. Such provocation might be interpreted as murder by loyal bereaved intimates."

"Then might we...?" I began, but Holmes halted abruptly and held out an arm to keep me from stepping further.

I looked carefully at a patch of still-trampled grass and the muddy patches where heavy metal circles had pressed into the riverbank. We were secluded from general view, in a place shielded by overhanging boughs, under a natural canopy. Almost a week after they must have been left I could still read traces of some heavy construction, probably a portable winch, and the places where a substantial bulk had been dragged.

Holmes, with his superior observational skills, quickly pointed out to me the various locations where flecks of blood had been preserved on the underside of leaves or on grass-stalks; the signs that a man had been ruthlessly flogged with staves here.

We had found the murder site.

At the Coroner's Inquest, the sensational news of the classical murder was impossible to conceal. Jury, press, and audience alike were shocked, confounded, and fascinated.

Dr Falwein's chief attestant was the consultant specialist Mr Sherlock Holmes. I pitied the medical man for having to curtail and control my friend's lengthy and precise descriptions and conclusions.

"So," Falwein valiantly summarised after Holmes had explained how his investigations had led us to Byron's Pool, "you discovered the scene at which the crime most likely took place."

We had already heard from Inspectors Sadler and Amett regarding their observations of that site and of Mortonthwaite's lodgings. We had also received testimony from the dead man's landlady, from the botanical gardens groundskeeper, and from the zoo attendant Staggett, confirming much of Holmes's own observations—even if he had first had to point out to them what they were missing.

"The interest comes from the methodology, not the findings," Holmes declared magisterially.

Falwein was there as magistrate, however, so he pushed on to the wealth of presented correspondence, so many exhibits as to require double-letters of the alphabet to denote them all. Here too his expert consultant was pleased to explain the purpose of the paper trail.

"There are three document chains. The first is protracted long-term correspondence with the late N. J. Nolley, dating right back from the occasion of Mortonthwaite's first publication, up to shortly before the Professor's demise. Of special interest was the rather vicious academic argument between Nolley, Mortonthwaite, and a number of other now-prominent scholars who had studied under Nolley."

A member of the jury interrupted to demand "what the big brains were squabbling over?" Holmes responded that the dispute, pursued through journals and academic circles, regarded modern interpretations of Greek and Roman literature and art around the subject of pederasty, the notions of the Greek *erastes* and *eromenos*[29] or the Roman *cinaedi*.[30]

Falwein was required to translate to his less-educated Isle of Sheppey jury panel that the scholars had all been arguing about definitions and practices of Classical inverts. A murmur of disapproval at this bad taste ran around the inquest.

Holmes testified on. "The second strand of correspondence was some terse and angry personal letters between Mortonthwaite and his principal opponent in that debate, Dr Norman Ledger, now a fellow of a rival college, master of late Roman history. This exchange descended on occasion to little more than name-calling and accusations about old feuds and incidents dating to their undergraduate days."

"Is this Ledger a suspect?" the foreman of the jury wanted to know.

"It is too early to say," Falwein controlled him. "It is for this court to determine a verdict of death, whether by natural or unnatural causes, and to recommend whether the police be instructed to prepare a criminal case."

Holmes proceeded. "The third set of documents—marked BD to CA in your register—are various enquiries and instructions from Dr Mortonthwaite to various craftsmen and merchants about the costs and technical possibili-

---

29   In the context of ancient Greek culture, particularly within the practice of pederasty, *erastes* (ἐραστής) refers to an older man who is in a love relationship with a younger male, known as the *eromenos*. The *erastes* is essentially the "lover" or "admirer" in this dynamic, while the *eromenos* is the "beloved".

30   In ancient Rome, some men who did not fit neatly within gender categories were called *cinaedi*. They were usually adult males singled out for their extreme effeminacy.

ties of certain purchases and commissions. Amongst these are quotations for the fabrication of a sturdy horsehide leather sack, the sewing of a draw-string bag from a provided animal pelt, the carving of clogs to a peculiar antique specification, the purchase of a portable crane-hoist suitable for lowering or retrieving heavy items from a river-bank, ordering of Royal Ordinance Survey maps of the Upper Cam, enquiries about the acquisition of viper and cockerel, and unsuccessful attempts to locate and purchase a monkey. In short, almost all of the elements of the crime that was actually committed on Whatten Mortonthwaite himself."

"Which makes no sense," Inspector Sadler declared from the floor.

Holmes shook his head ruefully at the policeman's lack of vision, but went on at Falwein's request to recap the classical sentence of *Poena Cullei*, including excerpts from the messages he had received from appropriate experts, including a quoted passage from one of N.J. Nolley's own texts.

"Mr Holmes, have you any explanation for this extraordinary death?" the Coroner asked in frustrated bafflement.

Holmes gathered in the full attention of the court and replied, "Of course. The material is incontrovertible. I must ask the inquest to admit some more evidence. Here are exhibits CK to DB, several pairs of work-boots confiscated by Inspector Sadler at my request. Here, exhibit DC, is the catch-record of the fishing trawler *Allison*. Here, the banking records of the late Professor Nolley, and here the banking records of Dr Ledger, both acquired for me through subpoena by Inspector Amett."

These additional items were admitted as exhibits, and then Holmes explained their purpose. "These boots were confiscated from a University society called the Followers of Ganymede. Dr Ledger was a founder member in the '50s. The original mythical Ganymede was a beautiful youth stolen away by Zeus to be his cupbearer, and said by some to also be his lover.[31] The prints of certain of these pieces of footwear match imprints discovered and recorded at Byron's Pool."

"It places men at the scene?"

"Indeed. Or at least puts their boots at the scene, worn by men of their weight and stride. As to the *Allison's* catch register, its relevance is to illustrate the diminished harvest brought in on the day after Mortonthwaite's murder. It suggests that for part of the voyage the smack did not have its nets cast but was instead occupied elsewhere than its usual fishing grounds. Comparisons with many other vessels along the Estuary coast indicate no likewise-diminished

31   Ganymede's Latinate name was Catamitus, from whence derived the general Roman term for a boy who was subject of a pederast's desires and the archaic English term *catamite* for the receiving homosexual partner. Classical authors were divided about whether Ganymede was indeed Zeus's lover, with Plato arguing that it was a Cretan invention to justify their social custom of *paiderastía*.

catch. Nor were any of the other boat crews so far interviewed able to recall seeing the *Allison* at its regular fishery. Further questioning of the *Allison's* crew upon its return again to port may be telling. There may be some special commission that these fishermen might wish to recall when they realise that there is murder involved."

Amett perked up attentively at that, and sent a hasty note out to his waiting sergeant.

"The financial records offer some interesting parallels. Sums of money withdrawn over nine months by Nolley match exactly with sums deposited a day or two later by Ledger. Over that time, the total exchange is £1,150."

There was a ripple of surprise at such sums passing hands.

"Do we have any reason for such vast payments?" Falwein asked.

"We have only inference," Holmes replied precisely. "From insults written by Mortonthwaite to Ledger, and from comments passed by Nolley's former staff, we might suspect but not prove a close relationship between Ledger and his old tutor; a relationship dating back to their earliest acquaintance which broke down a year before Nolley's death. It is then that regular payments from the Professor seem to have begun, right up to his suicide.

"I submit that Mortonthwaite regarded that suicide as tantamount to murder of a *patron* by his *patronus*. He too had strong affection for his old college tutor, and knew enough to suspect what had driven N.J. Nolley to his death. In his outrage and cold wrath he plotted for the putative murderer a terrible and classical death."

"It was Mortonthwaite who assembled the mechanism of the murder," I agreed, "but it was then he who died by it."

"The monkey," Holmes told me, and the court. "The stolen capuchin was the thing that gave it away. Ask the zookeeper Staggett, who has already testified before us today, to whom he mentioned the simian's loss, and his suspicions about who thereafter took the creature. Ask him now."

Falwein called again upon the unfortunate Staggett, who confessed that he had disclosed his suspicion to Dr Ledger. At Holmes's prompting Staggett additionally admitted to having once been a member of the Followers of Ganymede, "a harmless University dining club", though stressing that he was now a happily married man and a father.

"Upon learning of Mortonthwaite's odd behaviour, Ledger looked more closely at what his rival might be up to." Holmes suggested. "Ledger discovered that he was scheduled for a horrible execution. Doubtless Mortonthwaite had dedicated, devoted students of his own, who favoured his faction just as rabidly, who might deliver the beating and hoist the scaffold. It is a grim thing to uncover plans for one's own murder.

"However, Ledger did not elect to inform the police of a murder-plot. Instead,

"Today is... a step in the right direction."

the Followers of Ganymede laid their own schemes to usurp the revenge. Just before some plan to capture Norman Ledger was implemented, Whatton Mortonthwaite was seized instead. The execution the vengeful scholar had planned for his enemy was meted out on him."

The Inquest audience were silent as they digested these revelations. Holmes laid out the chains of evidence, stringing them into unbreakable ties that condemned men for murder.

That was the jury's verdict also. Dr Falwein heard the decision soberly and recorded it, with a referral to the police for a criminal investigation. Thanks to Holmes there would not be a long prosecution..

"Remarkable!" I told my friend as the courtroom cleared. "With nothing but lenses and test-tubes, you broke this case. You promised that such things could be done."

"But so far they have been done only by me," Holmes tempered my enthusiasm. "My boasts to Lomax and Stamford will require much more study than that, and by other men of science. Today is… a step in the right direction."

"And the exposure of foul plots by foul killers," I added.

Holmes nodded. "Whatever other rights a man should have, past, present, or future, they do not include the right to murder."

"Might we, then, eliminate murder through your 'whole art of detection'?"

"I doubt I could make that claim, doctor. We cannot erase human nature or the human condition. Let us rather aim to uncover every murderer. That is the purview of the investigating detective."

"And if you do, will there still be need for a consultant to intervene?"

Holmes pulled on his hat and faced the steady sea-wind blowing off the Estuary. "I fear that my services may be required for some time yet, Dr Watson."

THE END

THE ADVENTURE OF THE ILLITERATE INFORMANT

N THOSE EARLY months and years of my association with Sherlock Holmes, he introduced me to many odd parts of London and the characters who dwelled there.

Without his expert guidance I would never have discovered the Tunnel-Runners Guild, the Ferret Jugglers League, the moving market run by the Brothers Spigendorff, the self-proclaimed Knights of the Templar Vaults, Lemmy Clement's bare-knuckle boxing cellar in Queenhithe, Dolly Minx's network of flower girls (who so much troubled Wiggins' smitten street boys), the half-spaniel half-lurcher Toby and his taxidermist owner Sherman, inquisitive young Cartwright who was so useful at the Express Office, the escapologist Zarlini, the pigeon-fancier Strome, the 'retired poisoner' Crawford, and many other colourful people and extraordinary places. The regular citizen of our capital never suspects the strangeness and wonder that lies behind its façade.

As part of a regimen of recovery from my Afghan injury, Holmes would accompany me on long walks through the highways and byways of the city. The workshops and music halls were are familiar to us as the museums and lecture rooms. Any one of our forays might bring us to rat-haunted wharfs or to glittering palaces.

One early acquaintance was Mrs Degger, a shapeless old woman of indiscriminate nationality who held court in a squalid yard off Poultry Street and Old Jewry. From a pile of apple boxes that might have been a throne, she met with dozens, perhaps hundreds, of elderly women of the lower classes, exchanging gossip, dispensing advice, and mediating squabbles.

"Where the courts and constabulary may fail to curb internecine warfare in Cheapside and Cornhill you may depend upon Mrs Degger," Holmes assured me at our first meeting. "Mrs Degger, this is my great friend and trusted associate Dr Watson. You may rely on him as you would me."

I doffed my hat and offered polite pleasantries, and was offered in return some thick blend of soupy Indian tea.

Even then there were some six or eight cronies lounging around—literally in some cases, since the inhabitants of those cloistered courtyards thought nothing of dragging their furniture outside to make use of—and so our meeting with the odd arbiter was public and witnessed.

"Amongst her many other public virtues, Mrs Degger provides lodgings for a rather unusual fellow called Scouty, and acts somewhat as his carer and business agent," Holmes mentioned. "You may encounter the odd fellow sometimes at our lodgings, for he is a most reliable courier, known for his infallibility."

"Idiot, is what he is," muttered one of the attendants.

Mrs Degger turned on the commenter hotly, defending her charge. "And wot d'you know, Mollie Partridge, except as 'ow to turn your daughters out on the game of an evening? I'd like to 'ear you lissen to a message spoke but once and then be able to repeat it back word perfick every time. I doubts what you could even recall all o' the sailors as 'ave crawled on top of you this week, if you'd but bothered to get their names! Be off with you, and bethink your tongue and manners 'afore you bother decent folk again!"

The unfortunate Mrs Partridge retreated from this reprimand and the cat-calls of her peers. Holmes used the delay to explain more about Scouty.

"The fellow is somewhat strange, Watson, quite unusual his behaviour. Not an idiot, but an idiot savant. He cannot read or write. When spoken with he can scarce manage to formulate a sentence. Yet when instructed to listen carefully he can memorise long lists of information, be it a letter, a set of figures, or some lading manifest. Any time within that day he can repeat it back without error, but come the following morning it is gone from his head and lost forever."

"That is a very unusual talent," I owned.

"A very useful one, Dr Watson," Mrs Degger answered me. "Why, the number of businessmen 'oo pays 'andsomely to have Scouty deliver a message for 'em…! Discreetly too, for Scouty will only remember for them as 'e's been told to speak it to. Why, I'll warrant that Scouty is the most trusted courier in London amongst them 'as values the privacy of their communications, which is why 'e commands a fee of no less than thirty shillings for 'is time!"[32] Remembering her recent feud with her neighbour she added, "Catch Molly Partridge or 'er

---

32   This in an age when a shilling bought a twenty-word telegram delivered within 100 miles. Thirty shillings, £1/10/- would be worth around £225 today; but this is deceptive, because costs of living were so different in the 19th century. In 1880 the average wage for a common labourer was 12 shillings a week, a female labourer 8/- a week, or a boy 6/- a week, whilst a bailiff or other official might bring home £1 a week (with 20 shillings to the pound). The average household budget of a labourer was 18/4½d per week, usually comprised from more than one wage.

[Source for wage statistics: *A Short History of English Agriculture* (1909) W. H. R. Curtler, available online at http://www.gutenberg.org/ebooks/16594]

girls commanding a fee of more than a tanner[33] all in, 'an more likely as they'd settle for a penny upright!"[34]

I agreed that Scouty sounded like a talented and handy fellow, but declined to comment on Mrs Partridge and her daughters.

I did not have to wait long to meet the eccentric Scouty. Only three days later our page Billy showed him into our chambers to await Holmes's return.

"How do you do?" I greeted the shabbily-dressed lank of oddness that hovered on our rug clutching a grimy felt cap.

"Scouty!" he introduced himself, tapping his chest to indicate his ownership of the name. "Scouty."

"I'm Dr Watson," I told him. "I'm very pleased to make your acquaintance."

Scouty nodded carefully, as if unwilling to shake words out of his brain.

"I doubt Holmes will be long. He told our housekeeper that he would likely be back by three."

Scouty held up three gangly fingers and then laughed. "And I would certainly not wish to be censured for being late for tea!" he answered in the unmistakable tones of Mr Sherlock Holmes.

"Holmes!" I gasped, frozen with my teacup halfway to my lips.

I saw it now, how with just a few lines of make-up, a change in the way the jaw was held and the brows furrowed, Holmes had entirely inhabited the character of the illiterate informant. Not for nothing had Holmes been able to make his living in a thespian career before returning home to begin his detective endeavours.

"I apologise, Watson, for my unfortunate habit of trying my disguises out on you. It is a compliment to your critical and observational powers that I test my false identities in this manner. If I may pass unrecognised at the hearth of Baker Street then I might pass unnoticed anywhere."

"I would not wager against you," I admitted. A new thought came to me. "Wait! Holmes...! If you are the uneducated and mentally deficient courier upon whom the demi-monde have come to rely for its covert messages, then you are at the very centre of a web of espionage such as no investigator has ever achieved. The greatest secret messages of the criminals of London must be committed to Scouty's memory."

---

33   Sixpence, half a shilling. The term is variously claimed to be derived from Cockney rhyming slang "tanner and skin" = "thin", or from the Romany gypsy word "tawno" meaning "little one [coin]", or from the Hindi "aat anna" for eight annas, half a rupee; or from somewhere else.

34   A sexual encounter standing outside against a wall, for which the prostitute would charge but a penny. By the end of the Holmesian era, inflation had raised the rate to the 'tuppenny upright' and the phrase was used as an insulting way of describing a woman for her lack of virtue.

"It is true that certain details have been given to Scouty to parrot that might otherwise have remained confidential between criminal fraternities."

"And you, Holmes... who else might memorise such tracts of text and numbers and repeat them faithfully without error!"

Scouty's portrayer dismissed my praise. "Mnemonic tricks, an actor's capacity for lines, and a few cerebral exercises are all that was required. Many a 'memory man' on stage could manage as much."

"But none might turn those talents to learning the secrets of the crimelords of London."

Holmes began to peel away the onionskin webbing that formed the base of his disguise make-up. "Some of the insights I have gleaned have been useful in my understanding of the seedier side of our city. I daresay I am becoming better versed in the details of the despicable. My files have swollen significantly thanks to the access that Scouty affords."

"And none suspect that their innocent courier is the sharpest criminologist in England."

"I trust not, doctor, or it would go very poorly for me."

"Mrs Degger must know."

"Knows and profits," Holmes agreed. "Scouty is her retirement plan. It is a matter of mutual convenience between us; convenient for all except those unscrupulous men whose secrets Scouty is given to recite."

I filed Scouty amongst the many eccentricities and strange habits that my flatmate possessed, another feature of dwelling with a man who played with poisons, scraped his violin at all hours, insisted on keeping his tobacco in an old Persian slipper, and when disconsolate might use our wainscoting for pistol practice. Nor was 'Scouty' the only odd character that Holmes occasionally assumed in his comprehensive survey of the criminal classes.

Some months later, as I was answering some delicate correspondence on a family matter[35] and was not pleased to be disturbed, our boy announced the arrival of Detective Inspector Bradstreet to see Sherlock Holmes. On being told that his quarry was not at home, he had instead requested to speak with me. I set my pen aside with a sigh and assented to meet the visitor.

---

35   Watson mentions in *A Study in Scarlet*, set in 1881, that he has "neither kith nor kin in England". In *The Sign of Four*, set in 1888, Holmes deduces from Watson's pocketwatch that Watson's father and brother are both dead, and observes the signs of the late brother's alcoholism.

W.S. Baring-Gold's biography *Sherlock Holmes* (1962) posits that in 1883 this brother was "penniless, and very ill, in San Francisco," and that Dr Watson took an extended visit there to nurse him. However, this reading requires an assumption that the conversation in *The Sign of Four* wherein Holmes deduces the late 'H.W.'s drinking habit is either transplanted from some other occasion or amended to ignore the detective's prior knowledge of why Watson might remove to America.

Holmes began to peel away the onionskin webbing that formed the base of his disguise.

Bradstreet was an old hand from E-Division of the Metropolitan Police,[36] and unlike his peers he preferred a policeman's uniform to the plain clothes worn by Scotland Yard investigators. He settled uncomfortably on the edge of one of our chairs, peaked officer's cap on his lap. "Do you have any idea how long Mr Holmes will be, Dr Watson?"

I apologised that I did not, and suggested that perhaps Bradstreet might return some other time.

The inspector did not take the hint. "There has been a murder," he revealed, as if that might induce me to conjure up Sherlock Holmes.

"Holmes comes and goes as he pleases," I pointed out. "He is a consultant, not bound to the beck and call of Scotland Yard or the Metropolitan Branches. You might leave a note for him."

"We need Holmes for this. It will interest him, and he would be unhappy if we did not call him in at once for a body found on the mudflats below London Bridge."[37]

"Do we not discover one or two unhappy souls who have taken their lives in the river every year?"

"That's true, and unpleasant work it is for the lighter-men who work the boat-taxis to have to fish such horrors out of the water. But this body had his throat cut from ear to ear and he didn't die quickly or pleasantly. Fortunately we were able to hook him up before the tide took him and washed him down the estuary. We were able to identify the corpse."

"You sound to have made significant progress by yourself. You know the victim."

"And Holmes will hopefully be able to tell us the murderer. He must help us discover who accomplished the death of the informer Scouty."

---

36   E Division of the Metropolitan Police covered the part of London around Holborn, centred upon Bow Street Magistrates Court (once famed for its proto-police force Bow Street Runners). Their "patch" covered the prestige homes of the West End to the poverty-stricken rookeries of St Giles and as such was one of the larger Divisions, and one given to intensive 'practical' policing.

        In "The Man With the Twisted Lip", *The Adventures of Sherlock Holmes* (1891), Bradstreet reveals that he has been a police officer since 1861. He would therefore have seen radical changes in the developing London force. Two years after he joined, as part of professionalising the service, some 215 officers were arrested for being intoxicated while on duty. He would have participated in the 1872 police strike, and served through the highly-publicised 1877 Old Bailey corruption trial of three high ranking detectives that led to the Detective Branch being reorganised as the Criminal Investigation Department (CID) and its separation from the uniformed branch.

37   London Bridge was also part of E Division's territory.

I hastened with Bradstreet back to the Thames bank mudflat on the city-side of London Bridge. I had not explained to him what I knew about the real identity of Scouty the Informant, but the E-Division veteran must have sensed my urgency, even my restrained panic. "The tide is rising but will not cover the site for another hour," he assured me. "That is why I need Mr Holmes to come now to view the scene."

But Holmes could not come—not if it was his disguised body that lay with a cut throat amongst the detritus of the river.

A pair of constables kept watch over the scene and kept back curious on-lookers. Bradstreet and I dragged on waders and squelched over the foetid mud to reach the corpse.

The inspector gestured to the lanky figure that lay face-down on the grey ooze. "Some mudlark urchins found it this morning as they searched for win-kles washed up by the tide. The body was then as you see it now, with the boots, weskit, and jacket missing, but they may have been stolen before the body was thrown into the river or after it washed to shore."

I checked the ground around for imprints. There were many, for the police had done a thorough job of clomping about; Holmes would have chided them for marring the scene. But already those heavy regulation boot-marks were melting away into the soft river-slime. Any earlier tracks would have already vanished.

"The river-men often find things washed up here," Bradstreet said. "Carcasses of animals quickly disappear to the meat markets, but this is also a favourite spot for suicides to float in."

It would have been helpful to determine if the body had been deposited as the tide still came in or began to go out; Holmes would have known, and from that have been able to estimate from which bridge or shoreline the corpse might have entered the Thames.

I braced myself and turned the cadaver. The head flopped unpleasantly, so deeply had the neck been cut. Only the spinal column and the flesh and mus-cle behind it remained to join it to the torso. The body was covered in welts and contusions; result of a peri-mortem beating with lead pipes or similar, and of assault with pliers and hot poker. The victim had been tortured before the end.

It was not Holmes. The morphology and silhouette were right, and the face resembled the slack countenance he effected in his Scouty persona, but there the similarity ended. This might have been Scouty's double, but it was not my dear friend.

So where was Holmes? How had his lookalike come to be here, dead by the water? "How did you identify the body?" I asked Bradstreet.

"Some of the crowd recognised him, and one of the constables. Scouty is a well-known figure in Cheapside."

And Cheapside was a five-minute walk from London Bridge, a quick jour-ney up King William Street and left by the Bank of England onto Poultry Street. "We must go to Mrs Degger's home," I realised. "She was Scouty's keeper, his managing agent."

Bradstreet saw my reasoning immediately. "If something has happened to him, she would know about it. Or else the same may have happened to her."

We hastened to the grimy courtyard behind Old Jewry. This time the grim brick square was deserted. The apple box throne was empty.

I realised that I was unsure which of the ten doors that opened into the cramped yard belonged to the Degger residence. I was about to explain as much to Bradstreet when one of them opened and Sherlock Holmes stuck his head out. "Watson! The very chap. I need you."

"Holmes!" I cried. "I had thought…"

"And you too, Bradstreet. Come in carefully. Murder has been committed here."

Mrs Degger was dead. Her body was laid out over her bed, the counterpane reddened with her blood. She too had suffered a slit throat.

"Her assailants came by night," Holmes interpreted the scene for us. "She was already in her nightdress and had retired—witness the heating stone in her bed and the position of the covers she shifted aside. She answered a knock-ing at the door, but first took up that bullwhip you see discarded in the corner there. Her visitors—there were at least two of them, though one may have been hiding himself when she opened the door, pushed their way in. She took a slash at one; you may see the edge of blood on the discarded crop. She was buffeted back, falling where the stool is upended, and she lost her weapon. She retreated towards the bed, where a straight-razor lies in a dresser drawer, but was captured before she could reach it. She was pinioned here, one man hold-ing her arms behind her, the other before her with a sharp blade, perhaps an American Jim Bowie knife or something of a similar configuration."

I knew that Holmes was reading blood spatters and body wounds. He had an uncomfortable gift. I was glad to see him alive to exercise it.

"Were they looking for Scouty, perhaps?" Bradstreet suggested. "You may not know, Mr Holmes, but…"

"I am aware of his murder, Inspector. Look at these signs. Scouty had a nest out there in the hall, in the boot-cupboard under the stairs. He preferred it so. Hearing the commotion of intrusion, he came out to see what was happening, leaving his closet ajar."

"He wore no coat or boots!" I realised.

"His arrival forced the intruders to a decision. They murdered Mrs Degger then and there so that they could fall upon and seize Scouty. He struggled, as witnessed by the broken china there and the smashed chair, but it was two to one and they had come prepared. He was overpowered and restrained—that was when he kicked over the coal scuttle and got smudges of coal dust across the floor to leave some tracks. The invaders secured him; one of them wore size 10 docker's boots with a more worn left heel. Scouty was dragged away, presumably to be questioned about what he had memorised."

"But he had learned nothing?" I blurted, confused. "Had he?"

Holmes did not reply just then. "You are looking for a left-handed Upper Thames bargeman of about five feet ten inches and weighing around twelve or thirteen stone," Holmes told Bradstreet. "The wear on the boot is indicative of that profession and the persistent use of a punting pole. A right-handed punter would have wear on the corresponding right boot. The height and bulk are estimated by the distance apart of the treads and the weight by how crushed the coal fragments are. The assailant may still have coal dust on his person, clothing, or soles. I suggest a canvas of the Embankment steps where the water-taxi men gather."

The Inspector nodded gravely. "I must report this and get some constables to the scene. The Chief must be told. Two murders linked together, it is a bad business and will command the public's attention."

"You know where to begin," Holmes told him. It was a dismissal.

When Bradstreet had hurried off I demanded more information from my friend. "Holmes, I thought you were Scouty. How then...?"

"How is my double now lying dead under London Bridge? Because I am a fool, Watson. There is no bigger fool than a clever one!"

I saw that he was distressed. "What has happened, then, Holmes? What error have you made?"

"The unfortunate imbecile who was dragged from here and interrogated was also Scouty. More precisely, he was the young man whom I impersonated when I took on the persona and pretended to be an idiot savant. When I played the role he could do those amazing feats of memory which made him of such utility. The rest of the time the poor lad was just what he seemed, a dullard of stunted intellect whom Mrs Degger looked after for kindness—and for a generous commission of my Scouty earnings."

"Then they dragged away and tortured a helpless ignoramus, a poor fool who could hardly speak and knew nothing of what they asked him?"

"I have underestimated my adversaries, Watson. In my cleverness I forgot that they might be cunning too. A secret message with vital criminal information might be as interesting to a rival villain as to the intended recipient."

"And such a rival came last night to beat that information from Scouty; but he found the other Scouty, not you."

"I might have survived the encounter." Holmes shook his head. "I must eliminate these miscalculations from my activities. But first the murders of

Scouty and Mrs Degger must be solved. The perpetrators must answer for their crimes."

If anyone could do it, I was confident my friend was that man. I said so.

"Not I," Holmes told me with a fey and deadly smile. "The man to capture them is poor foolish Scouty."

I entered the saloon bar[38] of the Hare & Hound in Hampstead with some trepidation. It was a sawdust-strewn bare-bones drinking house full of bare-knuckle drinking men, burly labourers and brawny pugilists who would not usually welcome a visit from a well-dressed former army officer. Before I even got to the bar a pair of large, unfriendly bruisers blocked my way.

"I'm looking for Mr O'Bannon," I told them.

"And what business has the likes of ye with Miles O'Bannon?"

"I need to speak with him about my patient."

That nonplussed the sentries. It was not amongst the usual responses they received. "I am a doctor in general practice," I explained. "Last night a man was brought to my door and abandoned there, a badly injured man who had been beaten and cut up. I treated him and quite possibly saved his life. But either the man is a congenital idiot or he has sustained a serious head wound in addition to his other woes. All he will say is 'Scouty,' and 'Mr O'Bannon, Hare and Hound, Hampstead.' Naturally I have come to see if this O'Bannon is some relative or friend who can identify the injured amnesiac."

"Scouty?" someone said. "They said as that feller were dead."

"Shut up," a darker voice growled. "Bring the cove this way, boys."

I was escorted somewhat roughly to a nook beside the hearth, where a gentleman dressed for a sporting event lounged with a pint of stout. He had a gaudy silk scarf in his top pocket and a prominent gold fob-watch. "I'm O'Bannon," he told me. "What's this about our Scouty?"

I told him the story that Holmes had rehearsed me on. Most of it was the truth; I was a retired military surgeon who did occasional locum work at a Kensington medical practice. Occasionally I was disturbed in the night by an emergency case that had been dragged to the surgery. But of course, I had not really had an illiterate informer dumped upon me. "All he says is your name," I told the sporting man.

"Well now, that's very interesting, Dr… Watson, was it? And this Scouty is at your house now, you say?"

---

38   Most Victorian public houses were divided into a saloon, for common customers, and a better-appointed lounge for "quality" visitors. Décor, prices, and service varied accordingly.

"He is in a hansom outside this very inn," I replied. "You know him, then?"

O'Bannon nodded to some of his fellow drinkers. "Bring him in, lads. Let's have a look-see."

Holmes was pushed into the pub in his guise as the unfortunate Scouty. In addition to his usual theatrical make-up he had applied a number of livid bruises, some scabs, and a gory throat wound under a realistically-blood-stained neckerchief. "Scouty!" he cried at the manhandling.

"Scouty, is it?" O'Bannon asked. "Well, you look the part, but let me ask you this. What's the message, Scouty?"

Holmes blinked confusedly.

"He had it yesterday, boss," someone advised O'Bannon. "He won't know it today, even if he hadn't been beaten."

"He'd better know it, for I need to be sure it's him! Scouty, look at me, lad. Think carefully. Edward, Peter, Stephen..." The sporting man paused in his prompt.

"Scouty. Edward, Peter, Stephen..." Holmes hesitated, then blurted out, "Oliver, Matthew, Lillian...!"

"That's enough!" O'Bannon cut him short. "That's him right enough, for that's the start o' yesterday's message.

"Edward, Peter, Stephen, Oliver..."

"For Mary's sake shut him up, will ye? He can't be blurting out his whole list here! Bring him with us."

"A moment," I objected. "I cannot leave this patient in your charge without much more information. Who is this man and why...?"

"Scouty! Scouty!" Holmes cried, reaching out in distress as he was parted from me.

"Bring 'em both in the back," O'Bannon sighed. "Then we'll sort this out. Finnegan, O'Marr, Murphy, Denny, with me. Rest of yez, as you were."

We were bustled into a small side-room where Scouty could be questioned more. My feigned protests were ignored.

"Now Scouty, my boy," O'Bannon told him, "There's a good lad. Can you tell us what happened to ye last night, and to old Ma Degger?"

Holmes made him repeat the question twice in different ways, then suddenly broke into a pantomime of the murder of Mrs Deggar, drawing upon his knowledge of the crime scene for verisimilitude.

"That's what was done, I reckon," one of O'Bannon's boys blurted out.

"And did ye see who done it, Scouty?" the sporting man continued. "Did you see a face you recognised?"

"Scouty," repeated the informant. But this time he pointed and swivelled round the room, spinning as if playing some children's choosing game that might end fingering any one of the men present.

"Someone in here?" O'Bannon asked suspiciously. "Someone who knew you had the numbers memorised and where to find you to get 'em out of yez?" His brow furrowed. "One of our own?"

Holmes had explained the code that Scouty had been given to memorise, a simple enough secret message which began with the capitals of each name: EPSOM was the first racecourse on the list, the Derby at which the most betting money changed hands. The next names mentioned the racehorses that had been fixed to be placed in the top three at each race. The same message went on to cover the meets at the Curragh Irish National, Royal Ascot, and the Northumberland Plate, all that same week.[39] Finally there were words which translated to a long stream of identification digits such as were used for making deposits into numbered private bank accounts.

As Holmes put it, "Scouty delivered his 'tips' to several places from which wagers could be laid, before the event and on-track. The unfair winnings were to be taken into town and deposited in the nominated account. Using Scouty ensured that the investor cartel behind the betting fraud remained anonymous."

"But someone got greedy," I guessed. "Someone else with the codes might get to the bank the next morning, proffer the correct identification string, empty out the whole account, and simply vanish with the cash. A great temptation for a mid-level bagman who had to watch his bosses profit while he received mere scraps."

Hence Holmes having me bring 'Scouty' to flush out the malefactors who had ambushed, interrogated, and finally murdered the messenger in their frustration. Justice must be observed.

Holmes's wavering finger passed more slowly over the men in the back room, as if he were about to identify the villain who had tortured him.

O'Marr's nerve broke. "No!" he cried, and reached into his pocket for a weapon.

"You b____d!" O'Bannon reacted, and cannoned into his colleague before he could pull out a blade. "You betraying b____d!"

There was a scuffle. Finnegan joined with O'Marr versus O'Bannon, Danny, and Murphy. Holmes and I shuffled to the side to avoid the violence. I found it satisfying to see these brutes savaging each other for once.

As for Scouty, he simply strode to the door and sounded a police whistle.

Inspector Bradstreet's men burst into the Hare & Hound, closing upon the drinkers from all quarters. Trust an experienced officer like Bradstreet to carry out a mass arrest at a drinking den. The wrestling sportsmen in the back-room were separated and overwhelmed by the constables.

---

39   This detail places the story in June, wherein all of these races are held, usually starting with the Derby on Epsom Downs on the first Friday.

O'Bannon was dragged out spitting and swearing. His silk handkerchief was spotted from his bloody nose.

"Him too!" O'Marr cried as Scouty came back into his view. "He was part of it!" But then, overwhelmed by the collapse of his plan else by superstition, he cried out, "A ghost! A ghost! Mother Mary and the saints, I never meant to do it!"

Holmes played his part to perfection. He unwrapped his gory neck-scarf, revealing the realistic wound of paste, wax, rouge, and ink that crossed his throat. Holmes had packed the scar tissue with a tiny bladder so that it oozed 'fresh blood' as he flexed.

"Scouty!" he cried accusingly at O'Marr. "Ma!"

Another fellow from the drinkers detained by the police tried to break for it. Bradstreet came down on him heavily, truncheon across the back of the knees, and the boatman with the size 10 boots was taken too.

"No!" O'Marr screamed at Holmes. "I killed you! I slit your throat! You went into the Thames! You was dead!"

Holmes abandoned his performance. "And there is your confession, Inspector," he told Bradstreet. "Two murderers, and the opening thread of an investigation into race-fixing and major gaming fraud. Match the account number to the bank quick enough and you can seize the money and trace the agents and investors who made deposits or withdrawals. Make good use of what is revealed, for it cost two lives to uncover it."

I knew that Holmes blamed himself for the murders. Though he disguised himself in many roles, he put his Scouty identity away and never assumed it again. O'Marr had indeed killed the illiterate informant.

THE END

THE ADVENTURE OF THE ABDUCTED BARD

A LIGHT DUSTING OF snow turned the soaring spires and gothic front-ages of Oxford's Colleges into fairy castles. Holmes and I crunched over Hythe Bridge from the railway station, over the desolate and icy Castle Mill Stream, and turned left into Walton Street. The University city was unfamiliar territory to me, but Holmes had spent two years in study at Christ Church.[40] We cut across Gloucester Green, and passed the Martyrs Memorial under the shadow of the Ashmolean Museum.

I struggled to keep up with my companion. Holmes's long strides betrayed his impatience to arrive at our destination. Across St Giles' lay the turreted bulk of Goneril College,[41] where we were greeted by a lodge porter and hastened to the Master's chambers.

"Mr Holmes," the Master greeted us, rising from his desk to shake hands. "And Dr Watson. Thank you for coming up from London so quickly." He introduced his colleagues, the College's Dean and Bursar, and a flustered-looking academic who was Reader in Elizabethan Manuscripts.

"Given the nature of the problem I felt I should come at once," Holmes replied.

"You come highly recommended from the Master of Christ Church. He said you had the sort of mind that comes along only a few times in a generation.

---

40   Holmes recounts his first detective case in his Oxford days to Watson in "The Adventure of the Gloria Scott" (*The Memoirs of Sherlock Holmes*, 1893). Sherlockian biographer W.S. Baring-Gould offers additional detail in *Sherlock Holmes* (1962), explaining that Holmes was studying mathematics at his father's behest with a view to becoming an en*gineer; th*at Holmes's encounter with fellow student Victor Trevor and his subsequent investigation of Trevor's problem convinced him to instead become a consulting detective; and that Holmes quit his studies after his second year against his father's wishes, to take up his new profession. Baring-Gould also postulates an acquaintance between Holmes and Christ Church don Charles Lutwidge Dodson, Lewis Caroll. According to this biography, Holmes later completed a course of study in science at Gonville and Caius College, Cambridge.

     Baring-Gould further suggests that Watson was educated at Melbourne College in Australia and makes a case for Watson's upbringing in the Antipodes, but there is no Canon evidence for this part of Watson's history.

41   Watsonian misdirection appears to be masking the identity of the academic institution he and Holmes visited. Given his description of the geography it was most likely either Balliol or St John's College, or possibly Trinity.

Your decision to leave your studies unfinished was a great loss to academia."

"My studies continue," the self-appointed consulting detective answered. "I elected to pursue them in a different manner in a secular venue."

The Master was forced to accept that, although it was clear to me that none of the dons in the room could really conceive of a study life outside the confines of their University.

Holmes had little time for pleasantries, though. "You have lost a manuscript," he said, "A manuscript of potentially great significance."

"A manuscript of substantial value," the Bursar answered, fretting. "And it is not lost, it is ransomed."

Holmes held up one long thin finger to stem the tide of indignation. "I would prefer to hear the facts presented in sequence in a logical and orderly fashion. One of you must bring to bear that academic regimen in which you are tutored and recount for me the case as it developed."

The Master nodded acknowledgement and gestured to the Dean to begin.

The Dean polished his spectacles and replaced them carefully. "Some three months ago, one of our alumni contacted the College in some excitement. He had recently been given the opportunity to examine his late grandfather's library, with a view to cataloguing it. Amongst the documents and papers there, misclassified as an 18th century pamphlet, were two pages of a 17th century folio, crudely printed, possibly as proof sheets, and an additional two of handwritten material, all stitched together with twine. The cover-sheet pronounced it to be *The History of Cardenio*, published in 1652 by Humphrey Moseley of The Prince's Arms, St Paul's Courtyard."

Holmes breathed in hard, like a man who has smelled his Sunday dinner about to be served.

"This *History of Cardenio* is held to be a lost play by William Shakespeare," I mentioned. Holmes had spoken of little save it on our train up from Paddington.

The Reader in Elizabethan Literature burst in with agitated footnotes. Dr Chadbury was a stick-thin scholar of advancing years, with huge bushy eyebrows that seemed to belong on a different face entirely. "It was attributed to Shakespeare and John Fletcher, one of the late collaborations like *Henry VIII* and *Two Noble Kinsmen*. But it is mentioned only once, in a 1653 entry in the Stationer's Register, reported there in assertion of ownership by the sometimes-unscrupulous Moseley."[42]

Holmes had also covered that in his lecture. "Moseley was a major printer at the time. He had already published several compilations of Shakespeare's works without the author's permission, and was not above padding out his

---

42   *The History of Cardenio* is known to have been performed in 1613 by the King's Men, a London theatre company. The 1653 Stationers' Register entry is the work's sole written attribution to William Shakespeare and John Fletcher.

"Your decision to leave your studies unfinished was a great loss to academia."

editions with works now thought to have been borrowed from other writers."

"Yes," Chadbury agreed. "But that was standard business practice in the day, it seems. Moseley was well-considered enough that his peers elected him Warden of the Stationer's Company in 1659. His imprint exists on three hundred and fourteen surviving editions, including the works of Francis Bacon, René Descartes, and the alchemist Robert Flood. It is possible—entirely possible—that he produced, or planned to produce, an issue of *Cardenio*, with or without sanction."

Holmes dismissed a century of academic debate in favour of the present narrative. "You were contacted by your former student," he prompted Chadbury.

"*I* was contacted," the Dean clarified. "Dr Chadbury was at that time visiting Salisbury to consult certain archives of relevance to his researches."

"I should never have left Oxford," Chadbury mourned. "This might never have happened."

"What happened, though?" Holmes demanded, as impatient as any senior wrangler with a derelict undergraduate.

The chastened Dean cleaned his spectacles again and carried on. "Our alumnus expressed a certain concern he had about his discovery. In the first place, he could not certainly verify it. The provenance seemed sound as best he could determine, but he freely admitted that he has not the scholarly expertise to determine if his find was actually what it seemed."

"He took History," Chadbury interjected, as if reporting a shameful deficiency. "He achieved a Second."

The Bursar chipped in. "A further complication was that the entire collection was now in the hands of his grandfather's heir, our scholar's uncle, who was somewhat indifferent to the library and was considering selling the whole of it to an American investor."

Chadbury shuddered. "The entire assemblage might be lost to British scholarship. And if the existence of the *Cardenio* was known, even suspected…"

"I gather that there is little love lost between our alumnus and his uncle," the Dean confessed. "Anyhow, the scholar undertook to borrow the document so that it could be properly examined here at the College. If the discovery was verified then some arrangement might be made to endow the manuscript here at Goneril; to purchase it if sufficient funds might be raised. But much depended on secrecy; one might admit to deception."

"Under such circumstances there is some justification for precautions," Holmes judged. "What arrangement was finally agreed upon?"

"A two-week loan," The Dean explained. "I don't believe the uncle ever really understood the agreement he made, or even glanced at the contract of indemnity. Conditions were laid upon the transportation of the *Cardenio*—if *Cardenio* it was. A guard was to be kept upon the item during transit. A special display stand was commissioned that might protect the manuscript from harm. Only certain named scholars would handle the document, under the supervision of Dr Chadbury himself."

"The manuscript arrived under guard yesterday?" I verified.

"Under escort," the Dean agreed. "We set the stand up in the Cresswell Library and the Master and I were present as the folio was locked into its case."

"Describe the item," Holmes instructed.

Dr Chadbury laid his head in his hands. He had been absent when the papers had arrived. They had gone before he returned. He might never now see the document that could have been the crown of his academic carer.

The Dean had made closest observation, since he had been signatory of the receipt that had included a description of the item's condition. "There were two printed sheets and two handwritten ones. The typeset ones were bifolia, two eighteen by seven inch pages printed side-by-side front and back, intended to be folded to make four pages of a book. The paper was fibre pulp, rather frayed and discoloured, with one corner of the top-sheet broken off and missing. The holographic paper was very faded and nigh illegible, but appeared to be a cast list."

"There is better detail in our scholar's correspondence," Dr Chadbury promised.

"You have been careful not to name your benefactor," Holmes observed.

The dons looked uncomfortable. "Anonymity was a part of the request," the Master answered for them at last. "As the Dean has said, there was a delicacy to the loan. Our graduate preferred to remain in the background lest he incur the wrath of his relative."

"It is relevant data and must be laid before me. You cannot expect me to untangle your affair blindfolded with my hands tied behind my back."

"That's fair," the Dean judged, glancing in consultation with his colleagues.

They assented to name their student, who had graduated two years earlier. "Mr John Clay is a grandson of the Earl of Montguerre, and it was his Grace's library collection wherein the manuscript was found," the Master told us.

"The old Earl was a dedicated bibliophile," Dr Chadbury added. "His son, the present peer, has shown no such interest."

"An agreement was made with Mr Clay and his Lordship, and the manuscript was delivered," Holmes summarised to continue the account. "What time yesterday was this?"

"About four in the afternoon," supplied the Dean. "The *Cardenio* travelled across from Hampshire. It was installed as required by five."

"And then?"

"There was a certain degree of furtive admiration through the glass top of the display case. At six, the cover was locked over the glass—I believe by the senior porter—and the Cresswell Library was closed."

"Locked?" Holmes checked.

"Yes. The Cresswell houses a number of rare exhibits. It is secured by our night staff. No-one could enter the room past the porter's desk without being seen or heard."

"When was the library reopened and the manuscript missed?"

"The Cresswell is unlocked at eight, although seldom used before ten. But on this occasion…"

"I was very eager to see the *Cardenio*," Dr Chadbury interjected. "I returned by the late train the night before and came down as soon as I could next morning to inspect the find. Except… it was gone."

"Was the case lock forced?" I enquired. "Or was a key used?"

"The key was still on the senior porter's fob," the Dean assured us, "but there was no sign of forced entry. The windows were sealed, wired closed for the winter. The door was still locked. But the manuscript was missing."

"A search was made," I supposed.

"Of course. That was when we found the note."

Holmes leaned forward.

The Master produced a folder and passed across a single sheet of bonded writing paper. Inscribed upon it in good penmanship was the message:

'I have your *Cardenio*. Except it is not yours, and when its loss is discovered it will bring disgrace upon Goneril and financial ruin. Who will afterwards trust your stewardship or value your scholarship? There will be scandal. There will be litigation. Imagine the response of the broadsheets and the good name of the College dragged through the mire.

'I have your *Cardenio*. It is nothing to me whether it survives or not. I might burn it at a whim, or return it shredded to prove its destruction. I consider it sport to threaten the loss of such a literary treasure. Unless I am diverted from my ends I will be pleased to deprive the world of the Bard's lost work.

'I have your *Cardenio*. Though I might dispose of it to unscrupulous collectors for a small fortune I am minded instead to hold it against the College's future co-operation. For the moment I shall expect a daily fee, a retainer to preserve the work in good condition. Five hundred guineas is a good start. You will tape the bag near the base of the Martyrs Memorial beneath the statue of Hugh Latimer. Deliver the fee by noon today. Keep no watch.

'I have your *Cardenio*. I have your hopes, your futures, your academic and financial wellbeing, your whole lives at my disposal. I am without scruple and disposed to vindictiveness. I urge you not to test my capacities, for I own an excellent box of matches.

'I have your *Cardenio*. You shall hear from me again forthwith.'

"Well," I breathed, "that's an unpleasant sort of missive."

"Where did you come by this paper?" Sherlock Holmes asked.

"There is a cupboard in the pedestal of the document case. This was on the upper shelf," the Bursar told us.

"You paid the ransom?" I asked. "Or at least an instalment of it?"

"What else could we do?" The Master despaired. "But five hundred pounds—even that is a large sum to render at such short notice."

"Was a watch actually kept?" The tall memorial[43] is in one of the most public spots in Oxford, overlooked by Balliol, the Taylorian[44] and many other buildings. At midday it is an important meeting point and junction, whatever the weather.

"A judicious eye was kept from a safe distance," the Dean admitted. "The bag was taken up by a rough-looking tramp of a fellow. He shuffled off with it along Beaumont Street, turned right into St John Street, and vanished in the warren of back alleys off there."

Holmes took a description, but it might have fitted any itinerant beggar. Nor could we be confident that this scruffy fellow was anything but what he seemed, employed for a few shillings to deliver the bag to some other party.

"We proved to the thief that we are tractable to his demands," the Bursar grumbled gloomily. Evidently there had been previous debate upon the point.

The Dean was evidently of the contrary camp. "We yielded to allow us time to think, to consider our next course."

"And that course is you, Mr Holmes," Dr Chadbury concluded.

"We are rather desperate," the Master continued. "If you would name your fee..."

"Pecuniary matters are trivial," Holmes rejoined. "What is money compared to the possibility of another fragment of Shakespeare?"

I have noted my friend's usual indifference to literature and the arts, but

---

43   The gothic memorial was raised to completion in 1843 to commemorate the 'Oxford Martyrs' Hugh Latimer, Bishop of Worcester, and Nicholas Ridley, Bishop of London, who were burned to death nearby for their Protestant faith on 16th October 1555, and Thomas Cramner, Archbishop of Canterbury, who was executed shortly after.

        The edifice closely resembles the peak of a church spire, and for much of the early 20th century Oxford undergraduates were pleased to inform tourists that it was the top of a sunken underground cathedral and to accept small fees to allow access below through a nearby staircase entrance; these steps actually lead to a Victorian public toilet.

44   The Taylor Institute is the Oxford University library for European Languages, established in 1845.

there are certain exceptions about which he feels passionately. He is entranced by the female soprano,[45] by the well-played violin—and by the plays of the Bard of Avon. Indeed, he was intimately familiar with the works of Shakespeare, having performed several of them on stage during an eccentric youthful tour with a theatrical troupe.[46]

"Of what value is the missing material?" I wondered. "I mean, what would it sell for at auction?"

"It is priceless," Chadbury insisted.

The Bursar looked a little sick. "Some two hundred or more copies still exist of seven hundred and fifty editions of Shakespeare's First Folio, issued in 1623, seven years after the playwright's death. When new they sold for the princely sum of one pound. Now they are exchanged for more than a hundred and seventy thousand."[47]

"A unique item such as the *Cardenio* might fetch a lot more," the Master added disconsolately.

"But would be very traceable," Holmes pondered. "Yet that does not seem to be the motive of our villain. Or not his only motive." He pressed his index fingers together as he thought. "There is more to discover. 'The play's the thing…'"

The Cresswell Library was a small annex beyond the larger repository, reserved for post-graduate study and as a display room for rare books.

Holmes halted us at the door. He took time to examine the lock and hinges of the library entrance, even kneeling to study the scuffed worn floorboards. The Dean and Dr Chadbury had escorted us to the scene of the mystery; now they stood uncomfortably with nothing to do while Holmes shuffled about without explanation.

"There may be signs of illicit entry," I offered explanation. "Holmes has made a scientific study of the marks of burglary: scratches on the tumblers, oil-spots around the keyhole, that kind of thing."

Holmes snorted at my inexpert witness. "There are few signs that can help

---

45   One such performer was the gifted and notorious Mme. Irene Adler—the Woman.

46   Baring-Gould suggests that Holmes toured America as part of Sassinoff's Troupe in 1878-80, and that "his Malvolio offered the most adequate presentation of that character that America had ever seen up to that time." This tour may account for Holmes' occasional Canon reminiscences of the United States and for his knowledge of its people and customs.

47   In 2020, Christie's of New York auctioned such a folio for $9.9 million.

us. Any useful evidence has now been destroyed by the passage of many visitors." He looked up at the Dean. "Your domestic staff are to be commended. They have wax-polished this floor quite thoroughly. Had I been called in at once when the manuscript vanished I might have read from this floor whether anyone had crossed it after that night's domestic work was done. As it is, a day later, such traces are useless. Nor has any mark been left on the lock; I would not have expected a real professional to do so."

He rose and ventured into the library. The room had but one exit and was lit from the east by five tall mullioned windows with ancient leads and coats of arms, presumably of the Cresswell benefactor who had endowed the College. A series of glass-topped display cases were positioned out of direct sunlight. Three long study tables were set out centrally, with desks against the far wall. A huge early fireplace dominated the rear of the chamber, but only a smaller, more modern grate lighted the wide hearth.

I saw at once the lectern that had previously housed the stolen document. It stood in pride of place between two of the windows, a heavy mahogany stand some four feet high, topped with a wide box. The protective security flap had been folded back to reveal a glazed interior cover.

"The stand is specially made," the Dean assured us. "It looks to be wooden, but the upper compartment is actually protected by steel plate. The base is weighted with concealed lead to make it too heavy to be easily manhandled away. The lock that holds the solid top-flap in place overnight is specially designed and is supposedly thief-proof."

Holmes examined the furniture, taking special interest in the cupboard in the pedestal. A simple hinged front allowed access to a small interior space, too little for anyone to hide in, with a single shelf dividing it. The upper level was where the unpleasant note had been discovered after the theft.

"The ransom demand," Holmes checked, "how was it laid out here? Foursquare, or simply as if it had been tossed in anyhow?"

The Dean frowned to remember. "It was the Bursar who discovered it," he recalled. "I believe it was stood up on one end, as if leaned on the back panel."

Holmes nodded, apparently satisfied. He crouched right inside the cupboard and called for a light to inspect it by. Then he opened the glass top and rummaged around the velvet-lined display box.

"When the manuscript vanished, I called the manufacturer," the Dean assured us. "I wanted to know if some duplicate key existed that might have been used to access the lectern. They claim not. Indeed, they sent one of their craftsmen down to check that nothing had been tampered with."

"Who was the manufacturer?" I asked.

Holmes tapped a discrete brass nameplate on the interior side of the cupboard door, engraved with the name 'A. Fischer and Sons'. "Albert Fischer is a well-known quality cabinet-maker on Cornwall Road off Waterloo," he instructed me. "He is the shopfitter of choice for many of the superior London establishments, and his cabinetry is also used by the British Museum and Library." He paused for a moment before adding, "I might have expected better tenon and mortise work from him, though."

"You have discovered something, Holmes?" I ventured.

"When was this furniture delivered?" my friend asked the Dean.

"The day before the manuscript arrived—that is three days since. I'd need to ask the chief porter for details."

I looked more carefully at the lectern, suddenly suspicious. "Are you saying that this is not Fischer's work?" I checked. "That this is another cabinet—the wrong cabinet?"

"A thief substituted the real display case for a facsimile!" Dr Chadbury exclaimed in outraged tones. "The delivery was somehow thwarted and a different lectern brought to Goneril—one for which the thief had the key!"

"That is certainly a conclusion that our adversary would wish us to make," Holmes scolded the scholar. "Let us, however, consider all the evidence before postulating a theory."

Chastened, Chadbury fell silent as Holmes grubbed around the floor at the base of the cabinet. "There are water stains here," he said aloud.

That did not lead me to any immediate deductions. "How would water come to be spilled in this place?"

Holmes brought his magnifier to bear, following minute traces on the base of the polished lectern and damp patches on the carpet beneath. "Not spilled. Trickled."

The Dean shook his head in perplexity.

"You are not following," Holmes understood. "Find me a stack of papers, as like in size and shape to the missing manuscripts as you can. And also two small plugs of blotting paper from the side-desk there."

We hastened to obey, and watched as Holmes fumbled about in the cupboard for a few moments with the screwed up scraps of blotter. Eventually he rose, closed the lower cabinet, and laid our facsimile documents in their place under the glass.

"Fasten and lock the top, Watson," he instructed me.

I did as requested, then stepped back.

"I cannot adequately demonstrate the full method of this. We lack the time," Holmes told us. He opened the cupboard again and invited each of us to stick our heads inside and look up at the small tabs of folded blotting paper he had wedged into holes at either side of the rear of the compartment.

I took my turn. Holmes's strange additions were mere twists of sugar-paper no larger or thicker than a child's fingertip, lodged like pegs in circular indentations I had not previously noted.

"You must imagine," the detective told us, "that those wedges are not paper, but actually made of ice. Ice that gradually melted over the course of the day since their installation, trickling down and leaving the minor traces on base and carpet that I have just discovered. Eventually, when both plugs were fully gone, this would happen."

Holmes removed the blotter-rolls. Something moved inside the cabinet. We all heard it.

"Look for your papers," Holmes instructed me. I unsealed the top and peered through the display glass. The sheets we had laid there were gone.

"Some concealed mechanism?" the Dean blurted.

"Indeed." Holmes obligingly demonstrated his discovery. "Look carefully. When the ice-pegs melted, this section of the top-box hinged down under its own weight. The papers that lay atop the velvet slid down as if on a chute, vanishing through this slot at the rear of the pedestal. There is a concealed section a mere inch deep behind this cupboard, and that was where they fell. At the same time, a hidden note was released into the cupboard proper, to drop down at the rear of the upper shelf. That was how the ransom letter was delivered. There was a third, larger plug of ice here at the front. When that finally melted, perhaps an hour or two later, a counterweight drew the trap-door back to its horizontal position and a small snap-latch secured it there permanently."

"No burglar was required!" I ejaculated. "The whole thing was done automatically with cunning machinery and chips of ice!"

"Then… the document is surely not lost, but hidden in the compartment of which you spoke!" Dr Chadbury exclaimed hopefully.

"It may be," Holmes answered him, "but I suspect not. Dean, when you contacted Fischers' about the key, they expressed sufficient concern that they sent a man down to inspect their cabinet yesterday. To what address did you wire your request?"

"The… the workshop address on the delivery sales docket," the pale-faced don answered, recognising his error. "The receipt said to use that contact in case of concerns."

"The fellow they sent… He was from the rogue outfit who supplied this rogue contraption!" I realised.

"And thus he was well-positioned to inspect the cabinet and extract the vanished manuscript as he looked the lectern over," Holmes suggested. "But we can easily check. Here is the hidden catch that releases the cupboard back-board. And here, behind this panel, the blank papers of our recent experiment. But no *Cardenio*."

"It was taken later," Dr Chadbury raged. "From right under our noses!"

"But it was taken," the Dean mourned. "He has our *Cardenio*, as he boasted. What ever shall we do now?"

Despite the lengthening of the day, Holmes did not linger in Oxford but instead took the Great Western Railway straight back to London,

"You are eager to begin the hunt, Holmes," I observed. I was pleased to see my friend distracted from the morphine bottle and the cocaine syringe.

He looked up from John Clay's notes about the find in the Earl's library, as if surprised that anyone sat in the carriage compartment with him. "Either this is a fascinating forgery or a remarkable discovery. Do we have a hoax of Irelandian proportions, a revenge like Hamlet's, or a genuine revelation of undiscovered work from the world's finest author? Any would be worthy of study, but of course one must hope for the latter."

"You think the thief may have stolen a fake?"

"Men have deluded themselves before with fool's gold, Watson. The Samuel and William-Henry Ireland Affair of spring 1795 proved that. Did not the greatest literary men of the age gather at the home of the antiquarian Ireland to examine the Shakespearean documents he claimed to have unearthed? James Boswell, Samuel Johnson's biographer, was amongst those present who examined the proffered papers and considered them genuine, including the previously unheard-of play *Vortigen and Rowena*.[48] Poet laureate Henry James Pye declared them genuine. Francis Webb, then-secretary of the College of Heralds pronounced that the play either came from Shakespeare's pen or from heaven."

"It proved to be neither," I surmised.

"It proved to be the work of Samuel Ireland's nineteen-year-old son William-Henry—but not until many professional reputations were ruined. The bloom came off the rose at a debut performance of *Vortigen* in the West End, where the audience were moved to revolt and the critics to derision. Eventually the work and all the accompanying correspondence, poems, and drawings were proved to be forgeries. Ireland junior confessed all."[49]

---

48   Vortigen was a 5th century English warlord, recorded by Geoffrey of Monmouth as the King of England and as a usurper tyrant. His marriage to the Saxon princess Rowena opened the way for the Saxon and Angle invasions and occupations of southern Britain. Vortigen is best remembered now for his early part in the story of Kings Uther and Arthur Pendragon and for his unfortunate encounter with the youthful Merlin.

49   In the 1790s, author and engraver Samuel Ireland claimed his son's discovery of four Shakespeare manuscripts, two of them of previously unknown plays. Respected literary figures such as James Boswell and poet laureate Henry James Pye indeed pronounced them genuine. Influential theatre manager Richard Brinsley Sheridan arranged to present one of the new

"Surely expert examination of the documents would have exposed the fraud immediately?"

"It was an age before forensic investigation, doctor. And young William-Henry had been quite clever. He had cut and reused the blank fly-leaves from books of appropriate age. He used specially-mixed ink, which when heated over a fire took on a convincing brown colouration like authentic aged iron-gall ink. He rehearsed his penmanship until he was perfect. And he was clever enough to provide a scattering of authenticating papers and original errors to help sell the illusion."[50]

"Such a thing would not pass today, though," I insisted.

"You would be shocked and appalled by the extent," Holmes warned me. "When collectors will pay massive sums for rare manuscripts there is every incentive for the cunning artificer to take trouble in creating such things. Our chemistry is now better at discerning the age and composition of paper—there are tests to determine whether modern rag was used in the mix—and of breaking down the composition and age of inks, but the checks are not infallible. There has been considerable study of the calligraphy of forgeries also; I am considering a monograph upon the subject. The slant of the character, the crush of pen on paper, the quality and spacing of the lines can all be telling. But the detection of literary fakes remains an art, not a science."

"You only have John Clay's initial reports and observations to go on."

"Yes. He conducted as thorough an examination of paper, ink, and script as one might hope from an amateur, but one must rely upon his observations as accurate. He likewise examined the provenance of the papers in the Earl's collection as best he might, given his resources. His reports are through and coherent, belying the poor showing he made at his Finals."

---

works with John Philip Kemble in the starring role, but the unimpressed audience at the debut performance of *Vortigern and Rowena* responded with raucous mocking laugher. Then Edmond Malone, widely regarded as the greatest Shakespeare scholar of his time, published a four hundred-page exposé that conclusively showed that the language, orthography, and handwriting were not those of the times and persons to which they were credited. William-Henry Ireland, the supposed discoverer, then confessed to the fraud, admitting his own authorship of the fakes; scandal and acrimony followed, with disputes continuing for a generation. The documents now reside in Harvard's Houghton Library.

50   After eventual exposure, William-Henry Ireland shamelessly continued to exploit his forgeries in extra-illustrated printed confessions, incorporating copies of selected forgeries along with other materials, "aimed not to deceive, but rather to provide entertaining fare for bibliophile collectors." *Miscellaneous Papers and Legal Instruments under the Hand and Seal of William Shakespeare...* (1796), is interleaved with mounted forgeries of the complete *King Lear*, a small fragment of *Hamlet*, and an assortment of forged letters and documents. *The Confessions of William Henry Ireland: Containing the Particulars of his Fabrications of the Shakespeare Manuscripts...*(1805) includes manuscript sheet music for songs from *Vortigern and Rowena*.

"Does he speak of the contents of the manuscripts?"

"Not much. He was wise enough to recognise the extreme fragility of the materials and not to try and separate the chap-book without expert intervention. Hence we only have the front and back pages to consider. The first is a frontispiece announcing the name of the play, publisher, and authors—'Mr Fletcher & Shakespeare', and featuring a fine engraving of the presumed protagonist and his inamorata. The rear of the bundle is the obverse of the hand-written notes, which Clay posits as a foul paper for the play."

I was not familiar with the term 'foul paper'. Holmes instructed me that it was an Elizabethan writer's term for a first-draft hand-written copy, as opposed to a fair copy written out in a clean clear hand without additional corrections or abbreviations. Very few examples of foul papers from that period are now extant.[51]

"Clay is hardly an expert in this field, however," Holmes cautioned. "His assertion of authenticity is no guarantee of veracity."

"So this History of *Cardenio* may well be spurious."

"Its theft is convenient," Holmes suggested. "It at once intensifies interest in the find and denies the opportunity to verify it."

"You cannot think the Earl or his nephew might perpetrate such a fraud."

"There are many crimes committed in the drawing-rooms of the rich and powerful, Watson. But we need not yet impute such deeds to his Lordship or his kin. The History of *Cardenio* may have lain unregarded in the late Earl's collection for many years, bought in with some job-lot or another and never recognised until Mr Clay's recent appraisal. It may have been purchased in good faith, either by old Montguerre or by whomever he acquired it from. This may not be a recent fraud but an historic one, dating back to the time when every forger aspired to be another Ossian."[52]

"You also mentioned revenge," I prompted Holmes. "It is certain that the manuscript theft has put the whole College foundation under a shadow."

---

51   One such example from *Folger Shakespeare Library* Ms.J.b.8, containing lines from Christopher Marlowe's *The Massacre at Paris* (1593), is reproduced at https://en.wikipedia.org/wiki/Foul_papers#/media/File:Handwriting-Marlowe-Massacre-1.JPG

52   From *Fragments of ancient poetry, collected in the Highlands of Scotland, and translated from the Gaelic or Erse language* (1760) to *The Works of Ossian* (1765), Scottish poet James MacPherson published the English-language text of purported works of an early Gaelic bard named Ossian, son of Finn MacCool. These texts, supposedly gathered from native folk-accounts, were later believed to have been almost entirely fabricated by MacPherson himself. Samuel Johnson condemned him as "a mountebank, a liar, and a fraud... the poems were forgeries" and dismissed the story of Ossian as "as gross an imposition as ever the world was troubled with." By Holmes's era, Ossian was generally dismissed as a work of 18th century fiction. Some 20th and 21st century scholars prefer to argue for authenticity in MacPherson's source material. Experts continue to publish on the matter and apparently nothing can stop them.

"I am intrigued by our thief's monograph to Goneril," Holmes owned. "Whether intended to divert our understandings of motive from pecuniary to personal, or as an actual act of malice, twisting the knife, it is a singular feature. Few robbers leave well-penned notes in good English outlining their intentions."

"I know that you can read much from a man's writing."

"Indubitably. But in this case my reading is that the correspondent has gone to some trouble to conceal his nature by disguising his script. He would have me think him a man educated some fifty years ago, taught his cursives on the old school, tutored in childhood with an old-fashioned quill and retaining those habits into the era of the fountain-pen. It is a masterclass in deception, and I doubt many would have seen through it to question its veracity."

"A forger might attempt such a dissembling. But that returns to the unlikelihood of a peer of the realm perpetrating such a fraud."

"If the document cabinet could be intercepted en route and substituted, then so might the manuscript," Holmes pointed out. "There are several possibilities. It is too early to draw conclusions. But if revenge is the issue, the choice of forged manuscript is telling."

"How so?" I was unfamiliar with the background of *The History Of Cardenio*.

"Shakespearean scholars remain ignorant of the nature of the supposed lost play," my thespian comrade instructed me. "The other unknown play listed in the same early source is *Love's Labours Won*, which might be presumed to be a sequel, or at least bear some relationship to *Love's Labours Lost*, a play that has come down to us in the First Folio. But nothing in the early literature gives any clue as to the content of *Cardenio*."

"Another reason why even a few sheets of the text might be invaluable," I supposed.

"A simple cast list would make and break scholarly theories. There is only one other known instance of a literary character named *Cardenio*, a relatively minor player in Miguel de Cervantes's *Don Quixote*. The first part of that work was published in English in 1612. Shakespeare's collaborator Fletcher made use of Cervantes in several of his later plays. Scholarship favours Quixote as the source of the lost play, and that would present some basic idea of the plot."

"It is about revenge?"

"Quixote and Sancho Panza encounter the ragged mountain madman Cardenio and hear an account of the events that led to his condition. Cardenio was to wed his true-love, but was betrayed by his rich friend who also desired her despite having contracted to wed a girl he had previously violated. Cardenio's heroine was to enter a forced marriage but planned suicide. Cardenio went to interrupt the marriage but fainted when the bride relented and said 'I do'."

"And then it got bloody," I assumed.

"No. Cervantes' version ends with unlikely happiness, when the bride flees to find and rejoin the madman and the rich friend relents and weds his ravished previous love. It is a comedy."

I ventured that the subject matter did not appear that humorous to me.

"There is little amusing about this entire plot," Holmes brooded, staring out of the train window at the Oxfordshire countryside. "A stolen Shakespeare work is not funny. A literary hoax is not amusing. Our perpetrator, whatever he has actually perpetrated, thinks himself insouciant and clever. The jest does not sit well with me."

I have seen Holmes be cordial with murderers whose methods he has admired, but against the thief of *The History of Cardenio* he showed no such signs of mercy.

It was past ten in the evening when we emerged from the station onto Praed Street, our collars turned up against the new flakes of snow that were attempting to improve the grime of London. I had expected us to return to our quarters until we could make visits in the morning, perhaps beginning with the cabineter Fischer. Holmes had other ideas.

"There are some places and people we can only visit at this hour or later," he assured me as he directed our cabbie towards Shoreditch.

Holmes has a comprehensive knowledge of the back-alleys of our capital. I do not. I was lost less than two minutes into our foray on foot from Great Eastern Street. Either the Borough of Hackney does not spend its income on street signs or the residents of that parish delight in removing them.

We passed under several old brick arches, through grimy courtyards that looked like they had not changed much since Jacobean times, spaces filled with old rotting barrels and collapsed carts and piles of stinking refuse. A couple of times Holmes turned and carefully lifted his walking cane as if signing to someone whom I did not see. I confess that I was concerned about footpads and wished that I had been able to go home and retrieve my bull-terrier and my service revolver.

We eventually arrived at a worn staircase down to an anonymous cellar entrance. Holmes rapped upon the heavy door, an odd tattoo that might have been a code. A small hatch opened in the upper panel, and shortly afterwards the portal was unbolted to admit us.

It was the nest at the heart of the rookery. Stacked under the low barrel-roof were crate after crate of tangled clothing and building materials, china jars and piled furniture. A narrow passage through the detritus led us to a vast, cluttered desk lit by an old oil lamp, and the Dickensian character who

It was past ten in the evening when we emerged from the station onto Praed Street.

crouched behind it.

The ugly bruiser who had opened the door padded behind us, too quiet for my liking.

"Mr Shaddock," Holmes greeted the sparse-haired, hook-nosed creature who awaited us.

"Mr Holmes," our host responded. "You has done me the honour of coming in your own persona tonight."

"I'm hoping this need not be a visit regarding the disappearance of a re-mover's wagon of goods destined for Rosebery Avenue, or the contents of the Clerkenwell Cricket Club's trophy cabinet," my friend replied. "I have come tonight seeking information."

"I don't peach to the coppers, Mr Holmes. You knows that."

"Nor am I a member of Her Majesty's constabulary. They would not be al-lowed to offer you a one pound banknote for your valuable assistance."

Shaddock settled back. He stretched out a booted foot and nudged a rancid old tomcat off the chair opposite so that Holmes could sit. There was no third seat so I took station to Holmes's left, where I could keep an eye on the door-man to his right.

"If I wished to dispose of a valuable historic manuscript that had been ac-quired by unscrupulous means, whom would I best approach at the moment?" my companion asked. "Old Granger? Peacock and Stone? The Chinaman? Meadowlark is out of the country just now, and Pullen is incarcerated."

"What period?" Shaddock asked carefully.

"Elizabethan. Ah, I see by your attempts to conceal your reaction that you know of the item to which I refer."

"I never said nothing like that."

"Come now, Shaddock. You would prefer to deflect my professional atten-tion. I would prefer to get on with my present investigation. Let us collaborate."

There was more to-and-fro, more evidence that my friend could do ir-reparable damage to the goods-fence's business and possibly his liberty, and eventually the old rogue had to submit.

"As it happens, Mr Holmes, I am aware of such an item being offered for sale. Well, not for sale, exactly. For auction."

"What do you mean?" I blurted, though I'd intended to stay out of it. I was picturing some dark room filled with criminals each holding up a numbered card to bid as the stolen *Cardenio* was demonstrated.

"A sealed-bid sale," Shaddock clarified. "Each of the men Mr Holmes just named and a few others will contact their clients, the ones they know has a special interest in items of this type. The one as will pay most, they'll write his blind bid in a sealed envelope. When the bids are opened, the winning middle-man will pay the promised sum and pass the manuscript on to their principal—with a handsome surcharge."

"None of the bidders are ever in the same room," Holmes told me. "None of them are known to the others. Their clients remain completely anonymous. What is the deadline for bids, Mr Shaddock?"

"Nine p.m. tomorrow," the fence admitted.

"And how may additional bids be entered?"

Shaddock evidently considered denying that knowledge, but under the perceptive gaze of Sherlock Holmes his nerve faltered. He confessed that he was the agent to whom each of the bids was to be sent.

Holmes secured agreement for the College to make an offer to regain its stolen goods. Since the item was not on the premises and never would be, and there was no evidence that might secure any conviction, we accepted reality and took our leave.

"You knew he would be involved," I accused my friend as we departed that Aladdin's cave.[53] "That was why you came here."

"Shaddock was the most likely to be broker," Holmes agreed. He had us stand in a shadowed alcove where we might watch the old fence's door for a time. "If not him then Granger. Shaddock does not have the rich contacts to bring in the high-bidders on a stolen manuscript, but he is trusted by the men who do. Someone has been doing their homework, Watson."

"The thief has no intention of returning the document to Goneril College. Or of destroying it."

"The thief is playing a complicated and dangerous game. Entertain the possibility that the *Cardenio* manuscript is and has always been a forgery. Why forge one copy of the document only? Why not make six or eight identical duplicates, impossible to tell apart because they were all made by the same hand at the same time? Why not let each auction bidder believe that he and none other submitted the winning blind bid—and sell a fake to all of them?"

"The winner—or winners—would conceal their ownership of the stolen document. No other bidder would ever know of the multiple successes. And even if they did, what recourse would they have when they were knowingly purchasing purloined goods?"

"*Caveat emptor*," Holmes agreed with me. "Of course, that is speculation, but a possibility worth a little trouble to verify."

---

53   The tale of Aladdin from *'Alf Laylah wa-Laylah*, the Arabic corpus of Middle Eastern folk tales compiled during the Islamic Golden Age, was first introduced to European readers in *Les Mille et une nuits, contes arabes traduits en français* (1707-1717, 12 volumes) and was popularised in Britain in Edward Lane's *One Thousand and One Nights* (1840). However, Watson is likely to have picked up John Payne's *The Book of the Thousand Nights and One Night* (1882, nine volumes) or Sir Richard Francis Burton's *The Book of the Thousand Nights and a Night* (1885, ten volumes), which were much in vogue in the latter part of the Victorian era and influenced a fashion for Turkish and Arabic art, fictional settings, and architecture.

"We do not have long to do so," I pointed out. The sealed bids would be opened in less than twenty-four hours.

"We must hurry. I shall... ah, excuse me a moment, Watson." He paused and turned to address the shadows of the alley behind us. "I am Sherlock Holmes. My companion and I are armed and well able to defend ourselves, using lethal force if required. I suggest that you leave off your inept pursuit and find other more productive means of income. In any case I would be obliged if you either come out now and make your futile attempt to assail us or else go away and cease to bother me."

He waited a short while to meet any response to his challenge, but none ever came. Eventually we went home.

I slept later than I had planned the following morning, but Holmes had clearly been awake for hours. Mrs Hudson had already supplied a second rack of toast and another plate of breakfast meats.

I staggered yawning towards the table and only then became aware that Holmes was conferring with our houseboy Billy, receiving messages and sending others.

"What are you up to?" I asked our young page.

"Telegrams an' favours," he replied.

"Urgent ones," Holmes impressed on the lad, dispensing him a rasher of bacon to reward him for his efforts so far and to see him on his way.

Billy clattered out, earning a reprimand from our landlady on the stairs. I settled behind a plate of scrambled eggs and kedgeree and enquired again as to Holmes's doings.

"I have been gathering my evidence," Holmes announced as if lecturing at the Royal Society. "No single point is conclusive, but together they are suggestive."

I saw the pile of telegram message papers discarded beside his chair, and a number of Holmes's big clipping files opened on an adjacent buffet.

"I have borrowed sales ledgers from A. Fischer and Sons of Waterloo," the detective told me. "The signature commissioning the Cabinet was the Dean's, as was the note of hand that outlined the agreed specifications for the loaned document. Those specifications were for a robust lectern of the kind eventually delivered, identical in measurements, but not one of such mechanical cunning."

"That's how the case was substituted, then," I recognised.

"Another letter was received at Fischer's, in a hand very like the Dean's and signed in his name, directing the new cabinet be delivered to a different address, at a furniture shop in Headington, a few miles from Oxford proper. The cabinet was received there and duly paid for, cash upon receipt. I have just received a wire back from the proprietor of that establishment, informing me that a gentleman paid for him to take delivery of the item and store it until called for."

"Can he describe the gentleman?"

"Billy is dispatching my supplementary enquiry even now, along with another seeking a better description from a carter in Aylesbury who hired his cart and team to a carpenter's work-crew to deliver some furniture to Oxford on the day that the false cabinet was delivered. A special hire-fee was paid because it was supposedly an urgent job."

"The thief had to have accomplices."

"The sheer weight of the cabinet would require that, yes. I will be interested if the descriptions of the diligent carpenter and the Headington gentleman match up with that of Fischer's supposed craftsman who examined the 'emptied' case. Meanwhile..." he handed me another note.

"The thief has contacted the College again! Or is he a blackmailer?"

The letter had evidently arrived at Goneril with the last post yesterday, and the Dean had forwarded it hastily with the first collection today, which meant that by eleven it was on our doormat. I scanned the contents of the new message, written in the same neat hand as before on the same bonded paper.

'I still have your *Cardenio*, your reputations, and your College's future. Another £500 proffered by noon in the same way as before will stay my malice for another while, but we must consider what is going to become of Goneril and the manuscript in the longer term. What of the word and bond offered to poor Montguerre? What of the academic liabilities? What of the treasure you are like to lose?

'I have your *Cardenio*. Further instructions will follow.'

"This fellow is decidedly unpleasant and a gloater to boot," I commented.

"Do not underestimate the value of gloating, Watson. It is that flaw which has caused the downfall of many a malefactor. Indeed, this second missive with its triumphal tone helps confirm the solution to our mystery. No, pray do not ask me yet to unfold the story. You know I prefer to have my solutions neatly assembled before presentation."

"Very well, Holmes. You have your methods. May I at least enquire about your other messages this morning?"

My breakfast companion gestured to the papers under the sugar basin. "Some financial and biographical material on the main people associated with the case. A few theses from the Goneril College archives, couriered up overnight. Opinion from a couple of the best forgers I know, men at the top of their profession, on what would be required to create a credible Shakespearean facsimile."

"Forgers? Holmes!"

"I have had some strange apprenticeships to develop my clinical skills, doctor. You had to cut open cadavers. I had to make other experiments no less unpleasant. Anyhow, I am now more confident in the likely way that any forgery might be made."

"Do you still fear that the original *Cardenio* might have been diverted between the Earl and the College?"

"I fear... well, we shall see when we examine the actual document, Watson. We shall go and review it once you have finished your breakfast."

I almost choked on my mouthful. "You know where it is?"

"I know the present address of the man who is selling it," Holmes told me. "I hope that will suffice."

Dunn's Mercantile Hotel was an unremarkable lodging house off Seymour Street. It offered twenty-two bedrooms for travelling salesmen, mostly catering to ambassadors of the pharmaceutical and dentistry companies, but its best room had been booked for six weeks by a gentleman who was evidently in town filling in for a colleague who had suffered a light stroke.

"Mr Theobald is no trouble," the landlord's caretaker assured us. "A proper gentleman, he is, with nice manners indeed. A cut above, really."

"And he shares his name with the eighteenth century editor and author Lewis Theobald," Holmes noted wryly. "That's the fellow who claimed to have obtained three Restoration-era manuscripts of an unnamed Shakespeare play, which he edited, 'improved', and published under the name *Double Falshood, or the Distrest Lovers.* The plot is the same as that of *Cardenio* in Quixote, but the names are all changed. Most scholars dismiss the works as lacking veracity. The original material may have derived from John Fletcher; few see Shakespeare's genuine hand.[54] But it is a telling choice of pseudonym for our quarry."

The caretaker did not follow Holmes's literary digression. "His name is not apt," he valiantly tried to keep up, "because he is far from bald. Indeed, he has a fine mane of ginger-red hair."

"I suppose he left early this morning, having received a telegram."

54   Some 21st century scholars have proved more willing to reconsider Shakespeare's involvement in these "lost works". The 2010 *Arden Shakespeare* included *Double Falsehood* in its series of scholarly editions of Shakespeare's collected works, and its editor, Professor Brean Hammond, made a case for Theobald's play having Shakespearean origins. It has since been produced on stage several times, beginning with a 2011 performance by the Royal Shakespeare Company.

"Why yes, sir," the caretaker puzzled. "Strange you might guess that. And stranger still the message, which was all nonsense words, all letters just jumbled up like. It happens I oversaw it when Mr Theobald came for his post." He hastened to explain that occasionally his gentlemen guests received racing tips from pals, and that a couple of times he had ventured a "gainful flutter" on some message he had "overseen." He surmised that on this occasion some racing-savvy sporting friend of Theobald's had chosen to use some secret code.

"This was the telegram you tracked," I guessed.

Holmes now revealed the detail to me. "Once I had verified Shaddock as the handler of the stolen property and let him know that I was on to him, it was only natural that he would wish to warn his principal. Our vigil last night was in vain, so it was evident that he would wish to send a warning telegram first thing today. I placed Billy to hang around the nearest post office, to read off the address that Shaddock's hulking thug wrote on the sending slip. And here we are."

"And if Shaddock had chosen some other way to communicate his alert?"

"There were other measures in place too, but I need to bother you with such commonplace precautions. They will hardly make for a compelling narrative in your notebook. Sufficient that we have located the temporary digs of our manuscript thief, while he is up in Oxford collecting fees at the Martyrs Memorial."

The threat of police attention bringing disrepute to Dunn's Mercantile, and the exchange of a crown[55] were sufficient to win us entry to Theobald's "best room in the house." Holmes dismissed the caretaker and proceeded to examine the place.

Everything was neat and tidy. Three shirts hung in the wardrobe but most of Theobald's possessions were still in a suitcase. "He is not here much," I deduced.

"This is merely a mailing address and changing room," Holmes told me. "Look at this theatrical make-up kit, similar to my own. Doubtless the tramp outfit departed with Theobald. Here in this satchel is a Fischer and Sons delivery smock. And here—hidden under the bed—a sealed document box."

Holmes found a roll of precision tools in a bedside drawer and proceeded to use Theobald's own lock-picks to open his chest. Inside were not one but nine identical bundles of documents.

"The *Cardenio*!" I exclaimed. "Or... *Cardenios*."

"Our villain does not think small, Watson. And each of these is indistinguishable from the others. Let me see... yes, the paper appears authentic at first inspection, and the writing on the foul page is of appropriate style." He sighed unhappily. "They are most excellent forgeries."

55   In Holmes's time a crown was a 5-shilling coin, worth one quarter of a pound sterling. There was also a half-crown, worth 2/5, or 12½ pence in modern currency. Since 1991, commemorative crowns issued by the Royal Mint have had a face value of £5.

"Might not one be genuine? Or could all of them be copies of some real original that is not here?"

"The holographic script is well done. The printing facsimile is excellent. But alas, Watson, the language...! Shakespeare's genius is much harder to forge."

He flipped the engraved title page and the *dramatis personae* and intoned some lines of the prologue:

"'True love brings joys and virtues with its bloom
But sorrows and misfortune when it's lost
And so Cardenio comes upon his doom
And learns of love's damnations at his cost...'"

Holmes shook his head. "Fool's gold. Dross." He seemed more offended by the cod-Shakespeare than by the thefts or blackmail.

"We have discovered all, then," I consoled him. "This man calling himself Theobald..."

"Thinks he has been very clever. Thinks himself a genius to match the Bard! He believes that by taking a false name and hiring temporary rooms he can insulate himself, another faked identity like those he used to execute each of the other elements of his plot. But nobody can make a fool of himself like a clever man."

Holmes rose and pointed to the wardrobe. "He has erased the laundry marks on his shirts, as if I could not name the laundry by touch and smell alone. He has left us ample samples of his style of prose, not only in his execrable faux-*Cardenio* but also in his rambling ransom demands. He has shown a knowledge of College procedures and of the weaknesses and responses of its dons."

"You know this Theobald's actual identity, then?"

"I have read his graduate thesis, Watson. It was adequate, but afflicted with the same arrogance of opinion and overconfidence that we saw in his demand notes and in his hubris at emulating Shakespeare. You will recall that this entire project was initiated by correspondence from the manuscript's alleged discoverer, Mr John Clay."

"The late Earl's grandson? The alumnus of Goneril?"

"The fellow who might be best positioned to turn the screw on the unfortunate and disgraced academics who dared to award his work a second-class degree, and whose finances might benefit from eight or nine sales of black-market Elizabethan dramas. I have investigated his affairs, Watson; he no longer receives any stipend since his grandfather died. He is under a cloud for some family business that I have not yet discovered."

"We must have him arrested."

"We must catch him in the act. No other evidence will do here, Watson. Clay has been cunning in distancing himself from his plans. No point of proof exists good enough for a jury unless we can catch Theobald returning for his masterpieces."

"If he picks up the money from the statue as he did before, will he not next return here?" I anticipated. "His planned auction is tonight."

"We can but settle in and hope," Holmes told me.

We hunkered down to await John Clay.

But John Clay did not come.

"He is gone," Holmes told me the following day, after whatever exhaustive enquiries he had set in train were completed. "Clay scented the wind and knew that the game was up. He has cut his losses and departed."

"Leaving us with no firm proof of his misdeeds," I complained.

"Leaving us with the supposed *Cardenio* for return to Goneril College and verification as a fake. The University's reputation will be untarnished, duplicates and original documents alike proved worthless. And do not forget that Clay's name is now known, not just to the College authorities but to the Earl and his people, and to the Criminal Investigative Division at Scotland Yard. A vigil will be kept. Clay will not walk so anonymously in future."

"But he does walk away. He walks off with a thousand pounds extorted from Goneril to encourage him in his criminal career!"

"Rather say he hastens offstage, pursued by a bear.[56] Old Shaddock knows of the deception now, and how he risked and almost lost his reputation in support of a confidence trick. Shaddock and his large friend do not require the same standards of evidence as Her Majesty's courts. Mr Clay had better lie low for a time if he cares for his health."

I supposed that was better than no consequence at all. Nor was that the last time that Holmes and I would hear of Mr John Clay.[57]

"What will happen to the forged manuscripts now?" I wondered.

Holmes told me that Dr Chadbury intended to keep one for the College as a curiosity, believing it to be a superior facsimile.

But Holmes had no interest in a souvenir himself; the documents offended him.

THE END

---

56   Holmes refers to the famous stage instruction to Antigonus in *A Winter's Tale*, Act III, Scene 3.

57   Clay was well known to Holmes by the time of their clash over "The Red-Headed League" in *The Adventures of Sherlock Holmes* (1891), although the two had never met.

THE NEW YORK CRAKSTER

N **Friday 24th February 1888**, the luxury Cunard steamer *RMS Umbria* neared the end of her six-day passage from Liverpool to New York. It had been a memorable voyage aboard a memorable ship.

The *Umbria* was at that time holder of the Blue Ribbon, the unofficial award for fastest transatlantic crossing, with a record time of six days, four hours, and twenty-two minutes from Queenstown, Ireland to Sandy Hook, New Jersey, having claimed the title from her sister ship *Eturia*.[58]

Passengers enjoyed not only the speediest of passages but also the most luxurious. The Admiralty had chartered *Umbria* after the 1885 Pandejah war scare with Russia,[59] converting her into an armed merchant cruiser; on her subsequent return to passenger service she had been refitted with the most modern and highest-quality trappings of any ship of the line. Consequently, a first-class return ticket on *Umbria* cost £25 or $100.[60]

Notable amongst the elite voyagers who had embarked a week before were the Right Honourable Gerald Runnelly, Viscount of Morcar, and his new bride Lady Edith, née Woodley, of *those* Carstairs. The young couple were much-

---

58   The *Eturia* was to claim the title back again in June of 1888 with a time of six days, one hour, and fifty-five minutes, the last of the single-screw ships to take the record.

59   An escalating armed engagement in the opening months of 1885 between the expanding Russian Empire and the Emirate of Afghanistan led to a diplomatic crisis between Russia and Britain regarding the security of the British Raj in India. Britain prepared for war, including the leasing of a number of commercial sea vessels for military use, but the matter was finally settled through negotiation. The northwestern border of Afghanistan was defined and further Russian expansion into Asia was curtailed.

60   The further adventures of the *RMS Umbria* included a 10th November 1888 collision with and sinking of the Fabre Line cargo steamship *Iberia* near Sandy Hook, for which *Umbria* was blamed since she was travelling at the dangerous speed of 17 knots (20 mph, 31 km/h); the 12th April 1890 rescue of the crew of the stricken Norwegian barque *Magdalena*, which had hit an iceberg; a 17th December 1892 propeller shaft failure that left the ship adrift without power for two weeks in stormy seas and gale-force winds; her 28th June 1896 striking of and temporary grounding on the sunken coal barge *Andrew Jackson* in the Gedney Channel off Sandy Hook; charter in 1900 as a troop transport and hospital ship during the Boer War; and a thwarted 1903 Mafia bomb plot intended "to destroy the British shipping interest in the port of New York." The *Umbria*'s service finally ended with her scrapping in 1910, after 145 round trips to New York.

feted aboard, since they were gay and delightful and clearly in the first flush of their love. However, gossips noted that the Viscount's father, the Count of Morcar, had lately been associated with some banking scandal that might eventually lead to his incarceration and ruin; the newlyweds might well prefer to be a continent away from the unpleasantness that would follow.[61]

The crossing had become that much more memorable with the sensational theft from the *Umbria*'s safe-vault of a string of diamonds belonging to Ophelia Dunfordine, an heiress of the Dunfordine copper fortune. Fortunately the brilliant Morcars were able to discover the stolen gems, prove that the unpleasant Ohio sweatshop-owner 'Viggy' Vorterson was the thief, and return the necklace to the distraught Miss Dunfordine for her profuse thanks. Vorterson had made his fortune off working the lives out of others, so he had no need to commit such a theft except for spite or lust, but the evidence was irrefutable; Viggy jumped ship rather than face arrest and was last seen in his stolen lifeboat drifting towards Newfoundland.

"You need think nothing of it," Gerald told Miss Ophelia. "We were glad to help out. It was only a matter of time before a rotter like Viggy got what was due to him."

"How stupid would one have to be to hide such stolen jewels under one's own bunk mattress?" Lady Edith added, wonderingly. "And then, when caught, to have prepared no plausible explanation for how the gems might have got there?"

"We are all very grateful," the Captain of the *Umbria* assured his most favoured passengers. "I shouldn't wonder but that the Line will wish to give you a suitable reward for your efforts. An insurance claim for jewellery of that value would have proved expensive in future premiums, to say nothing of the bad publicity."

"We require no reward except to know that justice is done," the Right Honourable Gerald assured him. "Indeed, we have already turned down a very generous thank-you from Miss Ophelia. I'll say the same to your owners as I did to her: if you feel you must make some gesture of gratitude then donate some amount to a charity that does some good."

"We have no need of money," Lady Edith added, hugging her new husband's arm. "Not when we have love!"

---

61   The Countess of Morcar, mother of Gerald, suffered the theft of her famous jewel in "The Adventure of the Blue Carbuncle" in *The Adventures of Sherlock Holmes* (1892). Information about her husband's criminal dealing was exposed in "The Legacy of the Nottingham Crakster" in *Sherlock Holmes, Consulting Detective* volume 17 (2021), which also revealed the further exploits of the Countess' larcenous maid Catherine Cusack and Miss Cusack's pre-existing relationship with Jemmy Wilson, the titular Crakster. Edith Woodley of the Carstairs was mentioned in "The Adventure of the Empty House" (1903, collected in *The Return of Sherlock Holmes*, 1905) as the former fiancée of the Honourable Ronald Adair, the second son of the Earl of Maynooth.

With that jubilant conclusion, and the goodwill of every passenger and crew-member, the Morcars disembarked in New York. And there they vanished.

It was not until three months later that the recovered diamonds were discovered to be paste forgeries.

That same day that Gerald and Edith Runnelly disappeared without trace at the disembarkation dock customs point, Miss Mercy Wheaton of Wellesley, Massachusetts, resorted in considerable distress to a Sixth Avenue pawnbroker. She was newly-arrived from Boston with her brother Charles, but there had been some terrible mishap.

Charles, usually such a studious young man, had evidently fallen in on the night-train with some city-types who had convinced him to try his hand at cards. The novice had done rather well at first and had eagerly consented to raising the limits of the pot. Thereafter his luck had changed; he now owed his fellow players the phenomenal sum of three thousand two hundred dollars.

"Father will be furious, of course," Miss Wheaton confided to the bemused pawnbroker. "He'll pay, naturally, but Pa will be back in the Dakota goldfields right now and no telegram will reach him in time. These fellows want their payment right away and… they may become rough! They won't let poor Charles from their sight until they are paid their due. He is terrified. The only thing will be to pawn my necklace, just until Pa sorts things out. Here it is. I'm told it is worth at least twenty-thousand dollars."

The pawnbroker's examination by magnifying lens assured him that the delicate gold and diamond jewellery was worth at least five times that and probably more. However, he pretended reluctance and was eventually able to barter the naive and desperate girl down to the exact value of her brother's debt. Moreover, he set the redemption value at double its pawn price, with only a three-day limit on repayment before he could claim the item in lieu.

The young lady was in a difficult position and the proprietor would have liked to be kind to her, but business was business.

The unholy bargain having been struck, the documentation signed, and the desperate lady departed with her brother's ransom, the Sixth Avenue pawnbroker held his prize up to the light and allowed himself a broad grin of triumph.

Unfortunately, Mercy Wheaton had hardly left the shop when a dapper fellow in a pinstriped suit entered. "Inspector Flanagan of the Customs Service," he introduced himself, showing his identification badge. "I believe that you've just had a visit from the notorious 'Generous' Jane Jasper, have you not?"

The pawnbroker denied it, but Flanagan described Miss Wheaton quite perfectly, even to the dimple of her cheek. "Her face is her fortune, they say. I'm sorry to tell you, sir, that the necklace she pawned to you is stolen property. And not any stolen property, but property of the Dunfordine clan—the copper barons who own half of Ohio. The jewels were extracted from the safe of the *RMS Umbria* during its voyage from England. Here is the statement regarding the incident logged to the Customs and Revenues Service by the captain of that vessel."

The unfortunate pawnbroker looked miserably at the document proffered to him, though he did not read so far as the second page which described the necklace's miraculous recovery from its supposed thief and its restoration to the *Umbria*'s safe.

"I had no idea that the piece was stolen," he insisted worriedly. "I advanced her over two thousand dollars in cash and bearer bonds! What about my money?"

"This is not the first time you have been suspected of handling hot goods," Inspector Flanagan mentioned. "This is once too often, sir."

"No. No, it's only an accident! She was—this Generous Jane, she was very convincing. She was… I acted in good faith, officer."

"I'll need to take the necklace now," the Customs Agent went on implacably. "I'll write you a receipt, of course. You'll be hearing from the City Police Department shortly about what charges they'll bring on you."

"Wait! It wasn't like that. Look… officer… you seem like a reasonable fellow. Is there no way I can convince you of my honesty?"

Flanagan received the diamonds without speaking, as if in deep thought. He wrapped the gems and folded them into his inner pocket, then wrote out the promised official acknowledgement of property confiscated.

"I suppose I might be able to write you up as an honest victim of an unscrupulous operator," he conceded at last. "For a consideration." He picked up a rather attractive fob-watch with an unusual eggshell-blue dial and examined it with casual interest.

The pawnbroker knew an opportunity when he saw it. One pocketwatch and fifty silver dollars crossed the counter into the customs agent's satchel before Inspector Flanagan nodded, winked some assurance, tapped his nose, and made his departure without further comment.

Flanagan, or at least the fellow who had pocketed the Custom Agent's badge at the disembarkation docks, met with the plausible Generous Jane Jasper around the corner, and restored her necklace to her.

"Nicely done, Miss Mercy," he told her. "How many more pawnbrokers do you think we might manage before close of business?"

"Three? Four?" the young woman suggested. "And then dinner?"

On Saturday, a confused young woman made a mistake outside the Fleetwood Park Harness Racing Track. Her superior accent and expensive outfit betrayed that she was not a native of the Bronx but had travelled in via the Fulton Market steamboat or on the new train from Grand Central Station to Melrose. Her error was that the betting parlour she entered was not one of the respectable track-side establishments controlled with severe authority by the New York Drivers Club but one of the less reputable 'unofficial' gambling dens unregulated by the City and Suburbs.

It was an easy mistake for a novice to make. The police regularly raided and closed down the ad-hoc gambling hells, only for more such vice-dens to spring up again in some other local house or abandoned shop. On a race day, when the horses hauled two-wheeled chariots along Fleetwood Park's one-mile track, such bookies' squats were all too common.[62] The 'book-keeper's parlour' that this lost lamb strayed into was almost opposite the racetrack's main entrance, behind a futile disguise as a second-hand bookshop.

The betting place contained a mix of rough labourers, unemployed louts, holiday idlers, and one or two sporting gents from the metropolis. The 'punters' quickly identified the out-of-place newcomer by her bright frock and elaborate hat.

"I'm looking for Dinky," she explained—or evidently thought she had. "Where is he? Everyone knows Dinky!"

The toughs who were clustered round waiting for message-runners to arrive with the track results were quite amused. "Dinky's not here, darling," she was told.

"Then I need to speak to Ronnie. Or Harry. I have a message for them."

A more senior inhabitant of the betting works emerged from a backroom. "Are you sure you have the right place, miss?" 'Honest' Hank Dibney asked the lady.

"Oh yes. Vandy and Rocky told me to meet Dinky here. And dear Lenny

---

62   Harness racing, where horses race at a trot or pace, pulling a driver in a chariot called a sulky or spider, was a popular sport in the 1800s. In the USA most races were over 1 mile. The Fleetwood Park track, in what is now the Morrisania section of the Bronx, existed from 1871 to 1898; at its height it attracted crowds of 10,000 and was described as "the most famous trotting track in the country". By 1888 it was managed by the influential and exclusive New York Drivers Club, whose membership included a Who's Who of East Coast millionaires.

"I'm looking for Dinky. Where is he? Everyone knows Dinky!"

and Corny! They will be *furious* if I don't show up to cheer their horses on. I love watching them running around in their bright colours with their big-wheeled carts—silkies, they call them, don't they?"

"Sulkys, darlin'," one crude fellow corrected her. "Your silkies are under your skirts."

"Mind your manners, buddy," Honest Hank cut in. "Maybe you got the wrong place, lady?"

"I don't think so. Vandy and Rocky said, go to the gate and the book office will be right there."

There was a difference between a booking office, where entry tickets to the track were purchased, and a supposed bookshop where illegal betting took place. The bookkeeper might have mentioned it, but just then he evidently made some shrewd associations and his brows rose. "Vandy and Rocky?" he checked. "That'd be *Vanderbilt* and *Rockefeller*? Willie Vanderbilt and Bill Rockefeller? And Leonard Jerome the financier, and Cornelius Bliss who chairs the Republican state committee?"[63]

"Well of course!" the bright young woman breezed. "Who else would it be? But I have a message for Dinky."

"And who would Dinky be?" the bookie asked uneasily, aware that his impromptu betting parlour had gone strangely quiet.

The lady confessed that she didn't actually know dear Dinky's proper name, but he was "one of those fellows who wear the pretty silk shirts and crouch on those little two-wheeled spider things that the horsies pull."

From this the toughs and gamblers derived that Dinky was a driver, due to compete that very afternoon.

"That's right," the fair sporting damsel agreed. "I have a *message* for *Dinky*."

The 'punters' in the shop assured their visitor that she could safely leave her message with them and it would be forwarded to its recipient. At last she was convinced to relay her missive.

"Ronnie would have come himself, but he's having a spot of bother with his daddy," she revealed. "Evidently Dinky's instructions have changed. Dinky is

63   William Kissam 'Willie' Vanderbilt I (1849-1920), businessman, philanthropist and horsebreeder, was inheritor of the Vanderbilt family fortune. William Avery Rockefeller Jr. (1841–1922), of the prominent Rockefeller family, was co-founder of Standard Oil and part-owner of the Anaconda Copper Company which grew into the fourth-largest company in the world by the late 1920s. Leonard Walter Jerome (1817–1891), "the King of Wall Street", was a stockbroker and speculator, part-owner of the *New York Times* (the offices of which he defended with a Gatling gun during the New York Draft Riots); he was Winston Churchill's maternal grandfather. Cornelius Newton Bliss (1833–1911), merchant, politician, and art collector, served as Treasurer of the Republican National Convention in four successive campaigns and was Secretary of the Interior in McKinley's administration.

All four were harness racing enthusiasts, prominent members of the New York Drivers Club that ran Fleetwood Park.

to…" The uptown lady furrowed her brow in concentration. "I'm to say to him 'Pigs to sausages', which is such an odd thing to pass on, isn't it? And *then* I must tell Dinky to come second, not first. Evidently it's not Dinky's turn or something. Whatever, Dinky mustn't be first. That's the message. What do you suppose it means?"

"You don't know?" one of the gamblers asked.

"Ronnie didn't tell me. He just said to find Dinky and let him know. Do you know what it's all about?"

It was clear to the sporting men in the betting booth. The coming race had been fixed, but now it was to be fixed with some different outcome. They had always suspected that the great men behind the races were as crooked as themselves. Now they knew that the owners had conspired to alter the outcome of at least one trial this afternoon.

"Which horse does Dinky drive?" Honest Hank asked, trying to sound casual.

Everyone held their breath as the lady pondered the question. "He's quite a pretty one," she replied at last. "With an odd name. Duck… or Mallard or Pigeon or something."

"Turpin's Swan?" the bookie ventured. "Turpin's Swan driven by Davie Dunall in the 3.15 trot? But he's 5-1."

There was a stir of excitement amongst the men in the gambling shop. There were more than a dozen of them, including the three or four in respectable middle-class garb, city gents who enjoyed the excitement of off-track betting where there was no regulation or limit.

"Shut the door and bolt it," Honest Hank told the others. "Miss, why don't you just go into the back there and find a comfy place to sit? We'll let you know when 'Dinky' turns up and you can deliver your message then."

The out-of-place visitor was solicitously guided to a small shabby rear parlour and ensconced there.

"Now listen up," the bookkeeper told the men in his shop. "We've dropped onto a bit of fortune, by dumb luck. What we do with it is up to us."

"I want to put a bet on with you, for Turpin's Swan in the three-fifteen," one hopeful but not-too-bright gambler proposed.

"Don't be dim!" another scorned. "'E knows it's a done deal, so it is, if that dolly's message don't get through. Dunall won't know 'e's not to take first. Dunall can't 'elp but win."

"The other bookies won't know, though," a third man, one of the middle-class gamesters, pointed out. "If we go around the other shops, all laying wagers…"

"The price will go down right quick," Honest Hank warned them. "We have runners and touts to warn each other when there's a syndicate trying something. But there's another way, if you want to come in with me."

The punters were willing to listen.

"It's this. When we're a bit short to cover a lot of bets, we have a system where we share out the risk between us. It gets settled up after. Now if I was to take large wagers from each of you, at 5-1, and I mean *large* wagers, boys, then there's time for me to go to my rivals and get them to spot me. I'd turn my takings over to them and they only return them if the nag wins, because then I'd have to pay out to all of you. But that way the payout price stays high." The bookie shrugged. "O' course, I'd actually be paying you mooks out at four-to-one, not five. I've got to get a cut."

The gamblers reviewed the plan. It seemed sound.

"If we're doing this, it'll have to be quick," Honest Hank warned them. "The race is on in twenty minutes, and I have a fair few visits to make. Empty your pockets, boys! And not a word to any soul."

The betting men were more than happy with a risk-free wager. It was a dream come true, something for nothing. Between them they managed to assemble over three thousand five hundred dollars.

"Don't any of you leave this shop until the race is done," the bookkeeper warned the gamblers. "None of you can be trusted not to try and squeeze a bit extra above the rest, and that might blow the whole thing. Keep an eye on each other. And make sure that dame don't come out of that door. We can't have her passing her message on to 'Dinky'. Don't disturb her, but she don't leave, right?"

That was agreed. The den's proprietor and all three shop-boys hastened off to spread his liabilities, to the ruin of his competitors.

The clock ticked on to three-fifteen and the audience inside Fleetwood Park roared as the harness race began.

"We can go out now," one of the more experienced gamesters argued. "Bets are closed. We can grab one of the runner-boys and find out what the nags are doing."

There was general agreement. The door was unbolted and enquiries were made.

At the half-mile mark, Toodle-Pip was in the lead, with Jericho and Mama's Sweetheart close behind. Turpin's Swan ran fifth out of six racers.

"He'll be coming up towards the end," the punters told each other.

One of their number, a dapper young sport who had also quite fancied his chances with the lost damsel, emerged from the back room with the cup of coffee he had taken her. "I say!" he called. "The filly's gone!"

A hasty inspection of the rear parlour showed that the lady had departed by way of the window. The bookkeeper's strongbox was also absent.

Inexplicably, Turpin's Swan finished in sixth and final place. When the bereft and out-of-pocket gamblers looked for Honest Hank Dibney, who had accepted their wagers and who had leased the shop for that afternoon only, or for his shop-boys who had been hired on that afternoon for crisp twenty dollar bills, the bookkeeper and the lady were not to be found.

On Sunday, an anonymous stranger heard High Mass at the glorious new St Patrick's Cathedral on Fifth Avenue.[64] Although he appreciated the gothic beauty of James Renwick Jr.'s architectural marvel, with its bronze doors and recently-added spires, he was more interested in the men who occupied the best pews at the front of the massive nave.

These were the men of the Tammany Society, the Democrat election organisation that dominated New York politics through its command of the Irish vote. Their Manhattan headquarters at 44 Union Square was the hub of power in the city; its operatives and agents controlled the police, the courts, and the political nominations.

A decade earlier, 'Tammany Hall' had suffered a blow at the fall of William M. 'Boss' Tweed, 'Grand Sachem'[65] of Tammany, a politician so successfully corrupt that over his career he had probably embezzled over 200 million dollars.[66] Tammany had become synonymous with election fraud, including

64   In fact, St. Patrick's Cathedral in Midtown Manhattan, seat of the Archbishop of New York, is the largest Gothic Revival Catholic cathedral in North America, occupying a whole city block bounded by Fifth Avenue, Madison Avenue, 50th Street, and 51st Street. Its construction began in 1858, was interrupted by the Civil War, and finished in 1878, with its dedication the year following.

65   This is an Anglicised version of cognate northeastern Native American terms for a leader or representative elected by a tribe or group of tribes. It was co-opted as the title of the "boss" of the Tammany political lodges.

66   William Magear "Boss" Tweed (1823–1878), political leader of Tammany Hall, was once the third-largest landowner in New York City, a director of the Erie Railroad, the Tenth National Bank, and the New-York Printing Company, proprietor of the Metropolitan Hotel, significant stockholder in iron mines and gas companies, board member of the Harlem Gas Light Company, the Third Avenue Railway Company, the Brooklyn Bridge Company, and the president of the Guardian Savings Bank. From 1852 he was elected to the United States House of Representatives. In 1858 he joined the New York County Board of Supervisors He entered the New York State Senate in 1867. His membership of boards and commissions, his control of political patronage, and his power to grant civil contracts gave him supremacy over the New York political landscape.

In 1877, Tweed was convicted for stealing an estimated $25 to $45 million from New York City taxpayers, but later estimates ranged as high as $200 million. Unable to make bail, he escaped from custody and fled the country, but was returned to prison from overseas. He died as

"voting the graveyard",[67] with bribery and corruption, with violence against opposition, and with bilking the public purse. It had taken a decade for the new generation of officers to live down their predecessors' excesses, to rebuild their political machine, and to once again establish lucrative ways of personally benefiting from their pre-eminence.

That anonymous stranger watched the movers of the new regime carefully, making mental notes about who shook hands with whom, which men avoided eye contact with each other, and what order of precedence they claimed. It would be important later.

At the same time, an equally anonymous young woman turned up at the New Mission House at Five Points with nothing more than the rags on her back. The Mission House had the worst address in New York, being built upon the site of the notorious Old Brewery tenement at the junction that gave the slum of Five Points its name. The neighbourhood, built on low-lying poorly-infilled land that had once been the freshwater lake known as the Collect Pond, was bounded by Centre Street to the west, the Bowery to the east, Canal Street to the north, and Park Row to the south. It suffered an average of one murder per day.

The old Sixth Ward was packed with Irish immigrants and emancipated but impoverished Africans. In the Western hemisphere, only parts of London's East End rivalled it for population density, unemployment, disease, infant and child mortality, prostitution, and violent crime. Gangs such as the Dead Rabbits and the Bowery Boys held a grip on the neighbourhood.[68] Even the police and fire services literally fought with one another over ways to exploit the area.[69]

The Old Brewery had latterly been a seedy tenement, wherein the 1850 cen-

a debtor in Ludlow Street Jail.

67   That is, fraudulently entering people who have died onto the voter's register, thereby gaining a block of illegal votes to support chosen candidates.

68   For example, on July 8th, 1857, an estimated 800 to 1,000 gang members rioted, along with several hundred others who used the disturbance to loot the Bowery area. Order was finally restored by the New York State Militia, with eight reported deaths and over a hundred serious injuries.

69   This culminated in The Great New York City Police Riot of 1857 in front of City Hall, with open fighting between the recently-dissolved New York Municipal Police and the newly-formed New York Metropolitan Police.

sus reported 221 people crowded into in 35 tiny apartments. In 1853, women of the Methodist Home Mission action group had launched a public subscription to buy and demolish the site. The New Mission House, with its 58 rooms, provided practical charity where it was needed most, including housing, clothes, food, and education.

The unknown newcomer was made welcome there. She was provided with food, a bath, and a good second-hand dress to replace her barely-decent skirts. She declined a bed for the night, to the regret of the Mission matrons who believed that must signify her return to streetwalking.

In actual fact the young woman walked out of the district until she could hail a cab to meet up with the anonymous man who had visited St Patrick's.

"I think I have found the genuine article," she told him.

"Oh, so have I," he replied with a grin; but they were talking about very different articles.

"Is it going to be ridiculous and insanely dangerous?" she enquired.

"Would you love me if it wasn't?" he answered.

"Well… perhaps not as vigorously."

"So, then…" He kissed her and it was excellent.

Jeremy 'Jemmy' Wilson, the Nottingham Crakster,[70] and Catherine Cusack, his accomplice through life, had arrived in the New World. Now they had business to attend.

On Monday, the grand and glorious Metropolitan Hotel on Broadway and

---

[70]   Jemmy Wilson, the Nottingham Crakster, debuted in Sir Arthur Conan Doyle's almost-forgotten short story, "Selecting a Ghost", also known as "The Secret of Goresthorpe Grange", first published in *London Society* in 1883 before Conan Doyle became a successful and sought-after author with Sherlock Holmes. This account should not be confused with "The Haunted Grange of Goresthorpe-A True Ghost Story", an entirely different tale written by Doyle when he was eighteen, submitted to *Blackwood's Magazine* but never published until the year 2000.

In "Selecting a Ghost", the notorious Crakster defrauds rich mark Mr D'Odd by selling him a supposed spectre and robbing him. The term 'Crakster' is a Northern dialect synonym for a jokester and a 'crack' is a joke.

Jemmy Wilson returned to encounter Holmes and Watson in "The Nottingham Crakster" in I.A. Watson's story in *Sherlock Holmes, Consulting Detective Volume 12* (2018, ISBN 10: 1946183423, ISBN 13: 978-1946183422), also collected in *Sherlock Holmes Mysteries Volume 2*, 2019), and in "Legacy of the Nottingham Crakster" in *Sherlock Holmes, Consulting Detective Volume 17* (2022, ISBN 10: 195358909X, ISBN 13: 978-1953589095), and *Sherlock Holmes Mysteries Volume 3*, 2023.

Jemmy Wilson the Crakster should not be confused with the very different "Wilson, the Notorious Canary-Trainer" in whose 1895 arrest Holmes aided, to which Dr Watson alludes in "The Adventure of Black Peter" in *The Return of Sherlock Holmes*.

Prince received notification by wire of the imminent arrival of V.I.P. guests for their Honeymoon Suite. Mr and Mrs Francis Hey Moulton were due that very day, fresh from their European sojourn. All was to be made ready for them.

At noon, a line of taxi-carriages pulled up at the hotel's forecourt. The hotel's manager struggled to roust up sufficient porters to attend to the eight cabs delivering the domestic goods and shopping purchases of the happy couple.

The doormen and porters went to it with a will, however; the Moultons were lavish tippers.

The three-hundred-foot four-storey brownstone Metropolitan was the shining example of the city's 1853 New York Crystal Palace Exhibition 'hotel boom'. It boasted steam-heated rooms for six hundred guests and their servants, including family apartments with private drawing rooms. Designed in a "grand commercialised style reminiscent of Roman palazzos", including the largest plate-glass mirrors in the United States, its European furnishings alone had cost $200,000.

Like New York's other expensive hotels, the Metropolitan suffered a downturn during the Civil War, bringing the Leland Brothers, pioneers of America's first hotel chain, to near ruin. The business was revived through its takeover by the infamous 'Boss' Tweedy, and it was the hotel's old political mob connections that attracted it to its present visitors.

"Welcome, welcome!" the Chief Concierge greeted the young Moulton couple effusively. "The General Manager will be along shortly to make sure you have everything you need. The Owners will wish to be certain that your stay is perfect."

"That is most gratifying," Mr Moulton responded. "There is a little matter that would be helpful. I presume that there is a hotel safe where we might deposit some jewellery and a small sum of cash?"

Assured that the Metropolitan had one of the finest lock-safes in America, the Moultons deposited some thirty thousand dollars in silver coin, notes, and bonds as if it was a mere bagatelle. To this Mrs Moulton added a diamond necklace of the finest water, which for insurance purposes was listed at a valuation of $165,000. "The majority of our stuff will be arriving next week," Mr Moulton explained to the Manager as the travellers' property was installed in the safe. "Along with our main staff."

Beside the jewels and rolls of money, the Moultons added an envelope of papers and a scrolled chart of some kind, which they did not explain.

Mrs Moulton whispered something into her husband's ear and he nodded acknowledgement. "One other issue," he told the Metropolitan's solicitous senior staff. "We are here on business, not pleasure. We might as well have stayed in Paris if we had wanted only to amuse ourselves. I am here to exploit a financial opportunity, to arrange a little project, and privacy is essential for its success." He folded a thick wad of notes into the Manager's breast pocket. "I would appreciate discretion from all your people. No press, no rivals hearing what I am doing. *Especially*, nothing that could get back to my father-in-law. No word of who I meet or what is discussed. Secrecy, you understand. Commercial secrecy."

Since the wad was very generous, the Manager of the Metropolitan was pleased to guarantee such assurances.

So the Moultons took up the Honeymoon Suite, but all the discretion in the world could not prevent the staff from gossiping and speculating amongst themselves about the happy couple.

The Manager, whose job it was to know significant guests and who valued his position even more than the large gratuity he had accepted, still chose to report what he had learned to the Owners.

"There is a whiff of scandal regarding the Moultons," he explained. "It seems that only four years ago, Francis 'Frank' Hay Moulton was nothing more than a desperate prospector looking for gold in the Rocky Mountains. His partner was Aloysius Doran—yes, the same Doran who is now a railroad tycoon—who was then likewise caught up in the gold fever in those hills. Moulton courted Doran's daughter Harriet. But then Doran struck his fortune, made his millions, and his success story began.

"Well, after that, Doran had other ideas than allowing his daughter to marry a penniless grubber nobody. He broke off her engagement to Moulton and took her to San Francisco to live a life in high society amongst Old Money. Moulton went off to make his own fortune and prove himself, but his camp in New Mexico fell to Apache raiders and he was thought to have perished.

"When news of Moulton's death reached Miss Doran she ceased resisting her father's attempts to find her a more suitable match. She became betrothed to an English nobleman by the name of Lord Robert Walsingham de Vere St. Simon, second son of the Duke lassof Balmoral. The dowry was one million dollars! The Dorans moved to the Old Country and the wedding was arranged.

"Here's where it gets odd. Evidently at the very wedding, the bride was passed a note by a stranger. She vanished at the subsequent nuptial breakfast. Her wedding gown, veil, shoes, and wreath were discovered on the shores of the Serpentine River in Hyde Park, London. Lord Robert's new wife simply vanished.

"Naturally, the nobleman was distressed. When the police discovered nothing, a well-known enquiry agent was called in. It was this detective, Mr Sherlock Holmes, who uncovered the truth of the matter.

"It seems that Moulton had gone to Miss Hatty Doran back in San Francisco; they had secretly wed. Nor had Moulton died by the Apaches but had instead been their prisoner. He had escaped, somehow made his own fortune, and had followed the Dorans to England to reclaim his wife. On learning of her husband's survival, the double-bride had fled her bigamous matrimony with Lord Robert and escaped with her first and legal partner.

"Mr Holmes uncovered all of this. He convinced the Moultons not to simply vanish but rather to return and explain themselves to St Simon and Aloysius Doran. The meeting was uncomfortable, but the noble bachelor was unable to do aught but recognise that his marriage was illegal.[71] Mr and Mrs Moulton retreated to Europe and have spent the best part of a year touring its capitals. Relations with Mr Doran are said to be frosty, to say the least. And now the Moultons are back in the United States, and something is going on."

Mr Francis H. Moulton and his wife might have been surprised to hear of their return to their homeland. They were actually just then arriving back at Le Meurice on the Rue de Rivoli opposite the Tuileries gardens of Paris's First Arrondissement, having completed a stately tour of European capitals in a year-long extended honeymoon. Seething, turbulent New York was far from their minds.

Meanwhile, the supposed Frank Moulton had arranged an appointment with New York attorney Bradwell Tyler, whose exclusive firm mostly specialised in political and property work.

"I have some very specific requirements," the young man told the lawyer, "and I'm told that you are the best man in the city to get them done."

"My practice is a successful one," Tyler admitted carefully, "but I am very selective in my clients."

"Well, I trust you will select me," Moulton replied, passing over an envelope of crisp bearer bonds. "I pay top rates—for top rate work."

Nobody handed over such a retainer for simple straightforward dealings. "What are your needs?" Tyler enquired smoothly.

"I am seeking to acquire certain plots of land. I will need city ordinance permissions to develop them. I may need orders of compulsory purchase. I'll require licences and labour permits. I'll want building contracts, materials contracts—steel and brick mostly—and some workforce guarantees. In other words, I want a smooth ride for my business enterprise. And I need someone who knows how New York works, who can make the mechanisms of government turn for me not against me. Is that you?"

"It might be. What's your budget?"

---

71   Dr Watson disclosed the details of this case in "The Adventure of the Noble Bachelor" (1892, collected in *The Adventures of Sherlock Holmes* that same year).

"I expect my project to cost me around six million," Moulton revealed. "That is including all… easement fees, mind you. Any other ongoing costs that the city requires will have to come out of a slice of the returns thereafter."

Mr Tyler resisted the temptation to lick his lips. "Six million, you say? And you'll raise the finance by…?"

"I already have the finance. If you haven't done your background look at me before you agreed to meet then you're not the man for me. But you're a shrewd cookie so I guess you know I'm one of those brash, annoying, new-rich guys off of the goldfields. I made my fortune there, quite a pile, but now I want to turn that into a very large pile."

"And the nature of the business you intend? The reason for the plots of land you require?"

Moulton sat back, lit a cigar, and grinned. "Trains. Elevated trains."

"Trains?" the attorney echoed, thinking hard. The elevated railways had been one of the great fortune-makers of New York City in the last two decades. From being eccentric pipe-dreams they had become major economic drivers, opening up once-worthless farming land to new housing developments, bringing a fresh commuting labour force into the swelling metropolis.

Moulton pulled out from his waistcoat a handsome gold pocketwatch with an attractive eggshell-blue dial and checked the time before he went on. "Twenty years back, the Upper West Side was about half a dozen houses and some shacks," he pointed out. "Then the railway connected through there, and now? Street after street of new tenements, thousands of builders working round the clock to meet accommodation demand. The 3rd Avenue line to 129th Street at the Harlem River, the 6th Avenue to 128th Street run, 9th Avenue to 51st Street… look at what's happened. The population in those outlying areas grew four-or-five-fold. And the men in a position to exploit that development, well they became wealthy folks indeed."

"Those lines you mentioned are all merged to one company now," Mr Tyler pointed out. "The Manhattan Railway Company likes its monopoly."

"And they pay for it, I'd guess," the brash gold-miner answered cynically. "That's okay. I don't want to compete with their routes. I have a different direction in mind. And I'd guess that elected officials who don't object to campaign contributions from the existing firm won't object to other contributions from a new one. Am I right?"

Tyler agreed that the officers and politicians at City Hall—and Tammany Hall—would not be averse to considering financial support from the right project. "Especially if they have a say in who does the construction contracts and provides the labour."

"I thought as much. And you could help me through that tangle, eh? You could have a word with the right people?"

Bradwell Tyler admitted that he might be able to do that. "I'll need to indicate where you might want to drive your elevated, though. There are planning issues, public nuisance enquiries because of the noise and soot, zoning petitions…"

"Well, that'll come. First off I intend to acquire some land I'll need for the stations and the rail pylons, and enough of a share of the backcountry real estate that'll be opened up to develop some housing. I'll be acquiring that before word gets out of my intentions for a railway, before the ground prices start rocketing."

That was a shrewd move, but Tyler was disappointed that Moulton was smart enough to know it.

"I want you to make me some introductions this week," Moulton told the lawyer. "Impress me. Then, when I know you're sound and square, we can move on to the other stuff."

Whilst the East Coast Frank Moulton was dealing with a slippery attorney, his supposed-bride was speaking with the Ladies Committee, who oversaw things at the Five Points Mission; except that Catherine Cusack was presently not being romantic Hatty Moulton or a desperate, ragged street-girl, but rather the sober Mrs Eliakim Meigs, a staid veiled widow past her middle age.

"You will pardon me coming to you with such an odd proposal," she told the women with whom she met. "You may understand when I explain. I see that out behind your charitable Mission House you have a scrabble of broken land, derelict and overgrown, left over from the days when there used to be a brewery on this spot."

The Ladies Committee owned that such a plot existed.

"Well," Mrs Meigs continued, pausing to touch a lacy handkerchief to her eye, "that very spot was where my late husband Eliakim was born, in the year of Our Lord eighteen hundred and twenty-nine. It was a stables then, for Eliakim was of humble birth. Nor do we Christians revile a child born in a stable, for was that not how Our Saviour came into the world? Anyhow, Eliakim grew up there, in the brewery yard, grew up in Five Points, until he was drafted for the War. That was the first time he ever left New York, and he never returned. He fought bravely, won promotion—won me—and settled in Arlington after the conflict to breed horses.

"Well, Eliakim proved a good man and a good husband. He passed away last year. Now I am minded to provide for him a memorial at his place of birth."

Mrs Meigs indicated out of the window to the valueless wasteland behind the mission's neatly-cleared rear yard. "I wish to purchase a small portion of that rubble field—perhaps no more than ten feet square—upon which I can erect a monument. It would be of great comfort to me to know that Eliakim's birthplace was so marked and that his humble beginnings are not forgotten."

Mrs Meigs also mentioned a sum of money for which she might purchase the tiny parcel of land. It was a very generous amount for a ten-foot square of Five Points. "It is a matter of charity and expediency," the widow explained. "I see the work that you are doing here, a Great Work, and I would like to support it. But also, I do not like being in New York. I do not want to remain in the city for more than a few days. finding it too crowded and noisy for my comfort. Hence if a generous sum can expedite the sale of Eliakim's memorial plot then I am pleased to offer it. I hope that you will consider my request sympathetically."

It took the Ladies Committee less than ten minutes to agree that they were very sympathetic to the offered amount, and contracts were set in hand.

That night Jemmy Wilson and Catherine Cusack regathered at the Metropolitan, sloughing for a short while their many identities and apparent motives, and they spent a very pleasant evening in luxury and mutual contentment.

Tuesday was a day of meetings, starting with a series of introductions and appointments made by Mr Tyler to develop Mr Moulton's initiative. Moulton shook hands with a succession of city officials, councilmen, civil servants, civic planners, and legal experts. By lunchtime Moulton was invited to dine at Tammany Hall, under an elaborate gilded moulded ceiling as rich and ostentatious as any European palace.

Moulton was a very confident young man. He seemed well-informed about matters of business and engineering. He was politically naive; no newcomer to the greatest city on the continent could lightly jump into the shark-infested waters of New York politics. But nouveau-riche strangers came to the Big Apple all the time; most were swallowed up, but a few battled their way to the big table—or was that a trough?

Moulton's proposals were impressive enough to catch the attention of political worthies and avaricious investors. Enough notice was taken to initiate a separate and private set of enquiries regarding Frank Moulton's ambitions.

A note of credit from Merrow's Bank of London, sent in care of Mr

Moulton's Metropolitan Hotel address, suggested that a line of credit had been extended from the venerable and much-respected London financial house to the limit of one and a quarter million pounds—over six million dollars—as a provisional sum pending the full bullion transfer of three million sterling when transatlantic delivery was arranged. Leaked intelligence of such a significant resource amplified Mr Moulton's credibility and unlocked more doors for the hard-driving newcomer.

About the same time, agents for the Methodist and Episcopalian Church Commissioners agreed to a hasty bargain with the attorney of Mrs Eliakim Meigs regarding that humble patch of waste ground behind the New Mission House. All concerned seemed eager to complete the deed transfer before anyone could change their mind.

If Moulton was a key feature of the morning's meetings, he was absent for several of the conversations that took place that afternoon. Those discussions happened behind closed doors, though several of them included Bradwell Tyler. The attorney did not strictly adhere to his professional obligations of client privilege.

Councilman Weeks, who had been prominent amongst those greeting Frank Moulton that morning, summarised the issue quite succinctly. "The question, gentlemen, is how far to allow this fellow to proceed? He has the money, for sure, and he might have the moxie. But he's an outsider and I don't know as if we should let him in. There's a lot to gain from more elevated rail lines, and I'm not convinced if we'd get our full and proper due for a new route from the Manhattan Railway Company now they're a monopoly. Or even if they could raise that much capital to put up the line. But Moulton, he's an unknown."

"We might let him spend and then shut him down?" one of the aldermen suggested. "Take him for what we can get before he crashes and burns."

"We might. Or we could see how far he gets then lever him out if he succeeds. That's what happened with all the other rail pioneers in New York."[72]

"There is substantial profit in the right lines," Tyler ventured. "Over three million passengers a week ride the elevated right now, all paying a nickel fare a trip. That's an eight-million dollar a year enterprise."[73]

"We should keep on with Moulton," Councilman Weeks decided. "See where it goes. We'll have options when we see how this pans out. I'll check

---

72　Technical innovators of elevated railways such as Charles C. Harvey and Alfred Ely Beech were shuffled out of the way by legislation or take-over when the rail projects proved to have commercial application. However, Harvey retained enough political muscle to thwart Senator Tweed's 1871 bill that proclaimed the New York Elevated Railway Company's venture "a public nuisance" that would authorise him "as Commissioner of Public Works to tear it down."

73　About $255 million in modern times.

with the Grand Sachem. You did well to bring the kid to us, Bradwell."

The big city attorney had betrayed his client's confidence. He might have been unhappy to know that his rather ill-paid legal clerk did the same to him later that night, when the youth went to the Metropolitan's Honeymoon Suite parlour and reported everything he had heard at the meetings where he had accompanied his employer.

Wednesday brought the complication.

"I want to know what's what," the new player in the game insisted to the Metropolitan's manager. "I'll pay you for your help, or I'll ruin you. If I have to buy this pissant hotel and tear it to the ground I will, but I'll find out what I want to know."

The angry, rough-spoken westerner wore a hundred-dollar suit and had diamond cufflinks, signs of his recent fortune. His card announced him as Mr Aloysius Doran of San Francisco—Mrs Moulton's father.

"I can't give out information about our guests," the Manager answered, re-membering the fat fold of cash that he had received from Mr Doran's son-in-law.

"You can either have my banknotes in your pocket or a gun-barrel down your throat," the gold millionaire warned him. "Take some thought, son, and choose the treasury bills."

The Manager considered his options and elected to have the bribe.

Doran interrogated him on Frank Moulton's comings and goings, on the meetings the young man had held in his suite—with an engineer, an archi-tect, and an accountant—and on the things he had bought, which included a complete set of modern city maps. Doran was especially interested in the documents placed in the hotel safe, and handed over two hundred dollars then and there just to have a look at them.

The Manager was curious too, and he knew that his hotel's Owners would be keen to know what the confidential packet contained, so he consented that the gold-and-rail tycoon might have a "quick looksee."

Doran was uninterested in the "small change" that his son-in-law had de-posited, or even in the stunning diamond necklace, but he was very enthused by the plans and drawings that Moulton had brought.

"A rail line?" he recognised, seeing the technical pages and the preliminary cost estimates. "Frank is planning on setting down a new route." He traced the larger chart that he had unrolled across the Manager's desk. "To Queens County?"

"You can either have my banknotes in your pocket or a gun-barrel down your throat,!"

Queens County was the mostly-rural Long Island territory beyond Brooklyn, one of the original twelve 1683 counties of the Province of New York. It was largely undeveloped beyond the six crowded towns of Flushing, Jamaica, Newtown, Oyster Bay, and Hempstead, and growing Long Island City. Its only significant rail line, run by the unprofitable Long Island Rail Road Company, was ill-routed to commute a potential backcountry workforce into New York. There were serious commercial possibilities in a new, custom line right into the Big Apple's heart.

The large map had other useful information too. Sixty red-shaded patches indicated country and urban land that would have to be acquired for the project. Three much bigger hatched areas near Woodside, Glendale, and Fresh Pond represented smallhold farming acres that would be ripe for development once a rail line came through.

Doran made notes in his pocket-book, making sure he had everything down before he allowed the Manager to stow the documents again. He departed a satisfied man.

His next stop was to interrupt the lunch of the attorney Tyler. "You don't know me, sir, but you will. No, don't get up. I know you. I know you're working for Frank Moulton and I know you're a backstabbing weasel who reports on him to Councilman Weeks and Tammany Hall. So stop spluttering and let's get to business."

The surprised Bradwell Tyler was rather intimidated by the fierce, bushy-bearded westerner. Aloysius Doran had about him an air of restrained violence, as if his temper was but barely held in check and he longed to bloody his knuckles.

"My name's Doran," the attorney was told. "Hatty Moulton is my daughter. Francis Moulton wedded her in secret, without my permission, agin' my express wishes. Then he ruined her, and a good marriage to a gen-u-ine English Lord. I'd have given her everything, *everything*, but he took it all away from her. He betrayed me, and I'll destroy him for it."

"I can't speak about…" Tyler began, but was silenced by a massive fist crashing onto the table beside his plate.

"Just listen, mouthpiece. Frank Moulton has set himself a nice little business enterprise in hand here. I see that. I've seen his papers and his surveys. I've talked to his experts. He's further on than he's let you know and he's not as dumb as he's made you think. But I am going to bankrupt him!"

Bradwell Tyler swallowed hard. His lunch was not agreeing with him.

Doran continued. "You associate with some folks who don't daunt from giving a man a beating if he's got it coming, or making him vanish for good if that becomes needful. Well, I'm that sort of fellow too, and I have my own bold lads who are more then ready with knuckledusters or a firearm. I'll do whatever it takes to have that railroad project away from Moulton and in my hands.

"Now, I've seen Frank's plans. I know exactly where he needs to buy land cheaply. I know what spots he can't progress his schemes without owning 'em. I can snap them up as easily as him—an' before him. You, your job is just to slow him down so as I can do that. Slow him and you'll be well compensated. Very well compensated. Got it?"

Tyler nodded.

"And not one word to your cronies in City Hall," Doran warned. "You have some powerful contacts—I won't say friends—but so do I, and they're not in one city or state. Tammany has four or five senators in their pocket? I have a score, and I can buy more. They think they can snatch a railway line because they have some local pull? Son, I own significant shares in the greatest railroad companies across our nation! There are big railroad interests quite ready to swoop in and wipe out the little monopoly you've got going here. So don't make it a contest. Don't start what you can't finish!"

"You won't be able to... to destroy Moulton unless you make some local accommodation," Tyler ventured.

"That's what you think. All New Yorkers think they're the centre of the world. But you're not Washington, and you're not San Francisco, and you're sure as H__ not the U.S. of A., so you'd better get into your place, boy. *You*, specifically, will do what I tell you. Keep Frank busy on the paperwork while I grab his properties."

"I don't even know which land he wants yet."

"Good. Keep it that way until he tells you. Slow and easy. Right?"

After the forceful Aloysius Doran had left Tyler to his ruined luncheon, the ruffled attorney took a moment to have a drink and to consider his options. Tyler immediately ruled out alerting his client, but in the end his loyalties, or at least his fealty, were to the political machine that ran the city. Those ties had to prevail.

"Doran is a coming man, a powerful figure these last couple of years," Councilman Weeks admitted. "This is the first time since he got back from Europe that I've heard of him straying from the West Coast, but I guess family matters have brought him East."

"He seems intent on bringing his son-in-law down," Tyler warned.

"Well, that's not our problem. But losing a sweet deal like that new line could be, that stings. Fortunately, the Management at the Metropolitan have been able to verify what Moulton's route will be, and which bits of property he'll require."

The attorney's brows rose. "That means…"

"That they can still be snatched up before anyone else gets a chance to get hold of them? Sure. And whoever owns those plots owns the line."

"Doran has the same information. He'll be racing to pick up the real estate before Moulton can."

"And we can beat both of them to the punch," Weeks insisted. "I'll speak to the wigwam,[74] get some finance in place."

"It'll need to be fast."

"Speed is possible, with some money and political support. If anyone's getting rich from this new railroad into Queens County, it won't be Moulton or Doran."

That conversation did not take place in the presence of Mr Tyler's clerk, so the junior had to press his ear to the door so as to be able to report back to Frank Moulton on what he'd heard.

Thursday was a day of hasty negotiations.

Representatives of the city's Board of Works went out with speculative offers for an eclectic list of properties, with a bonus fee offered for swift completion. They were disconcerted to discover that many of the sites had been visited the previous evening. Offers had been made by Mr Doran's representatives, and some of the deals had been tentatively accepted.

Urgent messages went back to Councilman Weeks, and enhanced proposals were made to the various landowners' representatives—providing that the deals could be closed immediately. The City had the edge on speeding forward any transfer documentation, an advantage that put them ahead of Aloysius Doran for all his millions.

Mr Doran's agents were still in evidence, though, a swarm of lawyers and real estate men who were intent on thwarting the Tammany officials that sought to undercut them. Fortunately for the City, some of Doran's operatives were hired locals who were quite willing to accept a gratuity to turn on their out-of-town employer and hand their gains over to Councilman Weeks.

While all of this was happening, Mr and Mrs Moulton ventured out to Keens

---

74   That is, Tammany Hall. The term Tammany was borrowed from the Anglicised name of Lenape leader Tamanend, often then termed "The Patron Saint of America" for his peaceful politics of negotiation and his promotion of amity between Native Americans and the new colonisers. Tammany societies were established across the United States after the American Revolutionary War, of which New York's Tammany Hall was the most prominent. Local lodges of the Society of St. Tammany were termed 'wigwams' to commemorate their inspiration.

Steakhouse at Herald Square and negotiated turtle soup, two medium-rare cuts with a garnish of fresh peas, squashes, and tomatoes, and to follow a compote of forest fruits and iced-cream. Then they enjoyed a matinee performance of Bronson Howard's *Saratoga; or Pistols for Seven*[75] at the Garrick Theatre.

"I do enjoy a good comedy," Mr Moulton told Mrs Moulton.

"You also have a taste for drama," his companion pointed out.

"Oh yes. I confess that I enjoy a spot of the dramatic."

"And I enjoy you enjoying it," his lady replied.

By evening a number of transactions had been finalised. The City now owned one third of the sites shown on Frank Moulton's chart and were in active pursuit of the rest. Mr Doran's attempts at acquisition were being held up in tangles of red tape, by estate transfer laws and neighbourhood provisions, by property tax questions and sanitation queries, by title deed anomalies and financial transfer audits. You can't beat City Hall.

"The estate purchase costs have been higher than we'd have liked," Tyler admitted to his unofficial sponsors. He didn't mention that as the attorney who had processed most of the contracts his percentage fee would therefore be that much greater. "Three and four times what we'd have gotten the properties for if we hadn't been bidding against a millionaire. But it'll still be a worthwhile investment."

"It'd better be," Councilman Weeks cautioned. "I've put my head on the block for this one—which means that your b____ are on the anvil, Bradwell!"

"We can have the rest of the properties by three tomorrow," Tyler quickly assured the investors. "That's when Moulton will be coming to see me with the list of sites he wants to buy."

"I suppose we should let him make an offer," Weeks considered. "It'll cost him a fair margin above what he expected though. Around five times as much, I'd say, twice what we paid out. And a share of any future fares from his trains."

"He might see sense," Tyler reflected. "If not, then Aloysius Doran might settle for a part of the pie since he won't get the whole?"

"Maybe he and his old pa-in-law can have a bidding war?"

"Old Doran might cut up rough."

"This is New York. We can always cut up rougher."

---

75   Debuting in 1870 at Daly's Fifth Avenue Theatre, *Saratoga* launched the long career of Bronson Howard as one of the most successful American playwrights of the 19th century, and became one of his most performed comedies. In December 1978 it was even presented by the Royal Shakespeare Company at the Aldwych Theatre, London.

The last negotiation of the day was a bit trickier. Mr and Mrs Moulton returned from a most pleasant day in Manhattan, arm in arm and very much in love. They ascended to their Metropolitan Hotel Honeymoon Suite laughing and hugging.

A thickset man in brown tweeds rose from the chair where he had been waiting. "That's enough of that," he told them. "Jeremy Wilson and Catherine Cusack, you are under arrest."

"Gosh, officer," Jemmy Wilson replied, "I don't understand what you are talking about."

Their unexpected visitor produced a copper badge and identified himself as Wilson Hargeave of the New York Metropolitan Police. "I have information from one Inspector Slump of the Notting-ham-shire Constabulary of England, Great Britain, that you are the notorious thief and confidence man known as the Notting-ham Crakster.[76] This young woman is your accomplice."

"An accomplice?" Miss Cusack quavered. "What is that?"

"Come now, Wilson. All is discovered. Your supposed fatal tumble under the wheels of a carriage in England is known to be nothing more than another of your tricks, a ploy to flee beyond the arm of the law. It has failed!"

"Oh. I feel faint!" Miss Cusack warned, touching the back of her hand to her forehead and swaying unsteadily. Her other hand negligently rose to her throat, neatly covering the Dunfordine diamond necklace that she had worn for her evening on the town.

"No need for that, love," Jemmy told her. "I can see that Inspector Hargeave is too wily for that sort of trick. And unfortunately, from what I hear, he's about the only cop in New York City that we won't be able to bribe."

"Not bribe?" Catherine asked, wide-eyed. "What's wrong with him?"

"I believe in the law!" Wilson Hargeave snapped back.

"He does," Jemmy confirmed. "By the way, inspector, it's 'Not-in-gum', not 'Notting-ham'. The 'h' is silent, and the emphasis is on the 'Not'—as in this is not what it appears to be."

"What do you mean?" the policeman demanded suspiciously. He produced a snub-nosed pistol from his coat pocket, although Hosiah Slump had indicated in his long warning telegram that the Crakster never resorted to violence.

"I mean that there are things of which you are not aware. Might you consider delaying your very righteous arrest for just a few moments so that I can explain?"

"What is there to explain?" the detective demanded. "There is a string of outraged pawnbrokers and some sort of betting scandal at the carriage track."

---

76   Inspector Slump was on the trail of his nemesis the Crakster since before Jemmy's exploits in "Selecting a Ghost", which is also Slump's sole appearance in a Doyle narrative.

"We may pass over those," Jemmy assured him. "By the way, have you communicated with Mr Sherlock Holmes at all?[77] He might give me a reference. I recommend that you send him a telegram. I'll cover the cost."

"I don't see that I need to wire London. I have already verified that the real Mr and Mrs Francis Moulton are still in Paris."

"And we are very happy for them, to be in love in such a beautiful location. We considered heading there ourselves, but decided that France was not far enough out of the reach and interest of a certain criminal mastermind whom I may have offended by declining a job offer. New York might not be either. We may have to migrate West."

"Once we have picked up some necessaries for the journey," Miss Cusack mentioned. Her eyes twinkled. "And of course, assuming that you decide to let us go, officer."

"Why would I let you go?"

"Because you are an honest man who believes in the law," Jemmy told him. "And I discern from the old fish-line marks on your hands that you are an angler. Therefore you fully understand when it is right to cut the line and go for a bigger fish."

"A fish?"

"For 'fish' read 'crooked politician'," Miss Cusack advised.

"You see," the Crakster advised the detective, "if you take us in then you lose the opportunity of bringing down some wicked men who otherwise scoff at your law. Powerful men with powerful friends who believe that the police are their hired attack dogs and nothing more. But if we remain at liberty, my lovely companion and I, for just twenty-four hours more, then we hope to bring the whole crooked pile of smug thieving bureaucrats down into a rotten festering heap. If you don't mind?"

"You see, Inspector?" Miss Cusack smiled prettily, "There is room to negotiate."

Friday morning passed with a number of difficult calculations.

Inspector Hargeave wrestled with some knotty moral calculus, balancing his need for justice with his career prospects if he truly sought it. In the end he relented and sent off a tentative telegram for advice to that famous sleuth

---

77   Holmes referred "to my friend, Wilson Hargreave, of the New York Police Bureau, who has more than once made use of my knowledge of London crime," in "The Dancing Men" (1903, collected as "The Adventure of the Dancing Men" in *The Adventures of Sherlock Holmes*), set in 1898, ten years after our current narrative.

across the Atlantic, hoping for inspiration.

Councilman Weeks endured an uncomfortable meeting with the Grand Sachem of the Tammany Hall wigwam—that was, the boss of the powerful and corrupt political lodge. At Weeks' recommendation, Tammany had risked a significant portion of their cash-to-hand, the better part of a million dollars of city finances and their own war-chest. It was a risk, both financial and reputational, and whilst it might make Weeks if it succeeded, winning him a ticket to much higher office in Congress or Senate, perhaps even an eventual shot at a Presidential nomination, it might also ruin him, with painful and permanent personal consequences. The odds were incalculable. Weeks began to sweat.

In Five Points, behind the Mission House on Cross Street where the Old Brewery had once stood, a small crowd and a trio of curious pressmen gathered to watch the careful erection of an incongruous stone monument upon a ruined wasteland. The workmen had faced a difficult engineering task, to clear, level, and secure a foundation under the broken bricks and accumulated detritus where a stable had once stood, and then to raise a stone obelisk some ten feet tall in memory of the late Eliakim Meigs of that parish. They laboured quickly; this was, after all, Five Points, and they did not feel too safe with valuable builders' equipment and supplies in such rough and lawless surroundings.

"An old woman's folly," the reporter from the *New York Star* opined to his peers from the *New York Daily News* and the *New York Times*. "The stone will be stolen and resold by nightfall."

"Quite probably," the *Daily News* man agreed. "But maybe not. Look at the other side of the monument. It carries the names of every man from the Sixth District who was drafted and died in the Union War. It's a memorial to them too."

"That's interesting," the *Times* reporter agreed, discerning an angle. More affluent neighbourhoods had been quick to raise statues, masonry, or plaques to the heroic fallen, but no such subscription had been possible in this poverty-crippled neighbourhood. "The natives might just protect that, then. Even the gangs like the Dead Rabbits and the Bowery Boys."

"Believe it or not, the Widow Meigs has spoken with them," the *Daily News* reported, since he had been diligent enough to seek out and interview the eccentric relic. "A 'treaty' has been agreed. And an approach has been made to the War Office's Battle Monuments Department[78] to maintain it as a war memorial, with an agreed bequest."

At the monument's dedication by the chaplain of the New Mission, Mrs

---

78   This organisation was re-established as the independent American Battle Monuments Commission by the U.S. Congress in 1923, based in Arlington, Virginia, and Paris, France.

Meigs had made a short patriotic speech alluding to how the Army of the Union had been the making of her lamented husband. She never removed her heavy black veil, even for the *New York Times* photographer's plate of the ceremony. Paid peacekeepers in the grieving woman's hire, salted amongst the crowd, had discouraged heckling—the Five Points way. At the end of the event there were formal gift presentations made to a number of prominent local personalities.

All of this meant that when attorney-at-law Bradwell Tyler arrived two hours later to pick up negotiations with the Cross Street Mission regarding an otherwise-valueless demolition plot behind the Mission House he had a series of unpleasant surprises.

First, the Home Missions committee had already received a significant offer for the whole wasteland, which they had given their word upon and were unminded to revoke. Overcoming that commercial choice would require the use of the City's powers of compulsory purchase, always a nightmare of legal wrangling.

Secondly, Tyler was a day too late to prevent the transfer of one ten-square-foot section of that required property to other ownership. The Widow's plot was almost insignificant, unless one intended to build a vital elevated railway station and refuelling depot on the spot. Civic powers would again be required to gain the land, but this time complicated by its dedication as a war memorial with the consequent involvement of the War Office graves department,[79] the press, and the high feelings of the residents of Lower Manhattan.

Thirdly, and quite absurdly, the remaining scrap of the widow's ground that had not been covered by monumental granite had been divided up into mere six-by-six-inch packets of land and gifted after the dedication to some one hundred and twenty deserving residents, civil leaders, and local characters of Canal Street, Mulberry Street, and Park Row. Untangling deeds of ownership after all of that would be a nightmarish quest.

Bradwell Tyler returned to Tammany Hall in low spirits. Even if other agents had been successful in acquiring the necessary footprints to enable the elevated train along Orange Street and across the East River at the Broome Slip, Mrs Meigs' intransigence regarding her husband's memorial would cause

---

79   So opposed had the Irish Americans of Five Points been to the North's compulsory Civil War draft that from July 13th-18th 1863 there was massive rioting against Congress' draft laws. The confrontations, which included the destruction of draft offices, have since been described as the largest civil and most racially charged urban disturbance in American history. Mobs ransacked or destroyed numerous public buildings, two Protestant churches, the homes of various abolitionists or sympathisers, many black homes, and the Coloured Orphan Asylum at 44th Street and 5th Avenue, which was burned to the ground. President Lincoln had to divert several regiments of militia and volunteer troops after the Battle of Gettysburg to control the city. The official death toll was 119 or 120 people.

costly delays and political popularity.

"She won't budge," he had to report to Councillor Weeks and his committee. "Not without a push. Not unless we agree to replace that obelisk at Five Points with a thirty foot bronze statue of her d_____d husband outside City Hall, in the same pose as Lady Liberty!"

"That's ridiculous," scorned Weeks. "We'll have to resort to other means of persuading her."

"That will cause us some trouble too," one of the committee-men predicted. "Those pressmen have smelled a story now. We'd be front-page leader columns if we try to strongarm a feeble old grieving widow about a war memorial."

"Well, get it sorted *somehow*, Tyler," Weeks warned the shyster lawyer. "This has gotten too big to turn sour now." His face was unhealthily red. The back of the councilman's jacket was soaked with perspiration.

Having given her statements to the newspapers, signed certain legal Deeds of Trust with the Mission's attorneys and accountants, and made a loving farewell to her sudden new monument, Mrs Ephraim Meigs departed New York and was never seen again.

Black suited Miss Cusack, but the make-up and veil could be somewhat stifling. She was glad to return to other disguises.

Bradwell Tyler left Tammany Hall with a flea in his ear that felt like an elephant. Presenting Moulton's scheme to the committee and to key investors had seemed like a ticket to the big-time, the attorney's chance to step up in the Tammany hierarchy. Now that gamble was beginning to look like a bet too far. Nor did Tyler relish his three o'clock meeting with Frank Moulton, where he would have to explain some facts of life to the arrogant young entrepreneur. Still, perhaps he might work off some of his bad mood on his brash supposed-client?

However, the attorney's expectations were to be thwarted again. His clerk sullenly announced that Mr Tyler's visitor was waiting in his office—and then gave notice of quitting. It seemed that the much-abused young legal secretary had come into an unexpected windfall inheritance and could now afford to make his way on his own. He intended to move on to greener pastures.

The clerk did not mention that his fortune was come from payments for information to Frank Moulton, or that it was not Moulton who awaited Bradwell Tyler in the attorney's office.

Tyler discovered the substitution the hard way. Instead of the expected young businessman, it was Moulton's fierce and unhappy father-in-law, the gold and railway magnate Doran, who occupied his chambers.

"You miserable worm!" Aloysius Doran cried out as he saw Tyler. "You were warned! I told you not to cross me! And you run straight to Weeks and his cronies, tattling all about my plans. Well, I promised you'd regret it, and you shall!"

"Wait! I can explain…!"

Tyler backed away but the angry gold-miner seized him by the collar and pressed him up against a bookcase. "Explain betraying me? Explain ruining my revenge? Explain costing me the millions I'd have made when I took over Frank's scheme? Go on then."

The lawyer babbled out whatever justification he might dredge to save his skin: the deal would only work with Tammany Hall's goodwill, and he had secured it; there could be an alliance between City and tycoon to bring the railroad to fruition; the gains would be grand enough for all…

Doran shook him like a weasel. "Don't be a d___fool! You jacked up the ground prices and now there's other parties jumping in as well. The cat's out of the bag! It's going to be an unholy free-for-all. You wrecked my retribution scheme and forced me to take final measures."

"What… what do you mean?" Tyler stammered.

Doran pushed him away contemptuously, and slammed an object down on the attorney's desk. Tyler recognised that distinctive gold fob-watch with the eggshell-blue dial that Moulton had worn at their first meeting.

"I told you I knew men who would take serious actions," Doran declared. "Well now they have. They have! Frank Moulton's body will never be found."

"You… you killed him!"

"As for my Hatty, she'll never be seen again either. She's put away where I can keep an eye on her for the rest of her life. I'd have preferred bankrupting and driving to suicide the man who stole her from me. She might have come back to me of her own accord afterwards. But you robbed me of that, Tyler, with your devious underhand dealings and blabbing mouth."

A deathly chill shuddered through the terrified attorney. His bladder failed him.

"So now my attention is on you," Doran went on. "I'll give you twenty-four hours to set your affairs in order. To say farewell to your wife and child. That's my mercy to you—and the last I'll show you. After that I'll be putting out bounties on you. Not on your life. Not at first. On parts of your body. A tooth, a finger, a toe, an eyelid… different bits every day of the week."

"No!" Tyler gasped. "Please, sir…!"

"Let's see how long you survive, eh? And don't look to your City Hall friends to protect you. They'll give you up to me just like that to avoid a war. You'll be the sacrifice, see? The penalty. And don't try mewling to the police, either. You won't escape by turning State's Evidence on your pals. There's not a copper in New York that I can't buy." Dolan twitched his head to the side to give Tyler permission to flee. "Twenty-four hours, shyster. Then it begins—snip, snip, snip!"

Bradwell Tyler fled for his life, as if the hounds of Hell were already after him.

The alleged Aloysius Doran used the keys he had pickpocketed from the law-yer as he had manhandled him to open the office safe, from which he extracted a substantial bundle of cash and every single confidential document that Tyler held for the politicians of Tammany Hall and the departments of the city.

"It's like this, Mr Tyler," Wilson Hargeave explained to the distraught and fearful attorney that evening. "As I understand it, you have no proof that a wealthy gentleman from out West has placed some kind of bounty upon you. There's little trace of Mr Aloysius Doran even being on this side of the conti-nent. In fact he has witnesses who will place him in San Francisco."

"Doran is a rich man," Tyler protested. "He can buy witnesses and alibis."

"Doran is unshakable," Inspector Hargreave warned. "Unimpeachable. But the truth is that documents from your safe, confidential documents of immense commercial and political value, documents that evidently expose some very dirty dealings in City Hall, have evidently been distributed between the three leading crusading newspapers of New York. Those stolen materials might be inadmissible for criminal prosecution at the Bar, but the broadsheets can print what they want and fight it out in the civil courts. Doubtless such a clash will boost their circulation."

Tyler pressed his forehead into his hands. "They will all blame me. All of them. I'm doomed!"

"Well, you are certainly in a lot of trouble," Hargeave agreed. "That's why you chased me down, isn't it? You need an honest cop who won't give you up for a bribe of any amount, someone you can depend upon to get you safely into custody where you can cut a deal with the State's Senior Prosecutor. I'm touched that you thought of me."

The Metropolitan Police Inspector wasn't surprised, however. He'd been promised a bigger fish. Now he might parlay this catch into a whole brace of bigger fish yet; perhaps even a whale or two.

"I'll do what you want, tell you what you want, if you can protect me from Doran and Weeks," Tyler promised fervently.

"Well then," Hargeave answered with grim satisfaction, "I shall take down your statement, sir."

The first that Councillor Weeks knew about the theft at Tyler's office was when the evening newspapers appeared at Tammany Hall. A late sidebar mentioned the arrest and custody of the unfortunate attorney, and his sequestering at an undisclosed location off Long Island.

Whilst those front pages were souring Weeks' digestion, he received a summons to speak with the Grand Sachem himself.[80]

The leader of the New York Society of St Tammany had also seen the papers. They were laid out across his desk, crumpled where his angry fingers had gripped them.

"I can explain," Weeks gasped quickly, knowing that he could not.

"A scandal in the three biggest news-rags in the State," the Sachem mentioned. "A great swathe of our quiet dealings exposed. We were just coming back from the Boss Tweed days and now there's this. It will have national consequences."

"We can put it on Tyler," Weeks suggested. "We can bury it—bury him."

"That'll just keep the story running. And there's more." The Grand Sachem dropped two manila folders atop the incriminating newspapers. "Here is an initial appraisal from our Chief Accountant on the costings of Moulton's Queens Line. Moulton's estimates were ridiculously off. The budget would need to be at least five times what he proposed. Did you not have anyone check the figures before you dragged us into this?"

Weeks swallowed hard. "There was such an urgency, sir, to strike fast…"

"So you did not. This other document is a preliminary survey of the project by the Senior Engineer of the City's planning department. Amongst many other points he makes, he notes that much of the land you have bought for us is drained swampland, quite unsuitable to bear the weight of railway pylons. The Five Points station is planned to be placed on what used to be open marsh by the now-drained Collect Pond.[81] In other words, you have spent a million dollars, a million of our dollars, on worthless land that is actually,

---

80   This would be Richard Welstead 'Boss' Croker (1843–1922), who controlled Tammany Hall from 1886-1902, earning a sinister reputation for corruption and ruthlessness. Though frequently the subject of investigations he was never convicted, and eventually retired to Ireland.

81   The 48-acre, 60-foot deep Collect Pond was the main source of drinking water and fish during the first two centuries of European settlement in Manhattan. Once a pleasant rural feature used as a picnic site and winter skating rink, its waters were polluted by 18th century commercial enterprises including tanneries, potteries, a slaughterhouse, and Couldthardt's Brewery. The pond was landfilled in 1811 and middle-class housing was erected on the site, but buried vegetation produced methane gas and the new neighbourhood lacked storm sewers, causing subsidence. Houses shifted on their foundations, the unpaved streets were often buried in foot-deep mud with human and animal excrement, and mosquitoes bred in the stagnant pools created by the poor drainage. Richer residents fled the area by the 1820s, leaving the site to poor immigrants, mostly Irish Catholics fleeing the Great Famine. The notorious Five Points district developed in the valley that had once been a pretty and pleasant lake.

properly, *worthless!*"

The Sachem slammed his palm onto his desk, setting his inkpot rattling. Weeks dared not speak.

"It was a joke, Councilman," the Grand Sachem explained, his voice dangerously calm and low. "It was a prank. A confidence trick. A property scam on a massive scale, aimed right at us. And you fell for it. You pulled us into this bog and sank us to the necks."

"I told you, it was Tyler. We can…"

"You're right that we must put it off onto a scapegoat," the Sachem said. "Someone has to be to blame. Blood must be let."

"We can silence Tyler and make it seem that…"

"Tyler's out of our reach, thanks to a smart straight cop who we'll have to watch more carefully from now on. And Tyler's too small."

"Moulton… It was his idea, his supposed project that…"

"Moulton's gone. Dead, most likely. And Doran was never here, that we could ever prove. *Someone* must take the fall."

And Councilman Weeks knew that he was doomed.

Frank Moulton and his charming wife never came back to the Metropolitan Hotel for their things, but that dazzling necklace had never been returned to the safe after Hatty Moulton had worn it to dine out. The thick bankrolls deposited with the hotel proved to be almost entirely of blank paper, with only a few real bills folded as wrappers. The bearer bonds were clever fakes. The silver dollars were of lead. Even the letter from Merrow's Bank proved to be false.

The twenty real dollars actually in the vault did not cover the bill for the Moulton's lavish stay. That account went unpaid.

Attempts to forward the bill to Paris were completely ignored.

The homeless woman who had received charity at the New Mission House returned but once, in company with a young man, and then only to hand back the good second-hand dress she had been given and to leave a stuffed carpetbag filled with money for the benefit of others in need.

Nor were that and the Widow Meigs' generosity the only good fortune that the charitable institution enjoyed. Over the coming weeks, as land sales contracts that could not be voided worked their way to exchange of payments, a number of spontaneous donations from proceeds of sale came to the Mission from a wide variety of vendors. In fact most of those landholders profiting from the lucrative sale of property that should really have been valueless retained only a third for themselves, forwarding a another third of their gains to the Mission's good work; where that last remainder of the windfall went was never determined.

It was evening on Saturday, 3rd March before Inspector Wilson Hargeave had the pleasure of saying, "Councillor Weeks, you are under arrest on charges of embezzlement, blackmail, conspiracy to pervert justice, and tax evasion. To start with." This was afterwards considered the start of the detective inspector's considerable rise in fame, esteem, and influence in the New York Metropolitan Police Department, and of his part in its gradual reform.

By the day and hour that Hargeave clapped the cuffs on Weeks, the detective had also received a reply from Baker Street, London, a cable which read,

'WILSON IS A ROGUE AND A THIEF, BUT AN ENDEARING AND SINCERE ONE + STOP + YOU MAY HAVE CONFIDENCE IN HIS GENUINE WORD + STOP + HOLMES'.

That night Jemmy Wilson and Catherine Cusack dined out on Eggs Benedict, Lobster Newburg, and Baked Alaska at Delmonico's on 5th and 26th, although they signed the guest-book as Mr and Mrs Courtald. They left a handsome tip, since the food was excellent and the service impeccable.[82] Thereafter they took a stroll in Central Park, arm in arm under the stars, and enjoyed the crisp clear night.

"Well," Catherine said, laying her head on the Crakster's shoulder, "we have discovered America. What shall we do next?"

"I think we might say good-bye to New York for a while," Jemmy considered. "We have made quite a bit of noise here. If Professor Moriarty is bothering to listen for us then he will hear it. I imagine that we shall have to 'Go West, young woman!'"[83]

"That sounds exciting. Westward Ho! Do you have a destination in mind?"

"I was considering the Black Hills of Dakota," the New York Crakster re-

---

82   In 1860, The New York Times reviewed the famous restaurant thusly: "We may frankly say that we have never seen a public supper served in a more inapproachable fashion, with greater discretion, or upon a more luxurious scale." They may have meant "irreproachable". Patrons of Delmonico's included Jenny Lind, Theodore Roosevelt, Chester Arthur, Mark Twain, Arthur Sullivan, 'Diamond Jim' Brady, Lillian Russell, Charles Dickens, Oscar Wilde, J.P. Morgan, James Gordon Bennett, Jr., Nikola Tesla, Commodore Matthew C. Perry, King Edward VII (while Prince of Wales), and Napoleon III of France.

83   The Crakster is mimicking the then-common phrase encouraging Western expansion across middle North America, "Go West, young man!". The quote is often attributed to author and newspaper editor Horace Greeley (1811-1872), but this is nowadays disputed.

"Well, we have discovered America. What shall we do next?"

vealed. "There's gold in them thar hills, you know. And a great deal of bad men who want it."

"And you want to take it from the bad men?"

"Well, if you're game, o beloved one. How do you feel about a nice trip to a little town called Deadwood?"

THE END

THE RANSOMED MIRACLE

HE RANSOM NOTE was written in squared block capitals on cheap common stationary, delivered in a plain envelope by third post. It read:

IF YOU WISH TO SEE THE CHILD ALIVE
THEN YOU WILL VOTE AGAINST
THE WORKMAN'S COMPENSATION ACT.
INSTRUCTIONS WILL FOLLOW TO PAY £2000 AFTER THE VOTE.

Holmes examined the letter with his magnifying lens, held the paper up to the light, then smelled the correspondence.

"Well?" Inspector Farmer asked anxiously.

"You must be patient," Inspector Bradstreet advised the local officer. "Mr Holmes has his methods and takes his time. He cannot be rushed."

I covered my hand with my mouth to hide the quirk of my lips at the Scotland Yard man's words. Bradstreet was one of the old school policemen who had started out running in Bow Street; I was amused to hear him speaking so familiarly of the consulting detective to whom the Metropolitan Police so reluctantly but persistently resorted.

There was little else to be amused about. Eighteen-month-old Samuel Deverill was missing from his cot, abducted by night from a locked and sealed house. His life was feared for. The ransom note had been delivered in the time between Bradstreet convincing the Somerset constabulary to send for Holmes and our arrival by train at St Ethelreda's Manor[83] in sleepy Quantoxhead, Somerset.

"Will Mr Deverill accede to the demands?" I had asked the investigators in charge of the case when they had produced the message.

"Deverill is so distraught that it is hard to know what he will do," Farmer responded. "As a Member of Parliament he must be above such pressure, whatever

---

[83] St Ethelreda (Æthelthryth, Audrey) was an East Anglian princess who managed to remain a virgin despite two marriages and the fierce pursuit of her ruthless and amorous second husband; her chastity was evidently considered miraculous. The village and parish of West Quantoxhead was also called St Audries after the saint.

the threats. He cannot go against his party and its whip[84] without serious consequences, especially on so controversial and marginal a vote as for the *Workman's Compensation Act.*[85] It would break him. But so would losing the boy."

Holmes had declined to speak to the desperate MP and his wife until he had examined the primary evidence. We now stood in the empty nursery while Holmes evaluated the ransom document.

Since Bradstreet was taking my customary role of keeping the local police inspector in check while Holmes worked, I took the opportunity of looking round the neat bedroom from which young Samuel had been snatched. The chamber was one of three south-facing rooms on the first floor, above the dining room.[86] It had two Georgian windows of the type that shuttered at night, and they had been sealed and locked at the time the child was found missing. The main furniture apart from the barred crib from which Samuel had vanished were a nursemaid's bed, a pair of chests of drawers, a wardrobe filled with child's clothes and toys, a rocking chair, and a large rocking horse.

I drifted over to inspect those internal shutters. They folded back concertina-fashion into the deep recesses at each side of the windows. When closed there was a bar that swivelled down to secure them in place, with a small hasp through which a padlock was threaded to prevent the bar being lifted. No burglar who somehow jimmied the window-sash could even reach the lock, and the key for the padlocks remained with the family butler who secured the house every night.

From the window I had a fine view over the snow-frosted landscape, across the fields and woodland that formed part of the estate and to the start of the Quantock Hills. Westward past the trees I could glimpse the bleak silver strand of the Bristol Channel.

I checked the chimney as best I could. At this time of year a small fire still blazed in the grate. Just above the upper level of the hearth was a 'pigeon trap',

---

[84]   A whip (from *whipper*, a huntsman's assistant who keeps the hound pack from straying) is a voting instruction issued by a political party to its elected members, usually requiring obedient support to some significant policy issue. Defying the whip can lead to censure or even exile from the party ("losing the whip"). Political parties appoint certain elected members as enforcers, also called Whips, under a Chief Whip, whose job it is to ensure that other members "toe the party line" when a whip instruction is issued.

[85]   Liberal Unionist Samuel Chamberlain's *Workman's Compensation Act* 1897 replaced the *Employer's Liability Act* 1880, changing the burden of proof for labourers injured at work so that a worker need only prove that he had been hurt on the job. It was controversial in some quarters because of fears that it might lead to employers being overwhelmed with liability claims and because it was an unfunded mandate on the private sector.

[86]   American readers are reminded that in British convention the floor on street level is the *Ground Floor* of a building. The next level up is the *First Floor*. The nursery was on the second story (or *storey* in British) by American parlance.

a metal grill fastened across the broad chimney to prevent stray birds from intruding. I did not need to be Sherlock Holmes to see the depth of soot crusting the bolts that held the ironwork in place and know that it had not been opened in the recent past.

Nor need I catalogue the wardrobe or other containers. Enthusiastic searchers had already pulled out every toy and garment, hunting for the missing boy. Contents were roughly scattered over the carpet. I suspected that the nursemaid would not appreciate how clumsy officers of the law had rifled her private linen drawer and then casually tossed aside the intimate contents.

There was but one door, out onto the landing above the main entrance hall. All the family and guest rooms of the upper floor opened onto this one balcony except for two box rooms that were accessed via the servants' stair that extended to attics where the house's domestics slept. That layout was significant too. The butler locked the intervening doors to the back stairs at night, suggesting that no member of the household staff except the nursemaid should have access to the main part of the mansion after lights-out.

The nursery door had a rim lock on the inside but it had not been fastened at the time the kidnapping was discovered. Why would such a precaution be considered necessary?

Holmes stirred from his examination. "The man who wrote this note," he announced without preamble, "was right-handed, of some but limited education, probably of around thirty years of age. He may be known to the family. The stationery was purchased recently, likely for the purpose of sending this message. The ink-type is cheap and common, but note that amongst its uses is the filling of inkwells in public venues such as Post Offices. The message was written very shortly before it was sealed into the envelope. The envelope was addressed after the letter was placed inside."

Bradstreet's brows rose. "Come now, Mr Holmes. You will have to explain how you might possibly make such assumptions!"

"Not assumptions," I assured the Scotland Yard officer.

"Hardly," Holmes agreed. "Must I show you what is quite obvious to anyone who takes the time to view the evidence with analytical care? Very well. The writing on the note is by metal-tipped ink pen, the old-fashioned sort requiring one to continually dip it into a reservoir. It has a broad nib that cants depending on whether it is held left or right handedly; determining how it was gripped is child's play."

Farmer looked suspicious of such conclusions. Bradstreet rather resembled a fellow to whom the obvious had now been pointed out to him after he had missed it.

Holmes continued his lecture. "The use of capitals, possibly intended to disguise a hand that might otherwise be recognised, is also valuable in determining the age and education of the writer. The choice of how to render the letters A, G, K, N, M, and Y are all telling. Examples of all of those characters appear in the letter before us. Fashions of writing vary, but for most people they are set from the time they first learned their A-B-Cs, and from those variations one may glean an inkling of the age of the author—or at least the age at which he was taught his letters. Female writers tend to different pressures on the pen than male ones and are often taught a more flowing, 'feminine' hand."

Bradstreet might have cut in, but Holmes had not finished. "Professional secretaries and clerks become more precise in their execution of script over time. Regular writers become somewhat sloppier as constant repetition makes handwriting less neat. On this letter I see signs of a man taught literacy some score or more years ago who has used a pen since then with less frequency than one would expect if he were a more educated fellow."

"And the other guesses?" Farmer pressed. "About the Post Office and such?"

"Hardly guesses, inspector. The recent purchase of the envelope is indicated by its faint odour of lilacs. It has lately been shelved or racked beside scented stationery, suggesting that it was on sale somewhere. The trace scent would have faded if it had been long separated from its shelf-mates. The use of cheap standard ink of the kind put out as a courtesy to members of the public who need to use one of the pens chained to a shop desk suggests but does not prove that the note was written at a Post Office, probably the Central Taunton branch indicated by the letter's postal mark.

"That the letter was posted immediately may be proved by examining the traces of ink from folding the paper before it had been adequately blotted and allowed to dry. There is a particular undried ink imprint where pressure was placed upon the envelope to affix the stamp, and lesser signs where the pen pressed onto the envelope when the address was written while the note was folded inside. We might possibly infer that the writer was in haste to prepare and send his note to catch the third post. Enquiries at Taunton might establish a description of someone who rushed at the last minute to get a newly-written letter into the mail sack."

"We will... we'll see to that immediately," Inspector Farmer promised, astonished at this sudden lead in his investigation. He hastened from the room to pass on instructions.

Holmes turned his gaze upon the cot. In particular he was interested in a pair of grooves rubbed into the varnish around the base of the box between two of the vertical bars. "What do you make of these?" he asked Bradstreet and I.

The twin marks were scarcely visible, each a minor scrape on the curved bevel of the wooden tray that held the cot mattress. They were about an inch apart, up near where the child's head would have settled. "I confess I'm baffled," I told Holmes.

"Some kind of… of…" Bradstreet attempted, but he too could think of nothing that would explain the abrasions.

Holmes declined to offer any help to satisfy our curiosity. Instead he cast about the room, pausing once to examine the carpet beside the maid's bed and a second time to look at the sad tangle that had been left when the constabulary had emptied out the contents of the nursemaid's knitting basket. Finally he looked at the hearth much as I had done, except he also took the rake and pulled some ash from under the firegrate.

He fixed a jeweller's lens to his eye to inspect the fireplace cinders. "List the members of the household and then summarise events as they have been established," he told Bradstreet meanwhile. "Be precise about times."

The Scotland Yard inspector referred to his notebook. "Let's see. The family consists of Mr and Mrs Deverill, Mrs Deverill's widowed mother Mrs Swift, the missing boy Samuel who is not yet two, and a nine-year-old sister Veronica. Additionally there are seven staff: a butler and his wife the cook, a footman-driver, two general maids, a page, and Miss Clementine, the nursemaid who sleeps here in the nursery with her charge. Mr Deverill is the local Member of Parliament, a coming man in his Party."

"They are all present and accounted for?" I checked. After all, someone must have unlocked the house to allow the child to be extracted.

"All are here and being questioned. As to times, young Master Samuel was put to bed around six-fifteen last night. He was somewhat colicky and was given a spoon of watered brandy to settle him. Miss Clementine remained with him as he slept, keeping watch from her chair. She did not leave the room before she retired at around nine-forty p.m., and she slept soundly until she was suddenly woken at around twenty past four this morning."

I noticed that there was a carriage clock on the mantel, so presumably the nursemaid's attestations about time would be accurate.

"Mistress Veronica was sent to bed at seven-thirty. Her grandmother went up and read to her, leaving her tucked up at ten past eight. The adult family met in the small lounge for a light supper at eight thirty and then retired by nine-fifteen. It is Mr Deverill's custom to retire early when he is in the country unless he is entertaining. Sleddow, the butler, locked up the house and put out the lights by nine-fifty."

"Was he alone or assisted?" Holmes demanded.

"Alone. He is also the only keyholder, apart from a set that is locked in an escritoire drawer in Mr Deverill's bedroom."

"How secure is the house?" I wondered. "Could a burglar enter without a key?"

Trust a Scotland Yard man to have checked for that, at least. "All the windows were shuttered and locked. Evidently the wind comes in fiercely off the

Bristol Channel and the house is draughty unless it is properly sealed. There are three external doors, all of which were bolted as well as locked. The chute into the coal cellar has an internal padlock. The cellar is bolted. I don't say but that a skilled burglar couldn't break his way into St Ethelreda's Manor, but he could not do so without leaving traces of a forced entry."

That point made, Bradstreet continued his history. "Miss Clementine was woken by some noise. At first she thought it was 'Little Sam' coughing. She rose to check that the child was all right, uncovering a night-light that she keeps burning for such a purpose. That was when she discovered that he was not in his cot."

"What did she do?" I asked.

"At first she hoped that either Mrs Deverill or Mrs Swift had come into the nursery and taken the child to sleep with them for some reason. She therefore looked in first upon the old lady, and on finding her sound asleep she ventured to disturb her employers. Mrs Deverill was alarmed to hear that the boy had vanished. A quick check was made that Miss Veronica had not for some reason taken her baby brother to sleep with her; in vain. At this point the alarm was sounded—that is, the dinner gong that warns of fire or emergency—and the whole household assembled."

"I imagine so." I could well picture the spreading panic as family and staff searched the premises trying to understand where the missing child had gone. What greater nightmare is there than this?

"The house was found to be secure." Bradstreet paused to add, "That's what makes it certain to be an inside job, of course. Only one of the occupants of the house could have snatched the child, unbolted and unlocked a door or window to hand him out, and then sealed it again as if nothing had happened."

Holmes was less interested in the detective's conclusions than in his facts. "Times and events," he scolded Bradstreet.

"Yes, well… By ten to five it was clear that the boy had been taken. Mr Deverill raised the alarm with his field labourers and grounds staff, who live in a row of cottages down the hill there. He had them start searching the grounds and gardens. He sent off a man for the local constable and a rider to Taunton to summon a police inspector. He was… well, they remembered the Road Hill House tragedy."

The Scotland Yard veteran's voice dropped as he mentioned one of the Detective Branch's earliest and darkest cases. I was not familiar with the events he remembered, being a tender seven years of age at the time they occurred.

Holmes, that very compendium of crime, saw my confusion and enlightened me. "On the night of 29th June 1860, four-year-old Francis 'Saville' Kent vanished from a room where he slept with his nursemaid in a locked house. After a desperate search, his body was recovered from the cesspit of an outhouse privy. He had been stabbed and his throat was cut so deep as to almost behead him. The atrocity was reported by the press and garnered national interest and revulsion. An inspector of the then-new Detective Branch at Scotland Yard was dispatched to investigate. He uncovered a number of unsavoury things regarding members of the household, including adultery and abuse, but eventually concluded that the culprit was the boy's 16-year-old half-sister, Constance."

"No!" I gasped. "Surely not!"

"That was what the general public said then, too," Bradstreet told me bitterly. "A common policeman imputing such wickedness on a sweet young lady of quality? There was public uproar and the case was dismissed. The detective was broken, his reputation lost.[87] But five years later, Constance Kent's priest confessor convinced her to come forward and own up to her crimes."

"Yes," Holmes said heavily, but did not elucidate.[88]

I could see why the present circumstances at St Ethelreda's Manor might raise ghosts for a senior Scotland Yard man of Bradstreet's vintage. "Has the outhouse been checked?" I asked hesitantly.

"It has," Inspector Farmer confirmed, returning to the nursery. "I've had men in waders down there sluicing it out since this morning. Never have constables been so relieved to grope around in such foetid slurry and find nothing."

Holmes rose from the hearth and stalked out to the landing. "The room

---

[87]   Bradstreet mentions in "The Man With the Twisted Lip" (1891, collected in *The Adventures of Sherlock Holmes*, 1892), that he joined the police in 1862, a mere two years after these events, when the disgrace of the well-known and previously-lauded Inspector Jonathan 'Jack' Whicher must still have been fresh in his colleagues' minds and conversation.

[88]   The Road Hill House Murder was amongst the first to be widely reported as the investigation was ongoing, in an era where newspapers were first becoming powerful. Many readers wrote back to the broadsheets expounding their own theories about the case or commenting on Inspector Whicher's investigation. Some literary commentators have suggested that these events created or illustrated the thirst for the genre of detective fiction that began only eight years later with *The Moonstone*. Wilkie Collins' groundbreaking mystery novel is itself set in an isolated country house with a family laden with secrets, where a working-class policeman faces difficulties because of a social gulf with his "betters".

Constance Kent's confession led to spirited debate in the Houses of Parliament over the confidentiality of the confessional, and to claims that she was covering up for the true murderer, either her father or brother. She was eventually condemned to death but had her sentence commuted to life and served a twenty-year prison sentence. She was released from custody in 1885 at the age of 41 and moved to Tasmania under another name. She worked as a nurse and ended up as matron of the Pierce Memorial Nurses' Home at East Maitland, New South Wales. She died at the age of 100, lauded for her charitable works, good deeds, and community service. *The Suspicions of Mr Whicher or The Murder at Road Hill House*, Kate Summerscales' 2008 Non-Fiction Booker Prize-Winner, reintroduced the case to the modern public and led to a 2013 ITV dramatic adaptation (along with a short series of Inspector Whicher's wholly fictional sequel investigations).

can tell us nothing more, Watson," he called to me. "Let us see what we shall learn from the people!"

"That family tree is not quite right," Mrs Swift advised me as I tried to take notes. "Little Samuel is actually the son of Edward's older brother, not... Oh, give me your paper here. Look!"

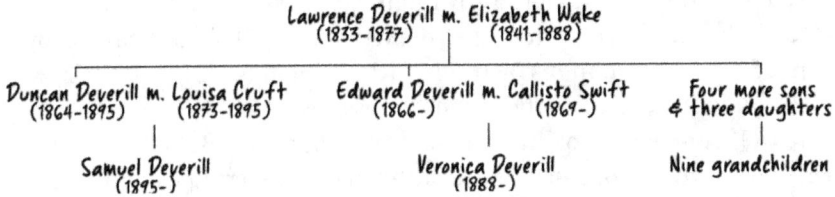

"You see? Duncan was the older brother, married to Louisa Cruft of *those* Crufts—you know, the Hampshire shipping people. Poor Duncan! He died of one of those horrid tropical diseases while he was visiting his Caribbean holdings. He never even knew that his wife back home was pregnant. And Louisa took the news of his death very badly. She became sick, and she didn't survive more than half an hour after childbirth. So Edward and my Callie, they adopted poor Samuel and made him their own."

"Samuel and Veronica are cousins by birth but siblings in law," I understood.

"That's right. She is very fond of him. You have no idea how upset she is about all this."

"You have the room next to the nursery," Holmes said to the old woman. "Did you hear or see anything unusual last night, before you were woken by the alarum?"

"I have trouble sleeping," Mrs Swift confided, "and so the doctor has prescribed me a little medication. One spoonful puts me right out and it takes an earthquake to wake me. Or, last night, Cally shaking me to ask if I knew where Little Sam was."

"You didn't hear the nursemaid looking in first to see if the child was with you?"

"I'm also getting a little deaf. I wish I could tell you anything useful, Mr Holmes, but really... all I can do is plead with you to find these monsters who have taken Sam!"

"It is a nightmare. A nightmare!" the Right Honourable Edward Deverill MP told us when Holmes interviewed him. His hand shook, almost spilling the whisky in his glass. "What am I to do?"

"You may begin by answering my questions clearly and precisely," my friend told him. "Begin with what you saw and heard last night."

"I saw nothing, heard nothing!" Deverill cried in anguish. "I saw Sam being taken up to bed. He was fussing and irritable and I was... I was pleased to have some peace and quiet! Lord...! And then I knew naught until I was woken by Susan in the middle of the night."

"You had no inkling that the boy might be at risk?"

"No. Who would do such a...?" The MP paused. "I should have known, of course. Samuel is rich in his own right. Richer than me."

"He is adopted, your brother's son," I observed.

"Yes. Of course we took him in, made him our own. But from his mother's Cruft legacy he will one day be a wealthy man." Deverill hesitated before daring to add, "If only we can get him back."

"The ransom note asked for a massive sum," Holmes mentioned. "Do you have two thousand pounds available to meet the demand?"

"Of course not. My resources are quite tied up, in commerce, in land, in property. If I liquidated them all I would still struggle to meet the amount, and it would take months."

"You said that Samuel also had some fortune," I noted. "Perhaps that is what the kidnapper is depending upon?"

"Then he is grievously in error. When Duncan married, his bride's family settled an income for life upon the newlyweds, a very substantial bequest and an annual bursary to support a daughter of the wealthy Crufts in suitable manner. In the event of Louisa's decease the legacy passed to any extant issue— Samuel. But until Sam comes to majority he cannot dispose of any assets from the bequest or draw more than the stipulated annual income."

"You are his guardian and trustee?"

"Indeed. But the terms of the trust are ironclad. I cannot dispose of his estate, even to meet a ransom demand."

"And if the child dies?" Holmes enquired ruthlessly with no regard for Deverill's feelings.

"Then the bequest lapses. The estate, all entailments, revert to the Crufts."

Holmes allowed that revelation to sit, and now asked, "How vital is your support of the *Workman's Compensation Bill* likely to be?"[89]

Deverill dropped his head into his hands and used language unbecoming a member of the House of Commons. "There is a narrow and uncertain margin.

---

[89]   The imminence of a vote on this bill places this case in the first half of March 1897, just before "The Adventure of the Devil's Foot".

None can be confident of the outcome of the vote. If I don't toe the party line there will be hell to pay! The Whip will come down on me like the hammer of God. I'll be done, cast out, if this vote fails because of me. And the tally may be that marginal!"

"Do you believe this abduction to be political in nature, Holmes?" I asked worriedly. Tempers were running high about the issues, with thundering leaders in the national newspapers and demonstrations in the capital. It was not too hard to imagine some radical or reactionary deciding to force the issue by threatening an infant.

"It seems to be," the great detective answered. "However, my enquiries have far from run their course."

It was some time before Mrs Deverill was calm enough to speak to us. "My angel! My sweet Sammy!" she moaned through her tears. "What has become of him?"

"That is what we endeavour to discover," Holmes told her severely. "The most useful practical thing you could do would be to render your testimony."

I offered a gentler persuasion, and between us Holmes and I drew out her account of the night before. The only new information was that Mrs Deverill was accustomed to walking around the house before bed, checking on the security of the doors and windows. "You hear such terrible things about burglars and beggars," she told us. "Edward thought me silly to worry so, but... look!"

Also of interest was the almost-vicious way in which the lady of the house assigned blame on Miss Clementine. "If Samuel were to be discovered this minute I would *still* want her out of my house!" Mrs Deverill declared. "Gone without references! How could she have slept through my angel being stolen? No—this is too much, too far! She must *go!*"

"*This* is too far?" I repeated. "It is not the first time that you have found fault with the nursemaid?"

"We have had significant trouble finding a reliable girl. This will be the third such person I have had to dismiss."

"What faults did you find?" I wondered.

Mrs Deverill stiffened defensively. "I'm sure that is a domestic matter of no concern to your investigation," she assured us.

"I would prefer to decide that for myself," Holmes interjected, interested now.

"Impertinence and overfamiliarity," the lady of the house declared, then clarified that she was referring to the nursemaids, not to our questioning. "Polly, the first, came with excellent testimonials but proved to not know her place in a respectable household. Emma was the second and I had suspicions about her honesty."

"I cannot assist you in the matter of your missing child if you offer me evasions and untruths, Mrs Deverill," Holmes insisted sternly. "The facts, if you please!"

Callisto Deverill blanched at his challenge, but it is very difficult to resist the penetrating gaze of Sherlock Holmes. "Polly was being overfamiliar with Edward," she reluctantly admitted. "Or he with her," she added bitterly. "I dismissed her in favour of a less attractive nursemaid."

"Ah." I understood the lady's reluctance to explain the circumstances. "And Emma?"

"Less attractive evidently does not mean unattractive," Mrs Deverill spat.

"But you have no reason to suspect Susan Clementine?"

"I have no evidence of any irregularity. But that does not mean that my husband has not succumbed to his weakness. In any case, the girl has proved unreliable in the one thing she is here for, caring for Sammy. My angel is lost! Lost!"

It took some time for us to calm Mrs Deverill again enough to continue with the interview. At last Holmes was able to ask, "You mentioned your habit of walking the house before retiring. Did you also visit the nursery last night to look in on Samuel?"

"Of course I did. My angel was unwell yesterday, suffering from colic. I had the doctor to him in the afternoon. I went up to check that Little Sam was settled at last."

"And was he?" I enquired.

"He was fast asleep, curled in his crib. Susan was sat beside him in the rocking chair, knitting. She had the impertinence to lift a finger to her lips to entreat me to silence so as not to disturb my angel—as if a mother does not know such a thing! I watched him breathe for a while, tucked under his sheets in his little frilled cap and gown, and then went to bed. And then... we were woken by... by..."

She became distraught again, and had little else to offer Holmes' investigation.

Miss Clementine was an attractive young woman in her mid-twenties; I could understand why Mrs Deverill might harbour suspicions about her husband around so neat and bright a person. But this nursemaid was a few years more mature than the previous incumbents and struck me as less naive and susceptible to seduction. She had also borne up tolerably well to the interrogations of Inspectors Farmer and Bradstreet.

"Must I tell my story again?" she asked us with a hint of weariness. "Well, if it helps. I brought Sammy up to the nursery just after the hall clock had chimed the quarter-hour after six. I gave him the teaspoonful of brandy and water that Dr Finland had prescribed and settled the lad in his cot. I sang to him for a short while but he was soon asleep. Then I settled down to watch over him, occupying myself with some knitting. After Mrs Deverill's customary visit I got ready for bed and retired—that would be around ten past ten, shortly after Mr Sleddow had come around and locked up. I had already closed the window shutters, of course, but he brings the padlocks that fasten them tight overnight. I read a little and was asleep by ten thirty."

"This is your regular routine?" checked Holmes.

"With small variances depending upon Sammy's moods, yes. Except for Tuesdays, which is my half-day, when one of the housemaids looks after him until I come back on duty."

"You were woken at four twenty," Holmes prompted his witness.

"Or a minute or two before. I thought I heard a cough. I may have been dreaming."

"The child's cough?"

"I assumed so at the time. Who else would it be?"

"It might have been a member of the family," Holmes suggested.

Miss Clementine's mouth tightened. "I have previously made it clear to Mr Deverill that night-time visits are not part of my duties," she told us curtly.

"I'm sorry that you had to make such a statement," I told her. It was a problem too common in certain affluent households.

"It was just a matter of being firm. I gather that previous staff have lacked such resolution. You will note that Mr Sleddow customarily locks the door to the servants' stair at night, curtailing access to the other staff's dormitories from the family rooms. But Mr Deverill also has a set of keys."

"Might anyone else of the staff have access to the keys?" Holmes wondered.

Miss Clementine considered the matter. "Well, Mrs Sleddow would presumably be able to get to Mr Sleddow's bunch, but I don't know that any of the other servants could. If Mr Deverill was visiting the servants' rooms and had his keys with him then I suppose that might possibly allow a wax imprint to be made, but I do not think that probable."

Holmes had more questions for the nursemaid: whether she had observed anyone taking a special interest in Little Samuel while he was promenaded in his carriage, whether anyone had attempted to strike up a conversation about the household or its routine, how much was generally known about the child's legacy… and what she was knitting last night when Mrs Deverill had visited.

Miss Clementine seemed as puzzled as I was at that last enquiry. "It was a cardigan jumper for my sister's child," she answered. "You will see the remains of it over the nursery floor, all dropped stitches and pulls after the police cast it aside in their searches. I'm… not sure how that helps your investigation."

"I was trying to understand why you would burn a quantity of cotton-wool and eiderdown in your hearth yesterday," my friend revealed to her. "I found the ash. Neither of those things are components of an infant's jumper."

The nursemaid's eyes widened in surprise, "How could you know…? But then, you are the famous consulting detective of Dr Watson's accounts. Well, if you must know, I suffer from extremely heavy monthly discharges." She blushed. "The cotton wool and down were contents of my hygiene bags."[90]

Holmes was unembarrassed by his interrogation. "Thank you, Miss Clementine. That is a very helpful explanation."

"Do you think you will be able to find Little Sam?" the nursemaid asked anxiously.

"Holmes is rarely thwarted," I assured her; but she seemed little comforted.

Sleddow was a short, stooped man who had been in service to Mr Deverill senior and to Mr Duncan Deverill before coming to work for Mr Edward Deverill after the older brother's demise. More properly, he had remained in service at St Ethelreda's Manor when the property had passed to young Samuel Deverill.

"I noticed nothing unusual when I locked up, sirs," he assured us. "Everything went just as always. The house was quiet until Mr Deverill sounded the dinner gong to summon assistance."

"Who responded first?" Holmes wanted to know. "Details, man, details!"

---

[90]   Sherlockians familiar with Dr Watson's notes as managed by his literary agent Sir Arthur Conan Doyle will observe that mention of such delicate feminine issues would have been instantly red-lined by *The Strand* editor George Newnes. Whilst medical men such as Watson and Doyle might not shy from mention of such bodily functions and the necessary but unspoken hygiene they required, and a nursemaid might be more practical and candid about such matters than most people, the inclusion of such a comment in our present account is a sure indicator of this story being drawn from that wealth of unpublished despatch-box cases which were never submitted to the Victorian editor's pen.

Sleddow considered the question. "It took me a moment to get my boots on," he confessed. "By the time I got to the servant's stair with Mrs Sleddow, the rest of the staff were on their way down—excepting Miss Clementine of course, who sleeps in the nursery. We passed through the connecting door and all entered the hall together. Mr and Mrs Deverill were already there with Susan. Mrs Swift was attending upon Miss Veronica in her room, making certain that she was alright."

"A thorough search was made of the house then?" I expected.

"Very thorough, sir. The footman and I even climbed into the attics and unbolted the cellars. Mrs Deverill had us turn out every closet and trunk, even the old cobwebbed packing cases in the wine cellar. We couldn't understand how young Master Samuel could have left the manor, you see. Not without an abductor leaving footprints."

Holmes looked up sharply. "There was snow on the ground. You looked for traces of passage?"

"Yessir. Me and Mr Deverill, we were the first to walk the perimeter of the property while the farmhands were being summoned. It had snowed lightly in the night, just enough to frost the ground, but we were leaving treads right enough. We didn't see any sign of other prints, such as a burglar might leave, whatever way they got into or out of the place."

"You are certain you saw no tracks?"

"Not at front door, back door, terrace door, or under any of the windows. The coal hatch was frosted over. For that matter, now I think on it, so were the joints of the window sashes. It should have been obvious if any were opened, if anyone had passed through them."

Holmes cradled his fingers and stared at them for a few moments. Then he returned to his questions. "You served in this house when it belonged to Mr Duncan Deverill and his wife. Has the establishment changed much since then?"

"Not substantially," the butler judged. "The present Mr and Mrs Deverill were frequent guests, being as he was standing for election hereabouts. When Mr Duncan Deverill went on his Caribbean business voyage and Mrs Duncan Deverill discovered that she was with child, and later when word came of her husband's illness and passing, Mrs Edward Deverill stayed to keep her company in her confinement."

"She was present during the tragedy of the childbirth, then?"

"Yessir. The midwife said there was nothing could be done to save the lady. It is a miracle that the boy survived. That was the words they used—miracle child. An angel blessed on us in time of tragedy."

"Samuel was not expected to live?" I surmised.

"The prognosis was always for a difficult birth, and Mrs Deverill's declining

"There was snow on the ground. You looked for traces of passage?"

health and morale were additional complicating factors."

"What would have happened to the Cruft legacy settled upon Claire Deverill had Samuel not survived?" Holmes probed.

"I believe that the balance of the assets would have reverted to the Cruft estate, sir. There was some loose talk of it both above and below stairs as Mrs Deverill's time of delivery approached and her life lay in balance. But then Master Samuel survived—a miracle!"

"And if the boy dies now?" the detective continued ruthlessly.

"I believe the legacy still reverts to the Crufts," Sleddow admitted.

I glanced over at Holmes. Here was another motive for kidnap—or worse. Some member of *those* Hamptonshire Crufts might do very well out of the demise of the missing infant.

My friend had other concerns to raise with the butler, though. "There have been some staff difficulties during Mr Edward Deverill's ownership of St Ethelreda's," he noted. "Miss Clementine is the third children's nurse in eighteen months."

Sleddow blanched. "Those were matters outside the scope of this investigation, sir."

"I'll define the scope of my investigation, Mr Sleddow," Sherlock Holmes warned him. "You are aware of your master's nocturnal wanderings?"

"I can't discuss such things, sir."

"A politician must appear beyond reproach," I recognised, "but a child's life may be at stake here. That must count for something. Come, Sleddow; get your priorities straight, man!"

It took us a while to winkle the sordid facts out of the butler, but at last he admitted the liaisons between master and maids. "That's why I started locking the servants' door," he confessed.

"But Deverill has a spare key," I pointed out.

"Yessir," the butler replied dispiritedly. "I believe however that the master's bunch is now kept in the bedroom escritoire—to which only Mrs Deverill keeps a key."

"What happens in case of fire?" Holmes enquired. "If all the exits are sealed, how could anyone escape?"

"When the gong is sounded twice together we are all expected to assemble in the hall. If the clamour is instead continuous I am to get the staff out by opening the rear external door at the base of the servants' stair, and then come round to unlock the other doors from outside."

"So there is scant chance of Mr Deverill unsealing the servants' interior door last night?" I recognised. "What of duplicate keys?"

Sleddow could say nothing of any such facsimile. He was reluctant to discuss details of his master's nocturnal perambulations. My hopes of a breakthrough in the investigation diminished.

But Sherlock Holmes seemed satisfied with the interview.

Constable Whatley had been the first police officer on the scene, being the local man based in nearby Quantoxhead. He opened up his pocket notebook, flipped to the relevant page, and outlined his actions.

"I was knocked up at 6.12 by John Claridge, sirs, 'im being one of the farm 'ands at St Ethelreda's, sent down to summon aid. I proceeded with him up to the manor, arriving at 6.24, by which time there was quite a search going on for the missing tyke—Master Samuel Deverill, that is. I interviewed Mr Deverill and the nursemaid and took a look at the nursery myself, conducting a quick search."

It seemed that Whatley had been responsible for the damage to Miss Clementine's jumper-cardigan-in-progress. Holmes asked some clarifying questions about the scene. "Was the fire lit? Were the cot-sheets in place or had they been removed?"

Whatley frowned to remember. "There was a bit of a fire, mostly embers, like it 'ad burned down over the night. It 'adn't been banked up again, if that's what you mean. And the crib? It was all neat and tidy as you please, like they'd made it ready for the baby to be put back in when they found 'im."

That seemed odd. A distraught nursemaid on finding her charge missing would hardly halt to make up his bed, and at the time the police constable had arrived, the search for the missing Sammy was still in full halloo. Did that indicate that the *abductor* had paused to smooth down the quilts as he took the boy away?

"You interviewed Deverill and Miss Clementine," Holmes observed. "No, don't bother trying to make report on that. Give me your notebook and let me read the account you recorded at the time. Hmm, I see that the nursemaid was somewhat distressed."

"Quite naturally, sir," Whatley pointed out. "Especially being as Mrs Deverill as much as accused her of allowing the child to be taken, or of being part of the plot. I know that Inspector Farmer is something of that opinion too."

The constable stifled a yawn and looked embarrassed. He had been on the scene from the time he had been called in the small hours up till almost noon and had then been ordered back to be interviewed by Holmes. He could scarcely have had three hours sleep in between.

"You cycled some distance along the road past the manor," Holmes read from the policeman's notes. "You were looking for the 'Peggles Camp'."

"Oh yes. Them Peggly Gypsies is well-known for stealing away babies," Whatley informed us. "Beggars and tinkers and puppet-show men, out for what they can get and no better than they should be! They'd moved on from where they'd been squatting when I got there—run off in the night, like as. I don't doubt but what the Inspector'll 'ave the whole county force out looking for them."

"I don't doubt it either," Holmes agreed. "Nor do I imagine he will have any explanation as to how the missing boy picked a window lock, flew out of his nursery, fastened the shutters behind him, then ran away to join the Romanys. But it won't stop him wasting time and manpower on the matter. Tell me, were there any traces of the Gypsies' passage in the snow? Or had they already packed up and left before that?"

The policeman had to allow that there was no sign that camp had been struck after dusk.

"Were there any other tracks on the road past the manor?" I wondered. "Before all the circus of the search spread that far, I mean?"

"Nothing I noticed, doctor, but it was still dark when I rode out." Whatley stifled another yawn.

We let him retire to his interrupted repose.

"I hold that it was the nursemaid," Farmer insisted. "How could anyone creep into her room and abduct an infant—a colicky infant who had cried for much of the day, at that—without awakening a girl sleeping less than ten feet away? She was in the pay of the abductors, you mark my words, and when we investigate her we shall uncover it!"

Holmes had already sent off a slew of telegrams, including those that might check Miss Clementine's references and establish her character. He frowned slightly at the local inspector's hasty conclusion.

"It's not necessarily her," Bradstreet argued. "This is political. It's not just about money, it's about perverting the course of Parliament. There are powerful concerns out there that have set themselves against the *Workplace Compensation Act*, and some of them have plenty of money and fewer scruples than they should. In London we encounter professional cracksmen and house-breakers who can sneak into anywhere, seemingly by magic. I expect that Mr Holmes can think of half a dozen specialists who might infiltrate St Ethelreda's Manor without ever betraying their intrusion, and be away with the babe. As for the bairn not waking, he had been given brandy to help him slumber."

"If it is political then that same money could have been used to suborn a domestic," Farmer countered. "We know that any of them might have wandered the house if they had obtained keys at any time in the past eighteen months. That is all that was required to extract young Samuel. We shall be looking carefully at the two dismissed nursemaids also, for either of them might have a grudge that could be exploited and might also have taken key-copies for their own use."

"Neither of you has explained how the child could be taken without leaving footprints in the snow," I reminded them. "Evidently the light fall began about half past nine, just before the house was secured, and continued until after everyone was asleep."

"The child might still be in the house," Bradstreet mentioned ominously. "An old place like this, there might well be a priest hole[91] or other secret place. If the boy isn't traced soon, I shall insist that we rip off the wainscoting and search for such a hidden chamber."

Holmes had conducted a measured survey for such things and was satisfied that no such lost room existed.

"If your kidnappers are so professional, then why demand so unrealistic a sum?" Farmer challenged the Scotland Yard man. "Why seek an amount so large that it cannot be raised? That smacks of an amateur effort, say from a servant with a grudge."

"Or the ransom is a distraction," I suggested. "Remember that there is a fiduciary motive for the poor boy's death. The note might be to make us believe we are dealing with an abduction when we are actually facing a heinous murder."

Holmes shifted in his chair. I perceived that he was not entirely in agreement with my assessment.

"It is the better part of a day since Little Sammy's loss was discovered," despaired Farmer. "He might be anywhere by now."

"It is snowing again," Bradstreet added gloomily. "If the boy has been hidden somewhere in the nearby countryside, a sick child exposed to the elements…"

"We can only hope for more correspondence from the abductors," I suggested. "If they set a time and place to receive the money they demand then we might set a trap."

"But first Mr Deverill must throw his vote in the House the day after tomorrow," Bradstreet objected.

"We should put Susan Clementine in a cell until she talks," Farmer recommended.

---

[91] During the 16th century persecution of Catholics in England, when harbouring a Catholic clergyman was considered treason and incurred a death penalty, many rich houses were equipped with small hidden rooms, 'priest holes' in which a visiting priest and religious items could be concealed from searching Protestant soldiers.

"We should wait patiently until I receive answers to my enquiries," Holmes interrupted us. "All that should be done has been set in motion. Only one thing remains. Watson and I must interview Miss Veronica Deverill."

"Do you understand what is happening?" I asked Veronica carefully.

The pigtailed girl sat on a cushion in the bay window of her bedroom, surrounded by her toys and dolls' house and an elaborate doll's crib complete with porcelain baby. She regarded Holmes and I solemnly and nodded.

"Tell us," I urged her, to make sure.

"Little Sammy has run away," she confided. "Everyone is looking for him. I don't suppose he packed any lunch."

"Run away," I repeated. "But he is too small to walk."

"That makes no difference," the child told me. "Golly couldn't walk, but he ran away."

"Golly?" I asked, puzzled.

Veronica pointed to her toybox and then to a bookshelf where two colourful illustrated volumes held pride of place: *The Adventures of Two Dutch Dolls and a Golliwogg* and *The Golliwogg's Bicycle Club* by Bertha and Florence Upton. I recognised the works. They were the latest popular children's books and the main character in them, a clever black-faced fellow with frizzy hair and red lips, had become the soft toy of choice. Every household that could afford it now contained a 'Gollywogg', and those of limited means created homemade knitted or sewn versions of the same.[92] "Golly came last Christmas," Veronica

---

[92] American cartoonist and author Florence Kate Upton (1873–1922) published her first and second Gollywogg books in 1895 and 1896 respectively, and went on to write and illustrate eleven more entries to the series. Her character caught on quickly in Britain; the knitted and stuffed dolls with their exaggerated Negro characteristics were the most desired stocking-filler of the late 19th century, at a time long before concerns of racism or blackface much affected popular opinion.

Upton did not copyright or trademark her creation. The term "golliwog" quickly became a general class of toy rather than one particular character of one particular author. The prolific Enid Blyton published three books about golliwogs and added the character to her popular Noddy series. Robertson's jam company adopted the golliwog as its mascot. In the middle of the 20th century only the teddy bear topped the gollywog for cuddly toy sales.

It is only in recent years as racial sensitivity has waxed that the golliwog's popularity has declined. A 2018 YouGov poll in the UK recorded 20% of respondents felt that sale of golliwogs was racist, versus 63% who felt it was acceptable. Many young people do not now know of the toy and the epithet 'wog' is used offensively as a term of racial abuse.

In 2023, police visited the White Hart Pub in Grays, Essex, in response to a customer complaint at being "racially distressed" by the 30-year-old display of five golliwogs behind the bar. Camra (the Campaign for Real Ale) determined not to list the inn whilst the items were on view,

explained, and then sadly added, "But he went away again a few days ago. Susan says it is because he is to have more adventures, and I shall read about them when his new book comes out."

"When your toy left, by what means did he depart?" Holmes asked the little girl.

"I don't know," Veronica puzzled. "He crept out at night. Like Sammy."

"It is quite possible that he did," Sherlock Holmes assured her. "Thank you for your invaluable assistance, my dear."

We overnighted at St Ethelreda's Manor, and the morning post brought a handful of replies to Holmes' enquiries.[93] He browsed through them over breakfast at the subdued family table. Mr and Mrs Deverill were not present, and Mrs Swift ate silently and departed. Bradstreet was evidently a late riser, but then he had worked into the night with the search parties, and had even chased Whatley's gypsies.

I read the envelopes as best I could, but only one had a return address printed on it, correspondence from the National Bureau of Births, Deaths, and Marriages at Somerset House. Another came in embossed stationary from a legal firm. A third bore the stamp of Sedgemoor Cottage Hospital, Bridgewater.

"I have received some useful data from a variety of sources," Holmes assured me. "I now fully understand the provisions of the Cruft bequest. I have confirmation of the governing trustees and benefactors of a number of local hospitals. I have testimonials from Miss Clementine's previous employers. I have a statement from the family's doctor in general practice. These, with the notes in P.C. Whatley's journal and the evidence of Miss Veronica Deverill should prove sufficient to untangle this affair."

---

and beer suppliers Heineken and Carlsberg declined to have their products sold there. The pub went out of business in May 2023, having made national headlines and provoked intervention from the Home Secretary.

[93]   We must assume that the admirable dispatch with which officials responded to Holmes' enquiries were due to his reputation and regard. In the 1890s there were three mail collections and deliveries a day to "the provinces" and five in London, excepting Sundays, so first class correspondence could travel from Somerset and back, 167 miles each way, returning to Taunton by mail train overnight, and be in tiny Quantoxhead the following morning. Telegrams were even faster but had the disadvantages of having to be brief, with payment by the word, and lacked privacy; the message was written out in plain text on an open sheet for any Post Office clerk to read, which made telegrams unsuitable for transmitting private personal, financial, or legal information.

"You can recover the boy? Find the kidnapper?"

Holmes nodded and returned to his ham and Scotch eggs. He preferred not to say more until he could gather the family together with the officers who had called us in.

I tried to swallow a bite of breakfast but in truth my appetite was soured by my concern for the missing child. I knew that if anyone might solve the mystery it would be my friend, but I felt sick and anxious.

"It is one thing to abduct a full-grown man but a quite different thing to take a helpless child," I muttered.

Holmes laid his plate aside. "My dear Watson! Your heart does you credit. Whenever I am in danger of forgetting the human element of our adventures you are able to remind me of the true consequences beyond the intellectual puzzle."

"A workman as assiduous as yourself must sometimes be myopic," I assured Holmes. "That is why he sometimes requires a companion to remind him of the wider world."

"And so you do, doctor. But you are also a medical man. You know that sometimes to heal a wound there must be cutting and blood, pain and loss for a greater gain. I fear that this case might require such a surgery."

I felt my stomach tighten. "But the boy is alive?"

"I have every reason to hope so; though I fear that restoring him to his mother will be a costly and unhappy task."

"See young Sammy safe and well, Holmes. Every decent parent would require that over any price or consequence."

Holmes turned to retrieve his breakfast. "You are my compass as well as my Boswell, Watson. I shall endeavour not to let you down—or Master Samuel."

An hour later, Holmes' assembly convened in the library. Deverill looked exhausted, as if the very hounds of hell haunted him. Well he might, given the choice between his son and his honour, between political ruin or being turned out of his home. "I have tried to gather the sum demanded in the ransom," he informed us, "but even if I go to the Jews I cannot raise so much in any sort of time."

Mrs Deverill cast a despairing look at him. Her mother gripped her hand and squeezed it.

"We have questioned all the staff again," Farmer promised the family. "Even the workers in the cottages. We are seeking the gypsies who were camped nearby, but so far without any luck. They seem to have disappeared."

"I have spoken with my colleagues and superiors in the Detective Branch," Bradstreet informed us. "Suspicion is growing that there is a political motive behind all of this—maybe even a foreign power."

P.C. Whatley, obviously out of his depth and extremely uncomfortable about it, tried to blend into the wallpaper.

Also present at Holmes' request were Miss Clementine and Mr Sleddow. The butler looked gloomy and resigned. The nursemaid was pale-faced and tense; as well she might be after the ordeal of interrogation to which she had been put. I worried that history might repeat itself and that a domestic might be scapegoated, as evidently first happened at the horrible murder at Road Hill House all those years before.

"It is time to draw back the veil on this sorry sequence of events," Holmes told us all. "I doubt that afterwards any of you will be very satisfied with the outcome, but the truth will out."

"Then the boy is… dead?" Farmer ventured.

Holmes was not to be rushed to his revelation. "We must go back some eighteen months to September 25th 1895, the time of Master Samuel Deverill's birth," he began. "Mrs Louisa Deverill, née Cruft, was weak and ill, devastated by her recent widowhood and the difficulties of her pregnancy. The prognosis was pessimistic. You looked over the medical notes, Watson?"

"I did," I confirmed. "It was thought, and rightly so, that Mrs Deverill might not survive childbirth. Without going into obstetric detail, there was good reason to fear that both mother and infant might perish. For that reason a Caesarean operation was considered, despite the significant risks that would entail. However, Mrs Deverill went into labour early before such a plan might be effected."

"A doctor and midwife from Sedgemoor Cottage Hospital attended at the birth here at St Ethelreda's Manor," Mrs Callisto Deverill stated.

Holmes nodded. "Quite so. Here is the certificate of birth for young Samuel, written and signed in the same hand as the certificate of death for his mother. You will see that the times are less than an hour apart."

"I don't see what this…" began Farmer, but Bradstreet shushed him to silence.

Holmes produced another birth certificate. "At the same time that Mrs Deverill went into premature labour here, Sedgemoor Hospital was tending to the charity case of a Miss Agnes Potter, who was likewise entering into the final stages of labour. She gave birth to a sickly baby boy who lived only minutes." The detective looked over at Mrs Swift. "You are a patroness of Sedgemoor, I believe," he said to the old woman. "Edward Deverill is now on the board of trustees."

"That's right," the MP replied before his mother-in-law could speak.

"Within four hours of the healthy Miss Potter birthing an illegitimate son who did not live, the sickly Mrs Deverill produced a miracle child who was healthy and whole despite the traumas of his nativity," Holmes observed. "The same two medical professionals signed all the relevant certification."

"What are you suggesting?" asked Mrs Swift coldly.

Bradstreet could snatch a motive as well as any Scotland Yard man. "If the Deverill boy had not lived, the Cruft fortune would be lost. But an heir was provided, and so he and his fortune fell under the control of his uncle, the foster-father who adopted him and enjoys all the advantages of young Samuel's fortune."

"I do not care for your insinuations, inspector!" Deverill thundered.

His tirade was interrupted when Holmes slammed down more papers on the table. "An examination of the banking accounts of the doctor and midwife involved will doubtless prove of profit, as will taking testimony from various staff at the cottage hospital at the time. But let us move on now to the question of Master Samuel's ransom."

The Right Honourable Edward Deverill managed to restrain his fury long enough to hear who was levering him to his political destruction.

"You see the received ransom letter here before you," Holmes told the assembly in the library. "I shared my analysis of it with the Inspectors upon my arrival yesterday. In brief, it was written by someone of limited education who does not regularly write with a pen, and who knew little enough of the Cruft bequest to assume that so vast a sum might be available to redeem the child. Of course, nothing in the note offers any sort of proof that the writer actually *has* Samuel in his possession."

"What?" I gasped. "You mean the demand is a hoax?"

"Somebody who was aware of the boy's disappearance decided that there was a chance to make some money, Watson."

"Or to gain a political advantage," Bradstreet insisted.

"No, Inspector. That demand was by way of another subterfuge, to mask a purely financial motive. I doubt that the writer even understood the full implications of that instruction. But we can confirm that with the letter-writer, who is in this room."

Holmes' words caused consternation and speculation, even before the great detective pointed one long, sensitive finger at the corpse-pale P.C. Whatley.

"Of all the people familiar with the crisis, few left the scene or gave up the search in time to post a letter in Taunton to catch the afternoon delivery. Few are more accustomed to filling in a notebook in pencil than in using pen and ink. The message was in capitals for fear that the officers in the case might recognise their subordinate's normal script."

"No!" Whatley cried. "You're wrong! I never...!"

"A check on stationers in Taunton and at the Post Office itself should verify your presence there," Holmes told the fellow inexorably. "For myself, the dozen minute signs of guilt you are betraying now are enough to confirm your actions. However, I shall leave it to Inspector Farmer to undertake proper enquiries for confirmation."

"Seb Whatley, step outside," the local inspector said in dark, wrathful tones. He saw the unfortunate, stricken constable into the hands of the other policemen in the house before returning to join the shocked throng in the library.

"If the note was not from the kidnapper, then who did take Samuel?" Mrs Deverill almost wailed. "And how?"

"For that information we must thank Miss Veronica," Holmes revealed. "It was she who told me about the disappearance of a beloved and treasured stuffed toy some days past. I can now tell you what happened to the missing Gollywogg."

"Golly?" Miss Clementine sounded puzzled. "What has he to do with it?"

"He was required as an alibi," Holmes explained. "Or rather, he was required to donate a substantial mass of cotton wool and internal stuffing to fill out a mannequin sewn into the shape and size of the sleeping Samuel. When the puppet was dressed in the frills of the boy's night attire he might look quite realistic, especially if someone was to operate a pair of canes under the quilts to give him the appearance of breathing. Of course, such canes might rub a mark on the varnish of the cot as they were manipulated under cover of moving knitting needles."

The nursemaid went deathly still. She swallowed hard. "Well," she said, "you are as clever as I feared, Mr Holmes."

"I don't understand at all!" Mr Deverill objected. "You mean that Susan abducted my son?"

"No!" the young woman protested. "I never."

"She means," Holmes explained, "that she instead retrieved *her* son. This is not the Susan Clementine to whom her references referred. That lady is actually working for the Hunter family in Birmingham, entirely unaware that someone has borrowed her identity for an adventure. Before us is Miss Agnes Potter, mother of the child who was substituted at birth for the stillborn Samuel."

"By George!" muttered Bradstreet.

Miss Clementine's—Miss Potter's—eyes flashed defiantly. "They stole my baby from me. Gave me chloroform for the pain, for an easy birth they said, and when I woke they told me that my boy was dead. They showed me his little mangled corpse. It took me a long time to find out what had really happened, where my true child had gone."

Mrs Swift trembled and looked away. Mr Deverill looked at his wife aghast. "Callisto... what have you done?"

"She tried to save you, Edward," Mrs Swift answered for her daughter. "To save your career, to set you up in Parliament as you wished. To free you from debt and ruin. Did you never suspect?"

"You stole my baby to grab your money!" Miss Potter accused the family she had infiltrated.

"And you came to get him back," declared Holmes. "The infant was sedated with Mrs Swift's borrowed sleeping draught and lowered from the nursery window to an accomplice before night came, before ever the shutters were locked, before the snow fell to betray any traces of a visit. The marionette was placed in the crib so that Mrs Deverill could attest to the child being there after all was locked up. Thereafter you needed only to dispose of the puppet in the hearth and all evidence of it was gone. You straightened up any trace of the apparatus when you made the bed. Then all that remained was for you to 'wake' and discover the boy was gone. By then the 'puppet-show men' supposed-Gypsies were well away, taking your son to refuge with... a sister? The one to whom you were to send the child's jumper you prepared?"

"I'll say nothing of that," the false nursemaid told us defiantly.

"You need not," I suggested. "If Holmes is right about the boy's true parentage—and Holmes does not make errors of that kind—then you are his legal guardian. You might have gone to court and claimed him without this charade."

"With what proof?" Miss Potter demanded. "Me, a disgraced unwed mother, a poor nobody, with no money for a brief, all but a Gypsy and a tramp, against the rich and powerful Deverills and Crufts? What chance do any of you think I would have had?"

"There is fraud here, and I don't know what other charges, as well as that fool Whatley's crimes," Bradstreet considered. "This will give the Chief Constable of Somerset a proper headache, and make my report to my superiors rather complex too."

Inspector Farmer winced at the account he would need to render. "Who do I arrest, then?" he wondered.

Sherlock Holmes declined to comment. "The boy is safe and well?" he asked Miss Potter.

"And loved," she replied. "I'll not give him up."

Holmes rose. "Then the rest is beyond the ambit of the detective sciences. Come Watson, we shall catch the 12.59 train to London!"

THE END

THE CONFECTIONER'S CAPTIVES

WATSON, BEWARE!" HOLMES warned me as we entered the small confectioner's shop off Sweetapple Lane.

I saw his hand dip to his greatcoat's hip pocket and realised that he was reaching for the revolver he kept there. Reflex more than thought sent me shifting my own hand towards my Beaumont Adams.[94] But we were too late.

A pair of scarf-masked figures sprang up from behind the sales counters, brandishing sawn-off shotguns at us. "Don't!" one of them warned.

They had us. We refrained from any further attempts to provoke a barrage of buckshot from the somewhat-antique but still quite deadly firearms now trained on us.

"What's this?" I demanded. "Are you mad? Firearms crimes are a hanging offence!"

"Shut up!" one of the two gunmen snarled. "Keep them 'ands high an' walk slowly into the back." He gestured with his barrel to indicate a small wooden door between the display shelves of sweet jars. It was such an incongruous thing to be threatened with firearms amidst the candies and boiled sweets of a confectioner's store.

"Do as he says, Watson," Holmes advised me. His gaze darted all over the room, taking in the cash register, the scattered sales ledgers, a row of shattered humbug bottles, and doubtless many more things that I could not perceive.

He also scrutinised the pair of scarf-swathed fellows who were threatening us. They were armed in common labourer's clothes, with donkey jackets and heavy work boots. Their headgear was cheap, a flat Northerner's cap and a cloth beret. Their accents were rough south-of-Thames London.

"Lock that shop door now," Flat Cap, who seemed to be in charge, instructed the other. His companion kept his weapon on us but sidled over to bolt the entrance and, perhaps for propriety, to flip the window sign to say 'Closed'.

Holmes and I were ushered into a workshop behind the salesroom. The brick shed was actually a manufactory; the tiny sweet shop was a mere add-on

---

94   The Beaumont Adams revolver was the standard British Army handgun from 1862 to 1880, favoured because of it was the first true double action firearm (cocked by either the hammer or trigger) and delivered a hefty 54 bore, .422 calibre bullet. It was replaced by the Enfield mark 1 as the army's weapon of choice in the year that Dr Watson was pensioned out.

to the main business of the Sweetapple Lane premises. The larger space was filled with four man-high boiling vats under a loading gantry, sweet moulds, cutting machines, and all the paraphernalia of a working confectionary production line. Here was all the apparatus for the making of barley sugars and bull's-eyes, gobstoppers[95] and cough candy.

Three captives were tied by their wrists around the support beams that upheld the balcony. All wore the aprons of factory staff; all were blindfolded and gagged with whatever material was at hand in the workshop. One of them was beaten to unconsciousness and a second seemed concussed. The oldest of them stirred when he heard us led in but could see or say nothing. A third armed and scarved man kept watch upon the captives with a firearm that had probably seen Waterloo.

"Check their coats," Flat Cap instructed his comrade. "These newcomers reached for their pockets when we caught 'em. They might be loaded."

A quick search discovered our weapons and disarmed us.

"Tie 'em and blindfold 'em with the rest," Flat Cap commanded.

"Your measures are unnecessary," Holmes told them. "You may not know who I am, but I know you. I can name each of you, I fancy. Mr Heskith Burden is easy to identify, even behind his cabbie's scarf and flat cap; the signs of his cab-driving profession are evident on his hands, boots, and trousers, and his accent betrays his address. In any case I make it a habit these days to know all licensed London Hackney drivers by sight; an old adversary of mine had a habit of suborning them or sending substitutes and I have grown cautious. And of course I know of your previous career."

Flat Cap jerked as if a snake had bitten him.

"The other two are harder to distinguish," Holmes went on. "They are certainly your sons, Samuel and William, whose malfeasance has formerly been limited to running numbers for certain Southwark bookkeepers and a modicum of debt collecting. I am inclined to think Billy the taller of the two, in the shabby beret, but I would not have confidently stated it before I observed his reaction to my identification. So you see, blindfolding us would be a futile exercise. You are discovered."

"Dad!" Billy gasped in horror as he was exposed.

"Quiet, lad. We came for answers and answers we shall 'ave. It looks like as these toffs 'as 'em for us. Like as they're in with Larkey and they know something good!"

"You are quite mistaken," I contradicted at a nod from my companion. "We know nothing of this 'Larkey' of whom you speak. But you have made the poor

---

95   A gobstopper, also known as a jawbreaker in Canada and the United States, is a type of boiled sweet. It is usually round, and usually ranges from 1 to 3 cm (0.4 to 1.2 in) across; though gobstoppers having a diameter as large as 3.25 in (83 mm) have been marketed

"Your measures are unnecessary," Holmes told them.

choice to level firearms at Mr Sherlock Holmes."

Old Burden flinched. "Holmes!" He shook his head and swore.

"None other," my friend cautioned them. "You had better decide whether to continue this confrontation. The consequences will only become more dire as your efforts continue."

"Tie 'em up, Billy," Burden commanded his son. "Good an' tight. And careful. They reckons as Sherlock Holmes is something of an escape artist."

I noticed that the three captives were all close-bound with packing straps from the pile near the carriage door. Closer up, I could see that all the prisoners had darkening bruises from vigorous interrogation and two were slumped to the foot of their restraining beams. The man nearest to me still bled from what looked like a broken nose. Only their senior was taking any interest in events.

Holmes looked around with interest of his own as we were bundled to the last pair of gantry supports. "I see that we have come to the right place, Watson. We are one step closer to recovering the stolen material."

"What material?" Billy couldn't resist asking.

"Why, the contents of the company safe at the merchant firm of Murdoch, Brattle, and Stodd," my friend replied as if it were self-evident. "The premises were burgled two nights since. The safe was cracked with gelignite. The haul included a stack of bearer bonds, some jewellery, and a number of confidential papers and personal documents. My colleague and I have undertaken to locate the thieves and recover the missing materials. That brought us here, of course."

Sammy kept his shotgun levelled at me while Billy fastened my hands.

"You knows about this place, then?" Billy pressed.

"I had my suspicions when the trail led us to the vicinity of Sweetapple Lane, which has formerly come to my notice as the native habitat of Mr Dromond Rook there." Holmes nodded to the eldest of the trio of ill-used captives. "My suspicions are now confirmed that Rook's business is rather more than the manufacture and distribution of cheap sticky confectionary."

Rook looked up frantically as he was named but he could make no objection to Holmes's revelations because of his muffling gag.

"The equipment for making confectionary is much the same as that for making explosives," Holmes noted. "Only the ingredients differ. I see—and smell—that we have found the source of the materials that burst open the Murdoch, Brattle, and Stodd vault."

"'E knows about the jelly, dad!" Billy blurted.

"If it's Sherlock Holmes, then 'e knows about all kinds of bloomin' stuff," old Burden answered acidly.

"Maybe 'e knows about our Nance?"

"And maybe you should keep your flappin' trap shut, lad!"

Holmes and I were well secured to the remaining gantry-posts that supported the platform from which ingredients were poured down into the boiling vats. To one side of us were pressing benches with their cutting machines, to the other were tables where the finished sweets were bagged and boxed. Behind us, under the balcony, were cases of ingredients and boiled candies stacked ready for distribution.

"Carry on the search," Heskith Burden ordered his sons. "Bring me any scrap of paper, any ledger what I 'asn't yet seen."

"What is this, Holmes?" I hissed under my breath as the searchers turned their attention away from us.

"It is one nefarious crew tripping up another," my friend supplied. "The ingenious Mr Rook there has found alternative use for his sweet-making apparatus. From what we see here he had turned his factory into an occasional gelignite-making laboratory. Probably a dynamite shop too. You may notice the slatted crates there behind the boxes of gobstoppers, which are open to the air enough that the volatile contents may breathe."

"There is gelignite here?"

"I warrant that I could pick out the exact composition from any sufficient sample. It appears that Mr Rook is in the business of supplying explosives on demand for illicit purposes."

"Rook was not the thief who burgled our clients," I understood. "He was the third party who made and sold the gelignite to the robbers." I looked over at the bickering Burdens. "It looks like he has some unsatisfied customers."

Rook was unhappy at Holmes's examination. He was even less happy when Sammy and Billy took up crowbars and began to wrench away the wooden half-panelling around the room.

"They are looking for a concealed space!" I recognised.

The younger Burdens rapped on walls and even lifted a drain-trap to inspect the rancid runaway of the soured remnants of the factory processes.

"Looking for more concealed hidden explosives," I guessed, "or else some hideaway for stolen goods."

Holmes sighed, as he does sometimes when he feels I have been obtuse. "Observe the nature of their search, doctor. Heskith Burden is interested in documentary evidence. He has gathered and sifted through sales accounts, delivery notices, and inventory purchase logs. In comparison, see how Samuel and William are set to search in large containers, packing crates, and suchlike. They are looking for hidden spaces substantial enough to contain a large single object."

"A large object such as... a person?" I speculated. I remembered Billy's unguarded name-drop. "Nance?"

"You just *shut* up!" Billy shouted, his face reddening under his slipped scarf.

"Now you have found the trail again, Watson," Holmes assured me. "You will notice that the somewhat-abused staff of this manufactory consist of the regrettable Mr Rook and two burly assistants to operate his machinery. And yet the account ledgers that Mr Burden is so zealously inspecting are written in a neat feminine hand. There is a missing staff member, I would say, a shop-girl who attends to the sales counter out front whilst the cooking is being done back here."

"The Burdens have come here to get her?" I asked.

"The Burdens have come here to rescue her," Holmes suggested. "Billy referred to the lady as 'our Nance'."

"That's because Billy 'as a mouth much bigger than 'is brains!" old Burden snarled across the factory.

Young William flinched at his father's displeasure. "Sorry, our dad."

The flat-capped senior shook his head. "I reckoned it was pure bad luck, us bumping into Sherlock Holmes himself like this. But now's I think it though, it might not be misfortune after all." He gestured to his sons. "Sammy, Billy, break out them sticks of dynamite from the box there. Gently! Rook's supposed to make good stuff that won't go bang without a detonator, but I don't want to go testing it!"

The taped bundles of seven brown sticks our captors hauled forth were like church candles with long trailing wicks. The rods of diatomaceous earth were soaked in nitroglycerine—that is nitrating glycerol with white fuming nitric acid—and covered in cloth. The substance is used medically, as a vasodilator for heart conditions, and I have prescribed it myself for *angina pectoris*,[96] but since Albert Nobel's 1867 patent of dynamite it has found a wider application. The fuse embedded in the stick connects to a blasting cap inside to detonate the whole with most potent effect.

"Rope a bundle to each of our guests," Burden instructed. "Then fasten the rest around the room. Sammy—*not you*, Billy. Use that spool of fuse-wire to tie 'em all together so as we can set 'em all off with one match."

Rook, discerning his captors' plans, began to struggle in his bonds. One of his white-overalled assistants squirmed feebly, moaning. Billy cuffed them mercilessly until they were quiescent again.

"They need not connect all of us," Holmes murmured disapprovingly. "In this proximity, the first bundle that the flame reaches will detonate sufficiently to set off all the rest. This whole building will come down."

"And us with it," I pointed out.

"You needn't go up in pieces," Heskith Burden told us. "That all depends. I need the brains of Mr Holmes 'ere."

"You assault us with firearms, bind us up, strap explosives to us, and then

96   That is, chest pain due to lack of blood pressure on the heart muscle.

you ask for a consultation?" I asked incredulously.

"There is certainly a problem to be solved here," my friend observed, looking around with interest. "This is no interrupted robbery, Watson. Look at the method of searching, at the signs of prolonged and savage interrogation upon Rook and his employees, at the lengths to which the Burdens are willing to go, even to the extreme of committing capital firearms offences." His eyes gleamed with anticipatory relish. "Present your problem, Heskith."

The old man narrowed his eyes suspiciously. "'Ow much does you know about me and Rook?" he began.

"You and he were once a team. You specialised in forgery and fraud. You were the artist, creating fake bank-notes or other items. He was the plausible front-man who spent them and got away with the theft."

"A long time ago," Burden muttered. His eyes reflected bitterness and weariness.

"Your work was adequate but not inspired," Holmes appraised bluntly. "It was only a matter of time before it was discovered and you were caught. I believe that Rook was apprehended trying to cash counterfeit bearer bonds at Merrow's Bank on Throgmorton Street. He did not give up your name, if I recall the matter correctly."

Burden glanced across at the battered and bound form of Dromond Rook, looking momentarily guilty at the torture he had inflicted, and then becoming overwhelmingly furious. "I was caught any'ow. Eight years hard for me and twelve for 'im."

"It was, as you say, a long time since. By the time you were released from Pentonville your sons were almost grown. You found honest day-work as a London cabbie. You have not come to my attention since."

I have seen Holmes rattle off the histories of obscure minor felons before, but it never fails to impress me how he can recall such details.

"Rook was released later, though with six months off for good behaviour," the detective continued. "He was not quite so reformed as his former partner, and has since supplemented his income with the passing of stolen goods and by advancing the occasional loan, to finance some illegal operation in exchange for a percentage of the take. It now appears that Rook's sweet-making business has also been a front for the occasional production of dynamite and gelignite."

"Surely he would have been caught before now if he was supplying the criminal population with high explosives?" I protested.

Rook shook his head in denial.

"'E don't supply the wrong element too often," Burden allowed.

"Ah," Holmes apprehended at once, "The majority of his trade is sales to 'legitimate' users, to builders or demolition men who prefer to avoid the stamp duty on officially-approved and regulated products. Perhaps a foreman or stores manager makes a little profit on the side by resorting to 'confectionary sources' rather than paying the full amount that appears on his company's ledger-sheet." He nodded to himself as he calculated how such a scheme might work.

He looked speculatively at the discarded ledgers nearby and then slyly back at Heskith Burden. "And where certification *was* required, it might be handy to have an old contact who could provide acceptable facsimiles at a reasonable cost. You are not quite so retired as you appear, it seems."

"We all 'as to make a living," Burden protested. "All right, so you knows our business. It's true I lately 'elped Rook out with a bit of certification paperwork on occasion, if the need arose and the price were right. But not that often—the 'Ville does no good to an artist's 'ands, I can tell you. And in reciprocation, Rook sometimes used our Sammy and our Billy to 'elp out with deliveries when 'e needed some extra bodies."

"And he also provided employment for Nancy, as a counter girl," Holmes surmised. "Your... daughter?"

"An' our sister!" Billy added wrathfully. "*Our sister!*"

"Do I understand that this young lady is missing?" I enquired. I began to understand the savagery with which the Burdens were conducting their operation.

"Our Nance, yes," old Burden agreed. "Seventeen years old and the nicest lass you could... And where is she now, eh? *Where is she?*"

I thought for a moment that he might fly again at this bound former partner, but he controlled himself at the last.

"What are the circumstances of her absence?" Holmes interrogated. "Where does this 'Larkey' come into the narrative?"

"Larkey!" Burden spat. "'E's one of '*is* customers. And Rook won't tell me where 'e is!"

From that garbled accusation I parsed that this Larkey was an habitué of the confectioner's shop, and likely a customer of the illegitimate manufacturing side of the operation. Despite ruthless interrogation Rook had not been forthcoming about the fellow's address, or more likely he had never known it.

"Davie Larkey and our Nance started walking out six weeks back," Sammy explained to us. "'E seemed respectable enough. Cut above, even. We di'n't know as 'e was one of Rook's dodgy kind o' customers."

"Well," old Burden allowed, "I knew as he weren't lily-white when 'e asked me to supply 'im with some tickets to some grand ball or other, so's 'e could flog 'em to society climbers what wanted to rub shoulders wi' the big nobs. But there didn't seem much 'arm in that. A cove 'as to live. We didn't 'ave any idea that 'e was in that deep wi' Rook's other business."

"Until today," prompted Holmes. The Burdens looked surprised that he might suggest that, so he added impatiently, "Had you been aware of difficulties before this, you would hardly have delayed your armed assault on your former partner's business premises."

"Right. Well, when we gets up for breakfast this morning, there's none made," Heskith recounted. "No Nance at all."

"We was worried as she 'ad eloped!" Billy contributed. "With Larkey," he added, as if that wasn't obvious.

"But she di'n't take none of 'er stuff," Sammy contributed.

"We couldn't find her," old Burden kept charge of the tale. "But then! In poles that Davie Larkey, cool as you like, and says, 'Nancy is in my power. I 'ave hidden 'er away,'—except 'e sounded posher than that, not like 'is normal voice at all—'I have hidden her away. No harm shall come to 'er—her—if you do as I require.'"

"We were that surprised we di'n't know what to do!" Tommy admitted.

"And just when we thought to grab 'im and give 'im a proper thrashing, he pulled out a gun!" Billy added.

Heskith senior gestured for them to pipe down so he could carry on. "It's true that Larkey 'ad a pistol. One of them swank foreign jobs. I 'aven't seen the like of it before, but very 'andy. And 'e knew what to do with it. 'E 'ad us all covered and no chance of jumping 'im. And if we did then... he 'ad our Nance."

"What was it that Mr Larkey required?" asked Holmes.

"He wanted some forging doing. But first 'e 'ad me tie up the lads so's they couldn't make a fuss, an' lock 'em in the boot cupboard."

"It was right tight in there," Billy complained. "And smelly."

"I'd not finished me breakfast," Sammy protested. "Me stomach was upset."

"Larkey wanted me to change the name on some 'andwritten invitation," Heskith reported. "A right fine bit of calligraphy with a proper printed coat of arms and gilded deckle edges. I did my best in the time I 'ad with the materials at 'and, but I don't say as it was perfect."

"What was the invitation for?" I wondered.

"Some big do tonight at the Duke of Steadhampton's place on Mayfair," he told me.

"And he already had an invitation?" I puzzled. "In whose name?"

"Some fellow called Plover. I 'ad to amend it to read 'Mr Charles Figg'."

Holmes waved that aside for now. He clearly wanted his information in a precise order. "At what time was the card prepared?"

"It was a difficult, precise job. I could 'ave spent a couple of hours on it and made it better, but Larkey seemed to be in a raging hurry. I was done around one-thirty or just after."

"We missed lunch as well," complained Sammy.

At about that time, Holmes and I had been tracing the contents of the

Murdoch, Brattle, and Stodd safe, questioning informants and sifting our way ever nearer to Sweetapple Lane.

Old Burden clenched his fists as he recalled events. "When I'd done to Larkey's satisfaction, I asked about our Nance, but all 'e'd say was that she was safe as long as we co-operated. I don't like to think about poor Nance, alone and terrified wi' that cad, but…" He glared again at the captive confectioner.

"Dad was too smart for 'im," Billy boasted. "'E hid 'is card scalpel in 'is sleeve when Larkey came to tie 'im up and all. Then when Larkey 'ad 'im trussed like us and was away, dad was able to cut 'is ropes and get us out."

Sammy took up the story. "Then we went straight to Iron George to…"

"*Sammy!*" Heskith snapped, silencing the young man's evident indiscretion.

"You acquired illegal firearms from an illicit supplier," Holmes noted. He did not seem surprised to hear of this Iron George's arms trade, but I knew that Holmes would take steps to curtail that kind of business in London. The Metropolitan Police take a very dim view of gun crimes—and their boots are every bit as good at trampling armed felons as they are at obliterating Holmes's clues.

"When Larkey started waving guns around, we knew we 'ad to take precautions too," Billy insisted. "'Specially 'cos we 'ad to come 'ere and find out what they'd done to our Nance!"

"But Rook and 'is bullies won't tell us where Larkey took our sister!" Sammy snarled. "No matter 'ow 'ard we thrashes 'em. Dad should let me cut some fingers off, I says!"

"We have conducted quite a search," old Burden conceded to Holmes. "As you see, we are becoming desperate. I confess as I am proper frightened for our Nance. She's a good girl 'oo wouldn't run away, and I don't know 'ow to save 'er from a black-'earted villain."

"You might have received better help from us if you had not strapped us with dynamite!" I pointed out.

"Well, I reckon it must sharpen up even Mr Holmes's mind something lovely. So if you wants to live, Mr Holmes and Dr Watson, I suggests you solves this case."

"Whilst we are tied to wooden posts and draped with explosives?"

"Just so."

Holmes shifted round to inspect Rook and his fellow prisoners. The confectioner was alert and very unhappy. "I will require an interview with your former partner, Heskith," Holmes insisted. "If I am to untangle this chain of events—literally with my hands tied—then I will need to question Rook next."

Old Burden gestured for Samuel to shift away the gag and pull out the rag that had been crammed into Rook's mouth. As soon as the sweet factory owner had taken a full gasp of breath he released a string of obscenities that were more remarkable for their volume and length than for their originality.

Heskith slapped him hard. "Shut your face, Dromond. If you 'aven't worked out this ain't a game yet then get it into your thick skull now! Our Nance is in right danger, and it's because of you not taking care to keep 'er from your dodgy customers. If aught 'as 'appened to her then I swears as you will bleed for it and die for it, as God is my witness! And if aught 'appens now because you didn't tell me an' Mr Holmes what we needs to know, then I will see you beg for mercy before you finally dies screaming! Got it?"

Rook bit back a snarl, spat some blood, and met Burden's stare. "I 'as already told you, you mad old fool, as I don't know where Larkey is. It's not my fault if your lass decides to take up with 'im. I'm sorry she's gone, for she's a nice lass and a good worker, but it don't make me responsible and it don't mean I knows anything. You comes in 'ere, waving your guns, beating up my boys, making all this mess—and now you're brought Sherlock 'Olmes into it! You and me, Heskith, we're going to 'ave a reckoning!"

"This is the reckoning, Dromond. If you don't..."

"I should like to conduct my interview now," Holmes interjected. "Mr Burden, if you would be so good as to return to your inspection of the documents you discovered, I shall take on the role of investigator with which you have tasked me. You may indulge your parental anguish and violent fear or you can allow me to determine facts, but you cannot do both."

The old man in the flat cap gritted his teeth and fell silent.

"You has to get me out of 'here," Rook told Holmes and I.

"Offering your testimony to Holmes might be the quickest way for that," I advised the confectioner. I was somewhat concerned for his health. In addition to the contusions of a rough beating he was also an alarming colour of purple, suggesting a very stressed heart, save for his bound hands which were alarmingly white. I judged that his two beaten fellows were possibly in worse medical condition.

"What does you want to know?" Rook asked Holmes sourly.

"Begin with your gelignite sales," the detective commanded. "What proportion of your actual business does that manufacture represent?"

"The better part, I suppose. But it's mostly bulk orders for construction firms, like you said. The railway crews are always wanting it, and those fellows digging out the Underground."

"And sometimes safe-crackers?"

"I don't ask for details."

"You do ask for references, though," Holmes insisted. "You must, or you might end up falling into the trap of an undercover policeman or crusading journalist."

"I work on recommendations."

"You sold a bundle to the fellows who raided Murdoch, Brattle, and Stodd last Thursday," I accused.

"I have nothing to say on that," Rook snarled.

"I don't care about that job," Burden objected to Holmes. "It's Nance and Larkey I wants to know about!"

Holmes was unmoved. "Perhaps if I mention that some of the papers abstracted from the safe at Murdoch, Brattle, and Stodd's were the property of the Duke of Steadhampton? Given the coincidence of the document which Mr Burden was asked to forge, Larkey having acquired an invitation to Steadhampton's society event from somewhere prior to that, and the break-in at the merchant shipping concern that Steadhampton was employing for his transactions in the Caribbean and Americas, one might suspect that we are chasing not two mysteries but one."

"You'll tell Mr Holmes anything 'e wants, Dromond Rook, or I'll start on your teeth!" old Burden threatened.

Rook slumped in his bonds. "It was Blind Henry's outfit," he confessed.

Burden frowned. "Blind Henry? 'E's usually empty 'ouses, or sometimes a Post Office! Since when does 'e do City firms?"

"Since 'e got paid to, I suppose! It was done to order, is what I gathered. But I don't exactly ask coves to fill out a questionnaire, does I? 'E wanted some jelly, 'e paid for some jelly, I gave 'im some jelly."

"That's usually the way of it?" Holmes verified. "Cash payments on pick-up or delivery?"

"What else?" sneered Rook. "That ain't a business what extends a lot of credit on trust."

Old Burden scowled. "You reckon as Larkey was the fellow what 'ired Blind Henry?"

"Well, Henry's employer knew enough to send him round to Rook for the explosives required for the job," Holmes pointed out. "When and how did this Davie Larkey become your customer, Dromond? Who recommended him to you?"

Rook hesitated. Burden gestured for his sons to act. Rook decided instead to answer. "'E came with an introduction from Nathan Cross."

Holmes clearly knew that name too, though it meant nothing to me. He saw the question on my lips and answered it. "One of the new generation of criminal middle-men who have crawled out since the fall of Moriarty's empire. He is something of a support service, a facilitator, a high-end fence's fence and criminal financier. At some point he was always going to deserve my attention, and now he has it."

Rook shuddered. "Don't tell 'im as it was me what named 'im!"

"We won't find Cross today," old Burden groaned. "Nor take 'im with only three guns. Chances are any'ow as 'e only took a fee to make an introduction."

"Cross sent Larkey to me to start. Larkey wanted a couple of dabs of jelly only, that first time. 'E didn't say why, paid cash on the nail, and went 'is ways."

"When was this?"

"Maybe three months ago. 'E's in the ledgers as a Mr Fabio buying two cases of Pear Drops."

"That's why there's no mention of Larkey!" Heskith Burden growled. He returned to the captured books with renewed interest. "Looks like 'e was a proper regular of yours. 'E was in every couple of weeks. Never a big order, only bits and bobs of 'Pear Drops' and 'Aniseed Twists'."

"That's 'ow 'e got to know our Nance," reasoned Billy.

"I didn't know about that," insisted Rook. "I di'n't know they was walking out till they'd been gallivanting for two weeks or more."

"This last order, though, three days ago," old Burden continued with the sales ledger, "This was a bigger lot. What's 'Butterscotch' mean?"

"It means a bulk supply made up into shaped blocks instead of sticks. The sort of explosive you uses for packing round something if you wants a shaped detonation or something special."

"What shape?" Holmes asked.

"A sort of disc, an inch thick and the size of a cupped palm. That was tricky and I charged more for it. Larkey wanted two score of the things."

"Did he provide a delivery address?"

"'E collected them 'imself yesterday."

"In what vehicle?"

"Just a normal dray. The package weren't that big."

"Describe the dray. The driver. Give me details."

"I di'n't pay much attention. It was a one-'orse cart. Green I think, with cream bits. There might 'ave been some writing on the side."

Holmes allowed himself a small smile. "The tracks in the lane outside. Yes, it was a sprung-chassis carriage with a wheelbase of five-foot-five. The cartwheels were steel shod with a missing rivet on the front offside rim."

"'Ow can you tell that?" Billy Burden asked, baffled.

"How could you miss it?" Holmes asked, in that disappointed way he has when the rest of us fail to take in details that seem glaringly obvious and trivial to him. "The driver was a plump fellow of late middle age who favours his left leg, possibly from gout. He smoked Lone Jack tobacco in a cheap clay pipe, whilst watering his horse. You must have walked in here the same way that we did. The tracks were quite distinct."

"Does that help us, Holmes?" I enquired.

"It might. The green and cream livery probably means it was hired by the hour from Fawcett's on Surrey Yard off the Blackfriars Road. He would have left a deposit with them, and possibly an address. The driver should know where he visited. If I can get down there and ask them…"

"You're going nowhere, Mr Holmes," old Burden interrupted. "I can't trust you on the loose. You stays 'ere till our Nance is found, or you goes boom. Nothing else!" He pointed to his son. "Sammy, get yourself to Fawcett's. Ask 'em about Larkey 'iring one of their nags-an'-carts yesterday. Don't take no for an answer."

The young man laid his antique shotgun aside and hared out of the delivery entrance at the back of the sweet factory.

"Why did you choose the pseudonym 'Fabio' to refer to Larkey in your accounts?" Holmes asked Rook.

"'Cos 'e looks a bit like a foreigner," the confectioner replied.

"'E does a bit," Billy agreed. "Sort of like a Dago, something like that. Of course the girls will swoon at 'im for 'aving a bit of a tan. I reckon that's why our Nance were so taken with 'im."

Holmes interrogated Rook and the Burdens for more description of the missing swain. They suggested a handsome man in his mid-thirties, of good build with slicked-back black hair. He had no facial hair but a natural 5 o' clock shadow on a prominent jaw. His most distinctive feature was a faded tattoo on his right forearm.

"Describe it," Holmes demanded immediately upon hearing about the mark.

Between Rook and the Burdens we got a fairly useful description of a knotted rope image over an irregular shape like "a rearing slug attacking a crumb", coloured in two horizontal bands of blue around a middle band of white, next to a blue ten-pointed star.

Holmes smiled like a predator. "Now we have something! I may have encountered something similar in my studies of tattooing. Release my hands. I need pen and paper."

Heskith shook his head. "No. I'll not fall for that, Mr Holmes. They say as you are dangerous and tricksy, and I feels better for you being bound to that pole."

"Release Watson then. Watson, do you recall your schoolboy geography? Could you sketch an approximation of the Spanish island of Cuba?"

I ventured that I could manage a very rough facsimile. I owned that the landmass does, viewed in a certain way, look like a gastropod looming over the small isle of Nueva Gerona as if to devour it. Burden was convinced to temporarily release me from my bonds at gunpoint so that I could trace an outline of Cuba as best I could.

The three men who examined my effort owned that Cuba resembled the "coloured slug tattoo" on Larkey's forearm.

Holmes was satisfied. "The 1848 flag of the Conspiracy of La Mina de la

Rosa Cubana, an uprising against Spanish dominion of the isle,[97] is two blue and one white bands with a blue decagram—that is, a ten-pointed star. Narciso López's unsuccessful rebellion ended with his public strangulation, but his emblem and colours remain popular amongst partisans today.[98] You will often find such images inked onto sailors and traders around the Caribbean and the Gulf of Mexico."

"Cubans might be mistaken for Spaniards," I reasoned. "Or some could pass as Englishmen if their complexion faded."

"The tattoo is usually worn by protestors against Iberian rule of the island," Holmes noted. "If I could see the work I might identify where it was created, by the techniques and needle style."

"Larkey don't sound Cuban," Billy objected.

"And what does you reckon as a Cuban sounds like?" his father asked scornfully. "Be about tying the doctor up again. No tricks, Dr Watson. I've got my gun on you."

Holmes ignored my reconfinement. He had other ideas to pursue. "If Larkey is a Cuban independence sympathiser that begins to explain much. His pale complexion suggests a prolonged absence from the Atlantic basin. He was possibly raised and educated in Britain, which would explain his unaccented diction. However, his enthusiasm for liberating his homeland might place his desire for gelignite in a new light."

"You mean 'e might blow something up?" Rook asked, aghast. "I means, not a safe or some empty building, but somewhere with folks in it?" I was reminded again of that curious patriotic horror that the common criminal feels for domestic and foreign terrorists. "I never would 'ave let 'im 'ave the stuff if I'd knowed…"

"You're a greedy fool and then some," old Burden told his former partner. "Always were. And now you've got Nance mixed up in this. What's Larkey want 'er for, Mr 'Olmes?"

We were interrupted by the abrupt return of Samuel Burden from his chase to Fawcett's on Surrey Yard. He had been longer than expected. It was now

97   López's uprisings from 1849 ended with his public garrotting in Havana on September 1st, 1851. His final words were "My death will not change the destiny of Cuba." His were only some of a long succession of uprisings and brutal suppressions against and by the Spanish regime—the Ten Years' War (1868–1878), the War of '68, the Little War (1879–1880) and the Cuban War of Independence (1895–1898) collectively claimed well over a quarter of a million casualties. The rebellion culminated after the Spanish-American War of 1898 with the separation of Cuba from Spanish rule.

98   That blue and white flag became the first flag of independent Cuba and remains part of the nation's heraldry today. The modern flag of Cuba is three blue and two white horizontal stripes overlaid on the left hand side with a red triangle containing a white star. This flag was also designed by Narciso Lopez and was adopted as the national flag in 1902.

almost evening outside.

"Well?" old Burden demanded, while Billy asked, "What kept you?"

"I 'ad to chase on," Sammy answered defensively. "I got to Fawcett's and needed to wait for the driver to come back in. And I 'ad to give 'im two bob to cough up what 'e'd done yesterday. Seems as Larkey made just one stop on the way from 'ere, at some dressmakers' place. And then 'e went to a yard off Union Street an' emptied his crate into one o' them lock-ups under the railway arches."

"So you went there," Holmes suggested.

"Right away, in case our Nance were there an'... and she needed 'elp, like."

"And your shotgun sitting 'ere in that corner," old Burden sighed. "If only you 'ad brains, our Sammy!"

"But I *did* go there," the young man insisted doggedly. "I broke open the lock and went inside—but it were empty."

"Larkey must 'ave shifted the goods again with a different wagon," Rook considered. "Smart."

"Holmes could doubtless learn where and how, if he was able to view the site," I argued, but old Burden wasn't having that.

"You should 'ave gone to the dressmaker's," Billy told Sammy.

"But I did that an' all!" the youngster protested, evidently feeling unfairly judged.

Holmes cut through the chatter and demanded to have the facts.

"Well, sir," Sammy explained, "When there was nought at the lock-up, I decided to try that dressmaker's on the way back. I was right afeared by then for our Nance, so I ran all the way. I spoke to the seamstress, Mrs Wallace—she does posh dresses for parties an' that, for rich ladies. 'Er workshop's full of 'em, though o' course they gets taken up to the West End an' Piccadilly and the like for selling..."

"Samuel!" the lad's father called him to order.

"Right, sorry. Yeah, well... Turns out Davie Larkey was there last week and yesterday and today. And our Nance was with 'im first time, and she were there today!"

"And you couldn't 'ave mentioned that right off, you dunderhead, instead of bleating about waitin' for draymen and railway arches?" Billy griped.

"I keeps trying to tell a proper tale but you all keep shouting at me and asking of questions!" Sammy objected aggrievedly. "So anyway, Larkey was there yesterday payin' for a dress what e' ordered. I mean a really swish dress evidently, an' seemingly for our Nance. 'Cos 'e brought 'er round there in the first place to be measured an' fitted for it, and today at two-fifteenish to try it on—this being one of them posh things what girls need lacing into, with them big..." The young man mimed a full hoop bell-skirt with a bustle behind."

"I keeps trying to tell a proper tale but you all keep shouting at me!"

"Our Nance was with 'im this afternoon?" Heskith puzzled. "She weren't 'is prisoner?"

"Sounds less like a kidnapping and more like an elopement," Rook chuckled through bloodied teeth. "A good girl, is she?"

Holmes's frown silenced the commentators so that Sammy could continue. "So Nance got into this dress—a blue dress, evidently, with… well, the lady described it a bit but I didn't follow most of it. It 'ad lace, seemingly. And some shoes to match, an' stockings and such, and… and underthings. It cost a guinea and a half! An' then Nance and Larkey went out to this carriage and rode off."

"What kind of carriage?" Holmes was always quick on the transport questions.

The seamstress hadn't known. She's been more interested in describing the ensemble she had created, "Fit for a princess, she said, but strange."

"Strange how?"

Sammy shrugged. "I di'n't quite follow that bit entirely. Seemingly them posh dresses 'ave some kind of wire frame under 'em, like a parrot cage, what 'olds the skirt like it was a tea-cosy. And this frame is covered with some gauze stuff between the wires. An' this dressmaker was told by Larkey to make every single one of them work like a pocket."

Holmes's brows rose. "*How* many pockets, Billy?"

"Forty, she said."

"Holmes?" I prompted.

"These shaped charges that you created, Mr Rook," my friend asked urgently, "the two score that Larkey most recently ordered—were they of the size that might fit into a pocket of, say, six inches square? Such that the gelignite might be slipped into an underskirt and connected to a chain fuse?"

I recoiled at the idea. "You are not suggesting that Nancy Burden's dress was laced with high explosives, turning the poor girl into a walking bomb?"

"I believe that Larkey had plenty of small samples from Rook beforehand to experiment with. That suggests a long period of planning and preparation. But then Larkey needed some details from the files held by Murdoch, Brattle, and Stodd. Shipping manifests? Financial transfers? Travel plans and itineraries?"

The Burdens reacted badly to the idea of Nancy wearing gelignite. "You 'as to find 'er!" Heskith demanded. "Remember, if *she* comes to 'arm they'll be picking pieces of *you* up for months to come!"

"Then we had best focus on the facts of the case," Holmes answered coldly. "Hypothesise that Larkey has some act of mass destruction planned at some society event."

"The Duke of Steadhampton's reception tonight!" I broke in.

"Most likely. You will recall that the invitation that Larkey brought to

Heskith Burden was made out to another guest, one who might reasonably be recognised by the footmen at the porch or who might have reported the loss of an invitation. Larkey needed a different name on an amended invitation to be allowed with his companion into the event."

"He plans to be there at Steadhampton's? Tonight? With Nancy?"

"Let us suppose that he does. A sophisticated young rogue worms his way into the confidence of a young shop girl. He beguiles her with love-talk and offers to take her to a fairy-tale party with dukes and princes. She has a wonderful new dress, so strange and different from anything she has known that she sees nothing strange in the odd gelid padding of her underskirt. She accompanies her swain to this glittering soirée, to see all the fine people in their finery dining and dancing.

"She is an attractive vision at this gathering, young and innocent and new. Might we imagine some gentleman is encouraged to take an interest, to go over and speak with her, flirt with her? A particular gentleman, perhaps, who is the focus of Larkey's campaign? And as Nancy talks with him, perhaps as he discovers she is an unlikely Cinderella at the ball, her wicked Fairy Godmother starts the slow fuse that is threaded in her gown."

"She blows up!" old Larkey gasped, panicked by Holmes's conjured vision. "She blows up and takes this fellow with her!"

"And a roomful of other guests," Rook added, calculating the effect of so much gelignite. "'Alf the bloomin' building!"

"We must stop this!" I insisted. "You must allow Holmes and I free. This can be prevented!"

Heskith Burden was still leery of Sherlock Holmes. "This might all still be fancy. Mr Holmes might be gulling us. It's not beyond 'im from what I 'ears."

"Then let Watson go," my friend suggested. "You and your sons could never pass the sentries on Steadhampton's event. He might be believed. If you will not release me then he is Nancy's only chance."

"'E mustn't give us away," old Burden insisted. "I'll need his word."

"Very well," I agreed, "but no harm must come to Holmes. Or these others."

A sly look came across the old forger's face. "Tell you what," he said. "We'll pay out three hours of this slow fuse 'ere. It gets lit when you go. It gets put out when you comes back with Nancy—and no-one else, an' no other way. That's the deal."

"You can't expect me to…" I began to protest.

Holmes interrupted me. "Lives are at stake, doctor. Trust that all shall be well if only you play your part. Listen carefully: this Larkey may be seeking some prey at the party who has a Cuban connection. When you get there, check the guest manifest for such a person. Speak with whichever military or constabulary officer is present to ensure security; given the guest list there is certain to be one. If you can, get to Steadhampton himself and explain the danger. When you locate Larkey, separate him from Nancy before he can activate any mechanism threaded into her ensemble."

"An' get my girl out of there an' back to me, not under police arrest as an accessory," Burden demanded. "You 'as three hours, Dr Watson!"

Freed from my unexpected confinement in the manufactory on Sweetapple Lane, I might have foundered about wondering what to do, about whether to break my word and call the police, about how to address the needs of an innocent young woman stolen away for murder by a foreign anarchist. Fortunately, however, I had Holmes's words to guide me: *Trust that all shall be well if only you play your part.*

That inevitably meant that my friend had some idea in mind. He had reason for dispatching me to Miss Burden's immediate aid. I could best serve his needs by carrying out the instruction he had given me.

I still paused for a moment on the track outside Rook's confectioner's to examine the ruts and splashes on the road, but I could read nothing of the tale that Holmes had deduced in passing of the events that had broken open the case. Holmes is remarkable.

On the main thoroughfare I was able to hail a passing cab and go with haste to Mayfair.

Steadhampton's mansion was a huge imposing place, more palace than house, with colonnaded portico and Classical frontage lit by dozens of torches and lanterns. A long queue of carriages waited to debark their passengers at the reception point.

I dodged out of my hired hansom and pressed through the wondering crowds that had gathered to watch the splendid social elite parade into the salons. I was halted near the entrance by a dour liveried footman, a giant of a fellow who was stationed to prevent access by any who lacked invitations.

"Let me through!" I protested. Lives were at stake. The unmoving lackey seemed as dumb and immovable as a block of wood.

Over the footman's shoulder I glimpsed the evening-dressed figure of Sir Tarrant Besting Q.C., one of Her Majesty's Assistant Directors of Public Prosecutions, the senior solicitors of the Crown Prosecution Service.[99] I called

---

99   The top posts in the Crown legal service, in the 1890s and today, are the Attorney General and then the Solicitor General. Beneath them is the Director of Public Prosecutions, the third most senior public prosecutor in England and Wales, who in Holmes's period also held the post of Treasury Solicitor. A variable number of Assistants undertake the bulk of the

out to Besting but the ambitious careerist has never liked Sherlock Holmes. The Assistant Director pretended that he had not noticed me.

"You have to let me past. I have an urgent message for his grace!" I argued, to no avail.

I was considering knocking the footman down when I spotted another familiar face amongst those ascending the front stairs. "Pike!" I called out. "Langdale Pike!"

The society newspaper columnist turned his elegant head and spotted me. He pointed his ebony-topped evening cane in my direction and spoke to one of the servants assisting guests up into the mansion. At that I was allowed past the obstructionist footmen to join Holmes's strange languid advisor on gossip in the highest circles.[100]

"Doctor Watson," he smiled, drawling my name. "May I assume by your desperate manner and lack of evening attire that something deliciously exciting is secretly occurring?" He looked around speculatively at the footmen who flanked us on the entry stairs. "Is Sherlock somewhere close by in one of his thrilling disguises? Shall he pounce at any moment on some devious malefactor?"

I briefly informed Pike that Holmes had sent me to prevent an atrocity. I made no mention that my friend, who would be so much better suited to the mission than I, was presently confined in a sweet factory wrapped in dynamite.

"A genuine damsel in distress!" Pike exalted. "There is no time to lose! No point in seeking out the Duke before it is time for him to come down. I understand from some confidential but reliable sources that he will be 'in conference' with Lady S_____ at this time, and the two of them would not welcome any

---

practical work, which in Victorian times was considered part of the *'cursus honorum'* towards higher government or legal office.

Q.C. is a formal abbreviation in the United Kingdom and the Commonwealth for the honorific post-nominal 'Queen's Counsel' (K.C. for 'King's Counsel' if the reigning monarch is male), for a lawyer appointed by the Crown to lead prosecution or defence in a major court case. In court, Q.C.s are entitled and required to wear the silken gown and peruke wig much beloved of TV courtroom dramas; indeed, becoming a Q.C. is colloquially called "taking the silk". In 1898 there were 238 Q.C.s, of whom only a third were in actual legal practice; today there are over a thousand.

Dr Watson has previously mentioned Sir Tarrant Besting in "Dead Man's Manuscript" (*Sherlock Holmes, Consulting Detective volume 1* (2010, also compiled in *Sherlock Holmes Mysteries* 2013, Kindle and Audiobook Only) and in "The Woman Who Collected Queen Victoria" (*Sherlock Holmes, Consulting Detective volume 13*) in stories by I.A. Watson.

100   Langdale Pike's sole Canon appearance is in "The Adventure of the Three Gables", *The Case-Book of Sherlock Holmes* (1926). It is usually assumed that Watson always referred to the gossip columnist by his assumed nom-de-plume. Langdale Pikes is a famous range of scenic hills in England's Lake District. W.S. Baring-Gould's biography *Sherlock Holmes* refers to Langdale Pike as 'Lord Peter'.

interruption, nor be in any state to organise a search of the premises. We had best proceed inside ourselves."

"Holmes believes that the fellow we're after may be Cuban, or have some connection with the place. Is there any guest who might draw his special attention? We might check the visitor-book."

Pike snorted. "My dear chap, how does Sherlock do it? I had to wheedle and cajole to get the merest sniff of what is happening tonight, and he has doubtless deduced it from licking cigar butts and the flight of birds! Yes, there is a special guest amongst the throng this evening. I am given to understand that Candido Ginovés del Cienfuegos, the Spanish governor of the Cuban province of Matanzas, is secretly present for a 'quiet meeting' with certain heads of state—a rendezvous that must not appear in the popular press or be known to their political enemies."

"But you know?"

"Such little secrets are my stock-in-trade, doctor, but I keep this kind of meeting to myself. They are not the sort of thing that interests the readers of my columns. Now that…" he pointed to a robust lady bulging out of a tight purple evening gown, "is far more my metier. Lady Brabington is wearing the famous Daxhunton diamonds which were formerly the property of the late Mrs Chesmere of Cheltenham. How generous of Mister C. to loan them to her!"

We hastened into the reception galleries, a long chain of halls where the guests met and mingled. The general flow of guests was towards the ballroom, but there were salons with divans and side-rooms for refreshments that diverted the visitors on their journey.

"Who is this Spanish governor, then?" I interrogated Pike. "What is his business here?"

"He is supposedly on a tour for his health, time aside from his tedious burdens of duty," my guide told me feyly. "If he happens to sail to England and meet with senior men in the Foreign Office, with ministers and financiers, at a discreet social event such as this, then it is mere coincidence. True, Alfonso XII's Spanish government would be delighted to strike some kind of agreement over the retention of Cuba, and at the United States' restraint from supporting an independence movement there."

"This Ginovés del Cienfuegos is present tonight to negotiate a deal to suppress Cuban independence uprisings?"

Pike shrugged. "If Britain leans on the U.S.A. to choke off support for the rebels then the long series of civil wars and revolutions in Spanish Cuba could be stamped down for good. Those fellows who wear the liberationist tattoos would not be best pleased."

Now I understood why Larkey might wish to destroy all hope of a back-room settlement in Spain's favour. One bright detonation would cull the better part of London society and send shock-waves round the world.

We hastened through the galleries, searching for the girl in the blue lace gown that the dressmaker had described; but Billy's description was sadly lacking, and all the young ladies present wore lavish evening costumes. Nor were the descriptions of Miss Burden's features much different from those of any of the other debutantes that adorned the proceedings. I began to wish that instead of Langdale Pike as my companion I had the scenthound spaniel-lurcher Toby or one of his get.

"That way," Pike told me. "That young woman in cornflower blue, chatting with the young Danbury sprig. Her dress is most certainly Mme. Lacroix's work, or rather of her principal seamstress Mrs Wallace, to whom your missing heroine was evidently taken to be clad. Also, the child herself, though a vision of female loveliness and coiffured by the best, has never been taught how to stand in those heels. Her deportment is lacking, though young Danbury appears more interested in her décolletage."

"That's Nancy? Then where is Larkey?"

Just then a handsome enough fellow of swarthy complexion returned to the girl, bearing a pair of fluted champagne glasses. He interrupted her chat with Danbury and saw the young hopeful off with practiced ease. Nancy exchanged excited comments with her beau, gesturing around her at the palatial mansion and the stately people.

"Is that your fellow, Dr Watson?" Pike asked me as we disguised our regard of the couple. "I believe I can put a different name to him. Two, in fact. He has cut something of a figure this season as the exotic and enigmatic Charles Figg, apparently a wealthy planter come from the Americas to find investment opportunities in London. A number of noble but impecunious families of ancient blood have considered him for one of their available younger daughters."

"Holmes mentioned that he must have been planning this for some time. I presume a secret diplomatic meeting for Ginovés must have required a lengthy set-up. Figg was the name he had inscribed on the counterfeit invitation."

"I did a little rooting into Mr Figg, of course. It is my living. He is also one Camilo Figueredo, who was sent to England in 1880 at the age of ten and entered into a minor public boarding school. He is the natural son of one of those Cuban landowners who perished in their 'Little War' rebellion that year. Evidently there was an endowment left for the child to be educated overseas."

"That might explain how he came to be a partisan of Cuban independence. On obtaining his majority he went home, acquired his beliefs and his tattoo, and has now come back to England under a different name to prosecute his act of terror in support of the rebellion against Spain. Nancy Burden and the criminal fraternity know him as Davie Larkey."

"Well, there he is. You are the man of action, doctor. What shall you do now?"

"See how the blighter is casting around the crowd, seeking someone? I must find a way to separate him from the girl, so he cannot access the explosives laced into her costume."

"How very exciting. In the meantime I believe I shall mention the problem to certain guests that I see milling in the throng. I am convinced that some of them will have the wit to address the situation. I might even enjoy disrupting Steadhampton's urgent conference with Lady Brabington for this." Pike grinned like a shark. "You have made my evening *so much* more interesting, doctor. Excuse me."

The odd gossip-monger glided away, louche and enigmatic, and vanished into the crowd. That left me with the immediate problem of Larkey and Nancy.

That difficulty became more acute as I saw a fellow in some kind of military dress glide across the floor to be introduced to the girl. From the amount of braid on the uniform and the number of medals on his breast he was clearly a very important personage—or believed himself so. I correctly assumed that this was Candido Ginovés del Cienfuego, and that the governor had been attracted by some ruse to come and meet the pretty disguised shop girl. Neither Cinderella nor her ageing Lothario would-be Prince knew that their meeting was engineered by the cold-blooded fanatical murderer who now made them known to each other.

I could not wait any longer. I went over there myself and addressed the girl. "Miss Burden. What a pleasure to meet you here, my dear!"

Nancy looked at me uncertainly. Her escort and the governor blinked in surprise at my uncivil intrusion.

"Do I know you?" Nancy ventured, trying to disguise her South Bank accent in this elite venue.

"I know your father and brothers," I told her. "I met them today, in fact. They are quite worried about you."

"Miss Burden has left her family's care," Larkey told me curtly. "She is presently my guest at this event, and she is eager to make the acquaintance of His Excellency. If you would therefore be so kind as to…"

"Mr Figueredo," I greeted him. "From what part of Cuba did your late father originate? And what was his surname?"

"What?" Ginovés frowned. "I though his name was Figg?"

"What?" Nancy echoed. "Davie?"

Whatever the bounder's name was, he was quick on the uptake. He was too close to Nancy for me to tackle away before he could grasp and hold up a thin length of cord that was fixed like a ribbon lead to Miss Burden's waistband—a ripcord!

"This string is attached to a great deal of explosives concealed in this girl's dress," Larkey warned. "If any of you move, if any of you call out—you included Nance—then I shall tug it and we shall all die in a devastating explosion."

I saw now that there were two rings attached to the dress at the small of Nancy's back above her bustle. Presumably one set off some kind of fuse-cord that allowed a timed explosion so that the murderer might escape. Larkey held the other one.

"Davie, what?" the girl squeaked, suddenly frightened. Her fairy tale had turned horror story.

"What does this mean?" Ginovés demanded.

"It's true," I warned him. "This cad has turned this poor young woman into a living bomb." To Larkey I said, "Have some decency at the last, you wretch! Set aside your mad fanaticism and let Miss Burden go."

"I fear that would not end well for me," the villain replied. "I have my mission."

So caught up in our drama were we that none of us even noticed the waiter until he leaned between us with a tray and offered us a choice of red wine or white.

And only I apprehended that the tall distinguished waiter was Sherlock Holmes.

"We want nothing," Larkey snapped to the 'servant'. "Go away!"

"Not even this?" Holmes asked him, and held up a small confectioner's sweet-cutting knife—the knife that he had just used to sever the gown's lethal pull-cord whose end Larkey still gripped.

There was no reason at all that I could not punch Larkey on the nose, so I did. As the villain tumbled back, Holmes hit him again with the wine tray, and then used more scientific methods of quelling the bounder.

"What?" Ginovés gasped. "Assassin? He was here to murder me? A *Beya-mesa*[101] rebel came to kill me!"

By now a crowd was beginning to form. Langdale Pike's promised intervention was not far behind.

Holmes seized the downed kidnapper's wrist and exposed the emblem inked there. "He was here to murder you, Señor, but he is not a rebel. As soon as I actually saw his tattoo I could tell the work was done in Spain, not the Americas. I would venture Porto or Vigo, judging by the technique. I suggest that 'Larkey' here was intended to be an *agent provocateur*. Your murder and that of so many British nobles and politicians would hardly deter our nation from seeking America's withdrawal from Cuban affairs. It would rather spur our foreign policy to compel it. Spain's cause would be furthered, the resis-

---

101   Three days into the Ten Years War that began in 1868, Cuban rebels seized the important city of Bayamo. In celebration and support, poet and musician Perucho Figueredo composed the song "La Bayamesa", which gave one name to the rebellion, and after independence became Cuba's national anthem.

tance's support entirely removed. All it would cost was the sacrifice of one ignorant diplomat by one cunning double-agent."

Larkey groaned but did not try to speak or rise. Nancy began to weep.

"We must find you other attire, Miss Burden," I coaxed the girl. I held her as she sobbed out her fear, shame, and heartbreak. "How did you come to be here, Holmes?"

"I freed myself from my bonds whilst you were being untied to draw maps of Cuba," the detective explained. "After that it was only a matter of waiting until you were dispatched here, while the Burdens were concerned with checking that you really did depart as expected. Divided they were conquered. You know my proficiencies. The Burdens are now all trussed up with Mr Rook and his staff, ready for the constabulary's attentions and that of medical men where required; although I shall speak in mitigation for the Burdens' firearms offences given the extenuating circumstances."

"In their own way, the Burdens have prevented a national tragedy," I recognised. "Perhaps an international one?"

The Duke of Steadhampton's large footmen belatedly came to secure the assassin. Sir Tarrant Besting finally had to acknowledge my presence, but his attempts to take control of the scene were ignored by the stern senior army officer in charge of the event's security.

"My own government arranged this?" Ginovés asked wrathfully. "To kill me? To make of me a sacrifice? *No puede ser. Ni hablar!* I shall speak to King Alfonso personally! I shall demand satisfaction!"

Holmes shrugged away the politics. We handed poor Nancy off to more tender attendants and spent a few moments satisfying Langdale Pike's curiosity.

"This is not a matter on which I shall ever be able to report," the gossip-columnist mourned.

"My own account must perforce be delayed until a time when its political ramifications are minimal," I consoled him.

Holmes had no more care for our writers' angst than for Miss Burden's anguish or the Duke of Steadhampton's foiled secret meeting with Ginovés. He produced from his pocket a paper bag of Rook's best gobstoppers, offered them around, and popped one into his mouth.

THE END

THE ADVENTURE OF THE ABSCONDED CORPSE

A STIFF CHANNEL WIND smashed breakers upon the Dorset coast, as if the sea itself strove to besiege our island nation. Flecks of spume beaded the windows of the motor car that conveyed Holmes and me across the narrow ribbon of connecting road from the mainland to the Isle of Portland. The waters at both sides of the causeway heaved and churned.

Ahead of us the silhouette of the naval base emerged from the mist. We discerned its yard cranes and fuelling facilities, the drydocks, the research buildings, the training camp; and beyond them the sturdy bulk of great warships at anchor. From somewhere overhead came the drone of a seaplane.

We paused for admission at a gated checkpoint. A striped barrier was raised and we were allowed into Portland Harbour,[102] base of our Home Fleet, one of the most secure military sites in existence.

"There are three successive checkpoints," our driver warned us. "They take access very seriously here."

As well they should. Portland Harbour is one of the biggest man-made harbours in the world, 1,300 acres of water shielded by four massive breakwaters close to three miles long, naturally protected by Chesil Beach to the west and mainland Dorset to the north. When it was completed in 1872 it was then the largest such installation on the globe. Since the advent of the Great War it had become a key part of our military efforts to thwart the Kaiser's mad plans.

"You cannot report anything you see here," Commodore Pinner warned us when we had navigated the layers of protection about the Naval base. He glanced especially at me "You cannot write any account for publication within a hundred years."

"You may trust Watson to use the finest of discretion," Holmes assured the project commander. "I might cite you examples of how he has maintained operational security on a half-dozen matters of national importance—but alas, I fear that *you* would not be cleared for such information."

Our driver had accompanied us into the meeting. Young Gleading was one of the War Office's couriers, tasked by his superiors with liaison between the Admiralty and the consulting detective dragged from reclusive retirement by a

---

102   From 1923 the site was designated His Majesty's Naval Base Portland. It continued in use until 1995.

world war. He proffered our documents and a letter of authority issued by his superior. "Mr Wiggins expects Mr Holmes and Doctor Watson to be granted every facility."

Mr Wiggins. It was still odd for me to think of our scabby-kneed street-Arab Irregular as a grown man, yet alone a middle-aged mandarin in the Civil Service, himself a father of young men who were now conscripted into the present conflict; but of course Wiggins was not only the protégé of Sherlock Holmes but of the late Mycroft Holmes of whom his brother had once said "He is the British government." Wiggins had risen through the ranks, from footman at the Diogenes Club[103] to courier like Gleading, and then though the tiers of the Civil Service to his present seniority. Holmes deemed him the most capable of the present crop of national administrators, and Wiggins knew where to resort when matters became impenetrable.

"Of course, of course," Pinner agreed uncomfortably. "It is just that this matter is d___d sensitive. D___d sensitive!"

Holmes declined an offer of tea from Pinner's civilian secretary, a smart young woman in sober grey workwear, albeit with a modern short skirt.[104] He was keen to address the case which had brought him so urgently from his Claridge's suite.[105] Even after all these years, the great detective's interest could be piqued by a seeming impossibility.

"We were told this was a matter of some urgency," he chided the project commander. "Lives have been lost."

Pinner's eyes went steely. He was well aware of the casualty list. "This way," he said tersely. "Miss Thorne, hold my calls until I return, unless it is an emergency. I will be in Boat Shed Two."

Pinner shepherded Holmes, Gleading, and I from his office, down an ex-

---

103   The progression of Wiggins from barefoot street urchin to adult footman at the Diogenes Club is not mentioned in Canon but has been a favourite idea of subsequent Holmes fiction. It was popularised in Billy Wilder's film *The Private Life of Sherlock Holmes*. Wiggins actually starred in the 1983 children's TV series *The Baker Street Boys*. Wiggins' further progression as Mycroft's emissary, and his entry into public service seem to be logical consequences of his career path and patronage.

104   Watson is referring to the wartime necessity of rationed cloth which led to skirts being simplified and shortened to six or ten inches from the ground, quite a departure from Victorian corseted dresses.

105   Holmes's residence at Claridge's Hotel in 1914 is attested in "His Last Bow" from *His Last Bow: Some Reminiscences of Sherlock Holmes* (1917). The 5-star hotel at the corner of Brook Street and Davies Street in Mayfair, London was founded in 1812 and by 1878 the first edition of *Baedeker's London* called it "the first hotel in London". It was.rebuilt in its present Grade II-listed form in 1897. Its long-standing connections with royalty have led to it being sometimes dubbed "an annexe to Buckingham Palace".

ternal stair and over to one of the huge covered hangars that fronted the dock. We passed another checkpoint and emerged into the vast engineering works.

A long vessel occupied the whole length of the chamber, hanging from cranes in a lattice of scaffolding, like the corpse of a great metal shark. "You know what this is?" Pinner challenged us.

"A submersible craft," I answered. "A submarine, somewhat like the German *unterseeboot* that has caused such devastation to our shipping of late." The Boche[106] had declared a policy of 'unrestricted warfare'—meaning they would attack neutral and civilian targets of opportunity as well as military ones. It was another example of why the enemy had to be stopped.

The vessel concealed from prying eyes in the long covered shed was somewhat worse for wear, weed-tangled and scuffed. I knew what fate had befallen it and doffed my hat.

Two days earlier this ship had suffered some kind of mechanical failure that had caused it to sink to the Channel bottom, with the loss of thirty hands.

Pinner beckoned over a bearded chap in a greasy service overall. "McCarl, these are the fellows from the War Office. Give them the rundown on the K-ship."

This was Senior Dock Engineer Lieutenant Argus McCarl, whose name I had seen on the reports that Gleading had shown us. He gestured at the dripping bulk that hung before us. "This is oor latest design, intended to completely replace the D- and E-class vessels we currently maintain," he instructed us in a brisk Scots burr. "She's significantly longer and faster than the *Nautilus* and *Swordfish* prototypes, which proved inadequate. This is the prototype for a whole new class o' submarines, the K-class, which are now being laid down and trialled."

"The K-Class is something new," Pinner chipped in. "They are designed to be able to actually keep pace with the fleet when they ride on the surface."

McCarl demonstrated the prototype like a child with a prized toy. "Three hundred and thirty-nine feet long, wi' a displacement of 2,566 long tons submerged, an' a surface speed up to twenty-four knots or a submerged speed better than eight.[107] Four 18-inch beam torpedo tubes, four 18-inch bow tubes, twin 18-inch deck tubes, two BL 4-inch Mk XI guns, one 3-inch gun." He pointed to the rear. "Twin three-blade 7ft 6in screws."

The engineer paused, presumably expecting some reaction to his encomium, so I responded, "Jolly good show."

106　　　This derisive common term for Germans in World War I originated in the late 18th century Parisian underground slang portmanteau insult '*alboche*', conflating '*Allemand*' ('German') and *caboche* ('cabbage-head').

107　　　That is 28 mph (44 km/h) and 9.2 mph (15 km/h) respectively.

"The K-prototype has a range o' 800 nautical miles at 24 knots," McCarl went on. "The ship's compliment is six officers and *fifty-three* ratings."

Holmes was quick to pick up on the emphasis that the engineer laid upon the crew number. "Your count came up short."

Commander Pinner made an embarrassed harrumphing sound and glossed over that comment for now. "The sea-test was scheduled to last three hours," he instructed us as we climbed up onto the gantry. "It was a preliminary practical trial, a short underwater run to test systems and seals."

"It should ha'e been a milk run," McCarl argued.

"But it went wrong," Gleading reprised. "The vessel lost power and sank to the bottom of the sea. Thirty hands were lost. The tragedy is classified; we cannot allow our enemies to know about this failure."

I was unhappy that the service of a brave crew of volunteer seamen might be erased. "How can their disappearance possibly be explained?"

"Records will be amended," Pinner told us. "Men will be accounted as being on ships that have been publicly lost. Lord knows there are enough of them. That is why we need the K-Class."

Since the *SM-U21* had sunk *HMS Pathfinder* on the 5th of September 1914, the Germans had conducted an all-too-successful campaign of terror at sea with their U-boats.[108] But Britannia still ruled the waves.

Holmes was more interested in the present case, and by the new technology before him. "Has a cause been determined for the prototype's failure?" he enquired.

"We've only had the salvaged hull back here fae nine hours," McCarl reported defensively.

Pinner justified the delay. "It took some time after the K-prototype failed to signal in before we could locate its actual position on the sea bed, and longer before we could arrange for it to be dredged and recovered."

"Times, man!" Holmes chided him, rapping his walking-cane down in irritation. "Facts!"

The Commodore suppressed a scowl; he was not used to be spoken to so sharply. "The test commenced at 0431 the day before yesterday. The ship signalled in and dove at 0515 and was expected to progress at best speed to a fixed position 22 nautical miles distant. The cutter *Diligent* was tasked with trailing it and offering support but could not track it underwater. From the position where the prototype was recovered, the K-ship suffered its problem

---

108   The U-boat campaign sank 1.4 million tons of shipping between October 1916 and January 1917. Thereafter Germany announced its policy of unrestricted submarine warfare and on 17th March German submarines sank three American merchant vessels. This led to U.S. declaring war on Germany in April 1917.

around 0600, having traversed six and a half nautical miles. When no report was signalled in by 0815, *Diligent* alerted us to the possibility of a problem."

"And then?"

"*Diligent* was tasked to search. When nothing was spotted by 0930 further assets were deployed. By then it was evident that something quite serious had happened. There were some previous problems with helm and diving planes, but those are now corrected."

"We thought they were corrected," McCarl hedged his bets.[109]

"You do have a preliminary analysis of the problems the ship faced, then," I pushed the engineer.

"At first we posited ballast tank failure or engine difficulties. The submarine uses two 10,500 shp Brown-Curtis geared steam turbines off a pair o' Yarrow boilers and four 1,440 hp electrical motors, but we'd previously noted that a problem with one sometimes trigged a parallel malfunction on the others."

"But…" Holmes pressed.

"But now ah've had a chance to look inside, I'd say a pressure valve on one of the steam venting stacks maybe malfunctioned. Cold water got into th' red-hot boiler and there was a rupture. The casing shattered, sending shrapnel across the engine bay and through bulkheads. At least that seems t' be the most likely cause—based on a *preliminary* analysis."

That won a nod of approval from my colleague. Holmes was always cautious about theorising ahead of his data. He gestured for Pinner to continue his account.

The Commodore scowled. "We had mariners down. The fleet was deployed. Eventually one of our E-class assets located the prototype, some two miles offshore, along the line it should have been following. We were unable to make contact with any crew."

"This would be 0122 yesterday," Gleading supplied from his briefing notes. Our War Office liaison was already learning how to offset Holmes's irritable response to lack of details. The years have not taught my friend patience or tolerance.

"Yes. We were uncertain then whether there were survivors or not. Whether the vessel was flooded or not."

"But it was," I noted. The damage on the retrieved prototype was all too evident. "At least a part of the submarine." It seemed preposterous to me to fit a steam turbine requiring large-diameter ports to be cut through the thick walls that kept out the sea under pressure, but I am not an engineer.[110]

---

109   The K-Class was notorious for its design. In May 1916 the actual prototype, *K-3*, suffered helm and diving plane issues and buried itself bow first in shallow water—with the Duke of York, the future King George V, aboard.

110   Engineers agreed with Watson, though. As *The Guardian* columnist Ian Jack summarised

The Commodore scowled. "We had mariners down. The fleet was deployed."

"The engine rooms were flooded," McCarl specified. "The for'ard section was sealed off from the inundated parts. The thirty men who died were trapped aft. Three officers and twenty-six ratings survived. The recovery was effected by 1540 hours yesterday."

And here we came to the reason for Holmes's summons. I pointed out the problem: "Fifty-nine men dove aboard the K-prototype. After its malfunction and recovery, fifty-eight were brought off, dead or alive. One simply vanished—while submerged in a sealed metal shell."

"Yes," Pinner answered grimly. "We are missing a dead man."

"And that isn'ae possible," McCarl insisted.

Holmes tapped his finger thoughtfully on the head of his cane and said nothing. The evidence suggested otherwise.

When Wiggins had asked for me to meet with Holmes and look at a mystery in Dorset I had been baffled by the details. As I regarded the cramped tube of underwater craft I was more baffled still.

"How can one simply lose a person aboard a ship like this?" I puzzled. The K-prototype was little more than a metal tube with a conning tower near its centre. There was only one hatch topside, and it was 'locked down' (in Naval parlance) before the craft dived.

"The K-class is a wee bit slow to dive," Lt. McCarl admitted. "It takes a full four minutes to secure to go underwater, which is probably too long if it wants tae avoid enemy fire. We're working on that. But once it is sealed, and especially once it's at any depth, it is impossible to leave the craft."

"The funnel vents?" Holmes enquired. "You said there had been a probable breach."

The senior engineer showed us the wreckage where Boiler One had detonated. I was amazed to see steel walls torn like tin cans, shrapnel embedded in heavy metal; but even then the outer skin had been fractured only a little.

in *From the K-class to the party boat, submarines have a history of disaster*, 4th November 2017, "The K-class were designed to be fast, so that when unsubmerged they could keep up with the surface fleet, and though they achieved that aim—no submarines matched them for speed until the nuclear age—it came at a terrible price. Only steam turbines could provide the required rate of surface knots; submerged, they used electric batteries and an emergency diesel. This complicated propulsion system gave the K-class a bulk and weight that made steering difficult, while steam's need for draughts of fresh air and smoke exhausts meant vents and two funnels—the only submarine ever to be so equipped. As one naval critic put it, the K-class had 'too many holes'. When a K sub dived, seawater poured through these holes if they weren't closed promptly or tightly, and sent the vessel and its frantic crew on an unchangeable course to the bottom."

There was no rent large enough for a corpse to be lost through it.

"As ye can see, the damage was extensive," McCarl answered. "That's why it's taking a while tae determine the initial cause. Also, it was a slow gory task removing th' bodies from this section. Some sailors died in the blast. Others probably drowned when the compartment was breeched. But there's nae hole sufficient for even a badly mangled body to be washed oot."

"Who is the missing man?" Holmes wanted to know.

"Leading Hand[111] Tenny," Commodore Pinner supplied. "He was Aft Communications Operator." It was explained to me that orders were transmitted from control room to engineering section via internal telephone, and that the radio operator doubled as the on-site 'relay point' in the boiler room. "Tenny was a youngster, newly promoted. His captain tells me he was a promising lad."

"When will the surviving crew be well enough for questioning?" I ventured.

"Soon enough. They are presently all being treated for oxygen deprivation. Once the engines stopped and the batteries failed there was no way of recycling the air. They were trapped for almost twenty-four hours in a space designed to sustain them for six."

"The, um, all the bodies have been... pieced together?" young Gleading checked. "It's not possible that somebody... miscounted?"

"Of course they've been..." Pinner snapped back. His frustration at the situation was palpable and his tolerance for inept questioning was no less than Holmes's taste for vague answers. "We are not fools, whatever the War Office seems to think! Every man signed aboard the ship. Every man received his orders. A Royal Navy vessel must operate under strict procedures; an experimental craft on a test voyage even more so!"

"When the prototype was recovered, winched from the sea," Gleading persisted, undaunted, "when the injured were taken off her, a tally was kept?"

"You imagine that the medics aboard *Cogent* and *Diligent* mislaid a patient? It's easy to see that you're not a seafaring man, or you'd understand how impossible it is to lose or hide someone, even a cadaver, aboard one of Her Majesty's ships."

"And this is wartime," Holmes considered. "Special vigilance is required. Special discipline is imposed."

"Just so," the Commodore agreed.

Even then, Holmes insisted on walking the interior of the wounded craft. From front to rear were a torpedo room, officers' quarters, and the cramped control room directly under the conning tower. Aft past a battered but intact division wall was the ruined boiler room, an engine and motor room, and

---

111   Leading Hand is the Royal Navy equivalent of a Corporal in the British Army or R.A.F., or a U.S. Army Specialist 4th Class.

crew quarters, all of which had been inundated by the flood. I could imagine the force of the boiler explosion from seeing the damage done to the supposedly-watertight bulkhead that had been a connecting corridor past the boiler room between control room and engine room.

"Several searches have been made," Commodore Pinner assured us.

"We checked the torpedo lockers. We searched the ballast tanks," McCarl insisted. "I e'en had them dredge th' oil reservoirs and fuel containers."

"There is some explanation," I promised the unhappy engineer. "You may rely on Sherlock Holmes to find it."

Holmes halted at the internal pressure door that had separated the living from the dead, grimly observing signs that someone on the flooded side had scratched for help. He checked the duty roster sheet on the wall of the bridge, the ship's log beside the captain's position, and a saturated signing-in log at the aft engineer's station.

He paused at one of the technical positions in the command room. "Something has been moved from this station," Holmes accused. "There is a gap on this shelf where another manual was stored."

"That's no mystery," Commodore Pinner assured us. "That was our code book, the cypher volume by which we presently encode our radio transmissions. It is a highly sensitive document. When the Captain faced the very real possibility of the ship being lost with all hands he would have ordered it to be destroyed. After all, there was a chance that the enemy, not us, would first locate the wreck."

"Those codes are priceless," Gleading agreed. "They could not be allowed to fall into foreign hands. Anyone who could translate our fleet messages would have a devastating tactical advantage."

"These codes would be specific to our submariners," Pinner qualified the caution. "But that would be bad enough. If Herman broke our cypher then he would hear technical and performance information that would inform him of exactly how effective our new K-Class is."

"Or isn't," McCarl muttered *voce sotto*.

Holmes passed on. He inspected again each of the eight ballast tanks in the ship's understructure, the sixteen fuel stores, and the "free flooding" areas that caused the submarine to dive.

At last, ignoring the increasing impatience of Commodore and engineer, he returned to that sad waterlogged section at the very rearmost past of the prototype, to the appallingly cramped bunkrooms of the ordinary seamen. I have travelled on military ships before but have always enjoyed the consideration accorded an officer. I shuddered to think of being confined in that meagre space, little more than a coffin, crushed in with dozens of other men under two hundred feet of ocean.

"This was Tenny's bunk?" Holmes supposed, reading off the identification tapes above each bedframe. "And this his locker."

We searched through the missing man's possessions, such as might fit into a cupboard nine inches by twenty inches by ten deep. There was not much space for personal possessions, but Holmes was interested in a sodden, unreadable mass of private correspondence, a pulped tintype, and a waterlogged pouch of chewing tobacco.

"And see here, Watson!" the detective celebrated. "Here in this trouser pocket, wrapped and knotted in a handkerchief."

"A ring!" I cried.

Holmes examined the find, a plain band with a small rectangular emerald-stone mounted on a bezel. "This ring is of a rather antique style. Wear upon the hoop suggests that the object is something of an heirloom; or second-hand at least. The kerchief in which the item was contained is a simple cotton square, plain and masculine; a man's accoutrement wrapping a woman's. May we venture that Mr Tenny had hopes of attaching the young lady of his choice?"

"None of the injured men made any report of Tenny having a fiancée, or of any lady he was courting," Pinner objected.

"Perhaps the ring was inheritance from a deceased mother or someone?" Gleading ventured.

"Kept in a plain handkerchief stuffed into a trouser pocket?" Holmes scorned. "Come now, under what circumstances would a young sailor pocket an engagement ring in his good uniform trousers if not to present it to a desired life-companionwhen his next leave allowed? We might have better proof had not boiler blast and the seawater incursion wreaked such havoc on the written materials aboard."

"We must find this young woman, Holmes," I suggested. "Not only should she be informed of her young man's likely demise but she might be able to give some clue as to how he could have vanished from a sealed ship."

"A sabotaged ship, ye mean?" McCarl muttered suspiciously.

Gleading caught the implication. "You believe that the missing man may have had something to do with the accident, the supposed accident that scuttled this vessel, Lieutenant? And that Tenny somehow escaped the disaster—perhaps absconding with the missing code book before the rear compartment was destroyed?"

Pinner emitted a sceptical snort. "It's a fine theory, and it neatly excuses many possible engineering failures in exchange for a traitor sabotaging a funnel valve or pressure gauge, but as I told you before, McCarl, it also depends upon the saboteur being able to vanish from a sealed ship at a hundred feet depth.

McCarl fell silent. A Lieutenant does not argue with a Commodore. Holmes took in everything.

"So many fine young men lost," Miss Pamela Thorne mourned as she finally served me the offered cup of tea. Holmes had dragged Gleading off for a detailed inspection of the prototype's outer hull, but I lacked my friend's uncanny vigour; at my age I was glad to sit in the warmth of the Commodore's outer office and interview his secretary.

"You knew them?" I asked the young woman unnecessarily. She was a personable and attractive girl, one of the few ladies on a closed naval base. Of course enlisted men and officers alike would vie to speak with her.

"I know most of them by name, a few to speak to. I handle the personnel records for the Commodore. Every sailor aboard the K-Class ships is a volunteer."

"Brave men," I admired.

"Fey men, after a time," Miss Thorne confided. "The K-ships are not acquiring a good reputation. This most recent difficulty is another in a long line of technical problems. The crews have taken to calling themselves 'The Suicide Club.'"

"Why so?" I enquired. Sensing her reluctance to speak ill of lost crew or to reveal classified information, I quickly added assurances of Holmes's and my security clearances and discretion.

"The officers talk," Miss Thorne confided in me. "And I type up the performance and development reports that go back to the Admiralty. You must know that there are serious flaws with the K-Class submarines now being laid down."

I ventured to ask what the difficulties were said to be.

"Apart from the issues with sealing off the steam stacks and air intakes— 'too many holes' is the constant criticism of the design—there is apparently also an issue with steering and planing. Manoeuvring controls are not what they should be. Visibility is poor, making navigation more difficult. There have been several minor collisions and two uncontrolled dives. But this is all new technology. There are bound to be teething troubles."[112] The attractive young

---

112   The K-Class is sometimes dubbed "the worst submarine in history". They were supposedly a marked upgrade on what had come before. In practice, the new submarines had persistent problems with navigation and airtightness. The class gained a reputation as being designated 'K' for 'Kalamity' or 'Killer'.

K-1 collided with K-4 off the coast of Denmark and was scuttled to avoid capture by the enemy. K-4 was later also hit by K-6 and later still ran aground. K-5 foundered during a mock battle in the Bay of Biscay, lost with all hands. K-2 caught fire on its first test dive. K-3 plummeted to the seabed with no explanation, which was doubly alarming since the Prince of Wales was

secretary shrugged apologetically. "What do I know? I just type the excuses."

"You do not have confidence in the K-ships?"

"It's not for me to say, Dr Watson. But I do know that every penny matters in this war, and those prototypes cost more than £230,000 apiece.[113] Think of all the guns and bombs that could be sent to the Western Front for that!"

"Did you know Leading Hand Tenny?"

"His identity photo in his file looks familiar. I'm sure I've seen him around, perhaps even exchanged words with him. The young seamen do swarm around the typing pool if they can, trying their chat-up lines."

"Tenny was evidently already spoken for," I revealed. "We discovered a ring amongst his possessions."

"Oh! Well that's an important clue, isn't it? I mean, if Tenny was planning to marry he would not intend to run away or anything."

"You thought he might have? But how could he vacate a sealed underwater ship?"

"I can't imagine. But then, I'm not allowed in the boat bays so I've never had a chance to understand the layout of those submarines. I will say this though: if the top brass wanted a man to disappear from one of those ships, I'm sure they could make it happen. Tenny could have been smuggled off during the rescue, disguised as a medic or something."

"Why might they do that?"

"I'm not sure. Maybe he was a spy? Maybe he was sent in by your War Office people to see what a terrible botch was being made of the K project?" Miss Thorne caught herself and looked abashed. "I'm only speculating. I'm sorry, Dr Watson. I should have kept quiet.

"Not at all. I appreciate your candour," I assured the engaging young lady.

---

aboard at the time. It eventually managed to claw its way to the surface—and was rammed by K-6. K-14 sprang a leak before it even had its trial voyage.

K-13 keeled over in Loch Gare during its seaworthiness trials. Extensively refurbished, it was relaunched as K-22, whereupon it collided with and sank K-14, which had just had its leak fixed. K-22 briefly survived its collision but then got hit by HMS Inflexible, which was in the area to help the damaged subs but was wrecked beyond repair. In the same manoeuvre, HMS Fearless was incapacitated by a crash with K7 and then impacted with K-17. K-4, seeing what was happening, cut engines to avoid a collision, but was broadsided by K-6, the sub that had previously rammed into K-3, which almost cut her in half. K-4 survived briefly before being finished off by a collision with K-7. K-6 later got stuck on the ocean bed. In just 75 minutes on that day in 31st January 1918, two submarines were sunk, three badly damaged, and 105 crew killed, all by "friendly fire"—without a shot being loosed.

After K-15 sank in Portsmouth Harbour before going anywhere, K's 18-21 were never completed. Their hulls were retained and modified for the new, more-improved M-class. M-1 was rammed by a merchant vessel while patrolling the Channel and M-2 sprang a leak and sank.

113   This would be about $35.5m today.

"It's just that... I've had to type so many condolence letters by now. 'K stands for Kalamity'—that's what the sailors are joking, but it is very black humour."

"I don't understand," young Gleading protested as he and Holmes rendezvoused with me in the senior mess hall. "I thought we needed to conduct an inch-by-inch examination of the K-prototype's hull?"

"That was what we told the Commodore and the Senior Engineer," Holmes instructed our War Office liaison. "That was a mere ruse to make them go away. Important and busy people have better things to do than spend hours watching two men crawling over a weed-choked wreck."

"Other sailors might be more inclined to offer testimony if their superior officers were not breathing on their necks," I understood.

The light of comprehension dawned in Gleading's eyes. "Those conversations you struck up as we were taking measurements...!"

"The measurements were of no relevance except to facilitate the conversations," Holmes informed him. "We now have a much better view of the state of morale around the K-project, of the sort of discipline it operates under, and of the way that the common seaman views its success."

"'K for Kalamity?'" I suggested.

"The crew is uninspired by the vessel's design and execution," Holmes allowed. "There is a certain fatalistic pride in making it work despite its shortcomings. This is the Royal Navy, after all."

"And those mentions of Tenny that you worked in to your talks..." Gleading caught up, "They were not accidental."

"Sherlock Holmes rarely does anything by accident," I cautioned the youngster. "What did you discover, Holmes?"

"That Tenny was a well-liked and well-known young man, respected by his peers. His recent promotion was considered well-deserved. He was a talented engineer from a humble background who, had he come from another stratum of society, would doubtless have risen quickly as an officer. As it was he would certainly have progressed through the non-commissioned ranks by virtue of his technical abilities and chosen specialism."

"He was a communications officer," I remembered.

"A submarine communications officer," Holmes clarified. "That is a rare discipline at present. Tenny actually helped to prepare the protocol manual that was destroyed along with the transmission codes when the vessel might have been lost."

"Did any of the chaps you spoke with know about his fiancée?"

Holmes frowned. "Almost all of his closest comrades died in the boiler explosion or subsequent inundation. However, there was evidently something of a common joke about Tenny's young lady, along the lines of whether she existed at all."

Gleading had been privy to those mentions too. "They thought he might be making her up, to mask a shyness or ineptness with girls. Nobody had ever seen her. Nobody had even seen a photograph. When a tool or document when missing, the ordinary seamen would joke that it had gone to meet Tenny's girl."

"But he had a ring," I pointed out. "Surely that suggests a romance. And probably that he had not yet screwed up the courage to 'pop the question'."

"And that he expected to encounter the young lady soon to be able to do so," Holmes pointed out more astutely. "The trial voyage of the K-prototype was not expected to be a long haul. A three-hour test underwater and then a swift surface return. Most of the crew might expect to be back in their bunks that same night. Some of them would anticipate leave."

"But not Tenny," Gleading objected. "I checked the logs. Tenny had his night off-base the day before the test, not after it."

"Perhaps he met his young lady but could not find the courage to propose?" I speculated. "Perhaps she simply didn't turn up? Or turned him down? Tenny crumpled the ring in a handkerchief, stuffed it in his pocket, hurled his dress trousers into his locker, and went about his work."

"We can never know," Gleading sighed. He had not yet seen what Sherlock Holmes could do.

I mentioned to Holmes what Miss Thorne had said regarding the official concerns about the new submarine research, and about her speculation regarding Tenny's possible covert intentions.

Holmes cradled is fingers and looked up at the mess hall ceiling. "Even a preliminary examination of Daniel Tenny's life dismisses the idea that he is anything other than a junior seaman rising through the ranks and making good. He has been at Portland for over a year, long before there were any difficulties with the K-programme. He was screened for sensitive submarine work, with background checks even into his parents and his school reports. His shipboard locker and his on-shore sea chest show all the signs of him being exactly who he appeared to be. Either that or the fellow was the world's greatest spy and I am a fool."

"But he might have been spirited away at the time the submarine was salvaged?" I checked. "As you like to say, 'When you have eliminated the impossible, whatever remains, however improbable, must be the truth.'"[114]

---

114   Holmes first made this statement in *The Valley of Fear* (1915)

"There are more improbabilities here than one," Holmes told me, almost gently. "The question is which improbability to verify."

Captain Happener was pale and ashen-faced, looking exactly like a commanding officer who had lost over half his command in the last two days. He lay in a small private room in the Royal Naval Hospital in Castletown, adjacent to Portland Harbour, which served as the base's sickbay. The remainder of his crew occupied the rows of beds in the two wards beyond.

"We made a successful dive," he told us listlessly in the tones of a man who had made this report too many times before. "There was some difficulty with the diving planes—the system is still new and requires a delicate touch—but we achieved a stable depth of five fathoms and maintained it. We set course by compass and chart to make our rendezvous in good time."

"There was no indication of serious trouble?" Gleading asked.

Holmes had examined the ship's log. "Not then, or at all before the explosion of the boiler rocked the ship," he answered for the stricken captain. "Mr Gleading, would you be so good as to interview the crew members indicated on this list? Establish which of them, if any, noted Leading Hand Tenny during the exercise. Ask them also about his putative fiancée."

"Gently and delicately, man," I urged the War Office liaison. Youngsters can have a tendency to go at it like a bull when questioning those who have experienced loss. As a military physician I knew the importance of dealing carefully with fighting men who have suffered painful casualties.

Happener watched Gleading depart with some relief, but he eyed Holmes cautiously, knowing that here was the man from the Ministry whose report could break an officer's career.

"I have no wish to taint a proper and thorough crash investigation," my friend told the stricken captain, "but if it eases your mind, I am convinced that your prototype met with disaster through other than sabotage."

"You think so?" Happener tried to sit up too quickly and I was compelled to ease him back to his pillows.

"Holmes has examined your vessel," I assured him. "In his academic days he studied as an engineer."[115]

"McCarl and his boffins tell me it may be days before any tentative conclu-

---

115   This assertion is in line with W.S. Baring-Gould's biography *Sherlock Holmes* (1962), which describes how Holmes came to move on from his initial formal studies of engineering at Christ Church, Oxford to take up a more eclectic and specialist course of study fitted to his chosen profession.

sion is drawn on that," Happener said.

Holmes sniffed. "Lieutenant McCarl is hoping that other investigation will offer up any but the most obvious solution: that it was mechanical failure that caused your tragedy, borne of insufficient quality control on an inferior design."

Captain Happener breathed hard. "What do you say happened?"

"There was a concatenation of three errors. First, the design of the closing mechanism which seals the boiler steam-vent funnels is clumsy and inadequate. It relies upon a copper plate and rubber seal to slide exactly into position on a piston arrangement which is all too flimsy. There is no physical or electrical test to ensure that the cover-plate is firmly locked into place before diving. Secondly, the rubber itself had become cracked and pitted from the heat of previous steam emission, making the seal imperfect, which allowed the first intrusion of cold sea-water into a still red-hot boiler chamber. And finally, when the explosion occurred, the internal bulkhead door between the engine room and the crew quarters was standing open."

"The blast ripped through the bulkhead between boiler room and engine room," I understood, "but the rearmost section was also flooded because of the unsealed hatch."

"I feared that was it," Happener admitted, referring to this third conclusion. "I had reprimanded the engineering Petty Officer for laxity on that account once before." His fists closed, screwing up the bedsheet. "Those engineering section men, they are a clan of their own, tight-knit and overconfident that they know best and... that is, they were like that...!" His voice trailed off in grief.

Holmes pretended not to notice the captain's emotional outburst. "Speak of Leading Hand Tenny."

"Tenny was a good lad. He had a good future ahead of him."

"Did he have family? A sweetheart?"

"A mother in Shropshire, I believe, but I never heard of a girl."

Commanding officers are the last to hear barracks jokes. "He was not intending to become engaged, for example?" I prompted. Serving sailors require their C.O.'s permission to marry.

"I've heard nothing about that. No request was made."

"Did you observe Tunny at his work during your test run?" Holmes enquired.

"No. I was in the control room or on the deck-bridge. He was in the engineering section, relaying my orders to the duty officer, Swanson. G_d, *Swanson!* He had a sick wife and four children...!"

"Which hand was responsible for relaying your orders over the telephone wire to Tunny?" Holmes continued remorselessly.

"Walsh; that is, Leading Hand Walsh. He's out there in the ward."

"Then it is to him that I shall refer my next questions."

Holmes had some other matters of detail to interrogate Happener about, but it was routine. I was glad when the captain was allowed to return to his rest. Oxygen deprivation is a nasty condition and sleep is part of the remedy.

The sanatorium beyond was like any military hospital anywhere, two long rows of patients along a 'Nightingale' ward of thirty beds, with a matron's desk at one end where watch may be kept on the invalids. I was gratified to see that it was well-ordered, clean, and calm there, so unlike the overcrowded and desperate evacuation hospital at Peshawar to which I had been invalided so many years before.

Leading Hand Paddy Walsh had the same grey complexion as his commander, but had his eyes closed and seemed to be asleep.

"It is no use feigning," Holmes told him. "You must answer my questions."

Walsh glanced across at his interrogator. Even I could read him trying to mask his disconcertion.

"You have so far avoided interview," Holmes discerned. "You do not regularly bite your fingernails but have done so in the last few hours. You are concealing information, and now you are beginning to comprehend the futility of it."

"I'm not well. I can't speak with y' now, sir."

"You were the communications man in the control room," Holmes went on remorselessly. "It was your task to pass on Captain Happener's orders to the engineering section."

"Yes, sir. That I did."

"And to whom did you relay these commands?"

"To Leading Hand Tenny, sir."

Holmes shook his head. "I did not ask to whom you should have spoken. I asked to whom you spoke."

Walsh swallowed hard. "It were Tenny, sir."

"I have seen the crew log, Mr Walsh. I have compared Tenny's usual entry and exit signatures with the one made the day before yesterday. It is an inexpert facsimile."

"Sir."

I saw where Holmes was driving. "You suspect that the reason Tenny's corpse was not amongst the dead was because… he was never there at all!"

Leading Hand Walsh looked upwards in despair. "We nivver meant no harm, sirs. I swears it!"

"The truth will be impossible to conceal as investigation continues," Holmes assured him. "It is unfeasible to maintain a secret amongst a surviving crew of twenty-nine men. Best to speak plainly now before more time is wasted."

"What is the truth, then?" I appealed to Holmes. He gestured long thin fingers at the bedridden sailor, bidding him to confess.

"We meant no wrong by it, sirs," Walsh protested. "Truth is, we all liked Tenny. We di'n't want him to get into any trouble. Not when he was so head-over-heels for that lass on his."

Holmes and I combined to get the proper story out of Walsh, aided and abetted by his mates in neighbouring beds.

"Tenny did have a girl," Walsh admitted. "He didn't want t' tell us who. A lot of the lads thought she was made-up, so as we wouldn't think Tenny weren't interested in lasses. But some of us reckoned she was maybe married, or more likely an officer's daughter. A mere leading hand wu'n't do well if he looked in that kind of direction."

"You did not see this girl?" I checked. "No letters, no photographs?"

"Tenny kept 'er properly secret. But we all knew how smitten he was with her."

"Too smitten," Walsh's ward-mate chimed in from the next berth. "She'd be why he was late back from shore leave. 'Unofficial' overnight leave, y'knows?"

A Royal Navy sailor on active service during wartime cannot sleep ashore except with his captain's permission. Happener had made no mention of any such dispensation.

Holmes shifted impatiently. "To summarise the facts: Tenny left Portland Harbour base for shore leave at 1800 on the night before the K-prototype trial. What time was he due to return, Leading Hand?"

"2200," Walsh conceded.

"When he failed to make his curfew, his friends fancied that he was dallying just a little too long with his fair mystery woman. It was simple to fudge the absent swain's return time to spare him an officer's reprimand or the censure of the Master-at-Arms or the Military Police."

"We *really* meant no 'arm by it," Walsh pleaded. He was even paler than his fellow sailors recovering from asphyxia. "We was just trying to keep him out of trouble, see? We thought he'd be five minutes late getting back, or ten. We kept on hoping he'd turn up in just a short while."

"But minutes became hours and hours became all night," I recognised. "Then it was morning, and the crew were expected to depart on the sea trial, and still no Tenny. And by then it was too late to report his absence without incriminating his ship-mates."

"It were me," Walsh confessed to spare his comrades. "I was the one who signed 'is name in the book, signed 'im aboard. We reckoned... well, we hoped that the lad had just got lucky with his young lady and 'ad lost all track of time. Such things happen in war. Sailors are men. Everyone liked Tenny; we was happy for him. But by then we had to keep 'is absence quiet. Desertion in wartime is a shooting offence, whether he meant to go absent-without-leave or not."

"So Tenny's bunkmates conspired to cover for his absence, to do his work," Holmes observed. "You knew that the voice at the other end of the telephone was not the usual communications specialist, but made no mention of it to your captain or to officers. The senior NCO in engineering knew, of course."

"We were all just hoping, if Tenny slipped back that night when we'd got in from the test... But..."

"But the test went horribly wrong," Holmes concluded. "One corpse was un-accounted for because that man had never been present when the K-prototype set sail. His comrades had sought to cover for him, but then disaster overtook them."

"Tenny was not a saboteur, then," I determined. "But then... Holmes, if Tenny was not aboard the submarine, if he never returned from his shore leave the night before, then where has be been since? Eloped? Deserted?"

"Now there we come to another set of fascinating questions, Watson. Come. We must take a stroll."

A blustering headwind bullied its way from the Channel, battering Holmes, Gleading, and I as we crossed the causeway and exited the Naval Base. Vicious sea-gusts tried to push us into the harbour. We braved the weather and pressed on into the civilian part of the Isle of Portland.

The promontory is some six miles long, jutting out into the British Channel and terminating at Portland Bill lighthouse. In better weather it would have been a pleasant place, with something of a market town feel to its grey-stone buildings and quaint cottages. But as an old soldier I could also see the marks of a settlement that has grown up around a major military site. The prevalence of public houses and dance-halls is always a tell-tale sign.

As we walked, Holmes had Gleading report on the results of the investiga-tions he had undertaken at the detective's behest. Holmes had devolved to him the less-important of the interviews, but the evasions that the liaison had been given by some surviving crew backed up what we had discovered from Walsh.

"Tenny was never on the K-ship!" Gleading understood at last. "That makes more sense now. I had thought his disappearance impossible, but it was so simple."

"Things often are—once Holmes has explained them," I chuckled.

Gleading had also been dispatched back to Commodore Pinner's office with additional enquiries. He reported on the questions of procedures and record-keeping that he had been tasked with investigating.

"You discovered who approved the shore leave list for the night before the prototype's test?" Holmes checked. "You brought me a copy of the document?"

"It was made up of individual sheets from various commanding officers, Mr Holmes. There was a summary topsheet initialled by Commander Pinner."

"Ah, so I see." The detective thumbed through the pages. "Most helpful."

We passed under the shadow of Portland Castle, Henry VIII's historical coastal defence against the French and the Holy Roman Empire; this area has long been a key part of our nation's military preparedness.

"Where are we going now, sir?" young Gleading finally ventured to ask. "You checked that I was armed. We might have brought MPs."

"A delicate touch is required," Holmes assured him. "You arranged for the precautions I outlined?"

"Of course. But if I knew what…"

"Holmes enjoys surprising his comrades," I warned Gleading. "It is a regrettable habit from his theatrical youth and seems quite unbreakable."

"Say rather that I prefer not to speak until I am certain of my conclusions, doctor," Holmes defended himself; but I thought I detected a mischievous quirk of the lip, for we had rehearsed this conversation many times in our decades of association.

He checked his watch. "Five thirty-nine. The day shift will have ended at the base. Civilian support staff will be heading home."

"And we keep watch. For whom?"

"Come now, Watson. If any man can apply my methods by now it must be you. You have seen and heard what I have. Engage your faculties."

"Holmes also likes to test his companions," I warned Gleading. "He finds it hard to understand how we cannot understand things which are so simple to him. He makes us run to keep up."

"We are looking for the deserter," the War Office liaison guessed.

"We are looking for the fiancée," I answered more astutely. "The reason why Howard Tenny failed to return before curfew, missing his berth on the K-boat's voyage."

"And?" Holmes prompted me.

"And we are walking towards her home, to meet her there," I predicted. "She works at the base and will be returning from her shift even now. You wish to observe her homecoming."

"And?"

"And she is the person who arranged for Tenny's convenient leave the night he vanished, and probably at other times before that. The person who typed out that topsheet for the Commodore's initialling and who might easily add another name to the list."

Gleading blinked as he comprehended. I suppose that must be how I look to Holmes. "Miss Thorne? Her initials appear as the typist!"

Holmes nodded. "Miss Thorne, Commodore Pinner's secretary. She was the person responsible for collating and summarising leave rosters. No trouble for her to add a young Leading Hand's name to the list of approved overnight shore stays."

"But Tenny wasn't approved for that," Gleading objected. "He was due back before lights-out."

"Read the very sheets you brought me, young man. You will see that our missing Leading Hand was added to the front page with permission to return the following morning."

"But his comrades expected him to be back before lights-out," I objected.

"That is what he had told them. It is likely what he expected. Miss Thorne evidently had different plans for him."

"He did not take his ring along," I realised. "He had no expectation of this visit with his girl being any different from others. It was not an occasion to propose."

"Indeed. He might have had no knowledge that his granted furlough was extended. The gate guards actually had no reason to remark his not returning that night since by their listings he was at liberty 'till morning. His bunkmates did not have the roster; they assumed Tenny was absent beyond his leave and they covered for him accordingly—until he really was."

Gleading shook his head. "It doesn't make sense. Why would Tenny hide his relationship with Miss Thorne? She is a much-sought-after young lady. If he had won her heart and hand..."

"The young lady required discretion of him. He showed no photograph of her, made no mention of her name. Had it not been for him secretly hoping to wed her, had he not asked his mother for his late grandmother's wedding ring in preparation, there would have been no sign of his relationship. Indeed, I doubt Miss Thorne was even aware of his intentions or his actions in regard to a matrimonial proposal."

"But why would the lady insist in silence?" Gleading persisted.

"Miss Thorne was at her desk today," I noted gravely. "She has not eloped. She made no mention of any intimate relationship with Tenny. Indeed, she presented herself as ignorant of him and indifferent to him."

"Yes. And I believe that she was at her desk for the last time," Holmes told us. "Here she comes now, heading for the home address registered on her security file. Remain concealed in this shop doorway until she has opened her front door. Then be ready to act."

The trim young secretary walked down Castle Street and turned into the side-road where she lodged. Holmes was wise to keep us concealed longer than seemed necessary, for she turned at the last and seemingly admired the view before producing her latch-key and turning to the door. She knocked before entering her own home, a strange set of raps like a code.

"Now!" Holmes cried, springing forward to seize Miss Thorne. "Gleading, there will be enemies inside!"

Wiggins had selected our liaison man carefully. Gleading kicked open the lodging-house door and leaped upon the burly fellow who lurked within. By the time I got inside to back Gleading up the scuffle was over and the stranger was down.

"What are you doing?" Miss Thorne cried as Holmes pinned her. "Let go!"

"Not until we have had the opportunity to divest you of concealed weaponry," my friend cautioned her. "And to retrieve the files concealed about your person, Fraulein Grafenstein."

The struggling woman froze in place. "You recognise me," she said at last.

"Now that I have seen you up close and heard you speak unguardedly I am certain of it. Your English is very good, but to the trained ear there is a Teutonic undertone that your best tuition has not overcome. And having met both Adolphus Von Bork and his uncle Count Von und Zu Grafenstein, the familial resemblance is self-evident. The pronounced nasal configuration, the shaped orbitals, the dynastic earlobes are quite unmistakable."

"Your service to my father was long ago. I had hoped that you would not discern any family resemblance."

"You feared that I would eventually place you, though, which is why you chose to make one final visit to your office today and then to depart with as much classified information as your raiment could conceal."

"You asked me to have two women close by when we picked up Miss Thorne," Gleading realised. "To search her!"

"She is a dangerous adversary," Holmes warned, "no less meticulous or patriotic than her cousin, whom you may well remember, Watson."[116]

"We must search the house," Gleading insisted. "There may be more enemies within."

"We must be cautious of booby-traps," I instructed the War Office sprig.

Once Miss Thorne—Fraulein Grafenstein—was in proper custody of her female warders, and the fellow that Gleading had downed was firmly cuffed and restrained, Holmes himself led us on an investigation of the 'lodging house'. Gleading gleefully collared a second thug who guarded a cellar stair, and Holmes made short work of the lock that secured the basement.

---

116   The Great Detective thwarted the spymaster Von Bork in "His Last Bow", wherein Holmes references saving Count Von und Zu Grafenstein from "the Nihilist Klopman".

He opened the sealed door swiftly and silently, so we were able to over-power a third man who sat at ease there reading a newspaper. This man was not as burly as the others, but his sleeves were bloody.

Behind him, tied to a chair, was the source of those bloodstains, the battered and scarcely-conscious Leading Hand Tenny. I hastened to loose his bonds and offer emergency treatment.

"I... I told them nothing...!" the captured sailor gasped to us before he passed out.

As I treated Tenny, Miss Thorne's guards brought her down into the cellar where we made fast the henchmen that Gleading had downed. Holmes made an additional check of Fraulein Grafenstein and removed a series of lockpicks from the seam of her coat.

"Your masters in Berlin and your family in Klagenfurt[117] will be disappointed by your failure," Holmes told the supposed secretary. "You came a long way and got so close to the code-books you desired."

"Tenny is a communications specialist!" realised Gleading. "He knew the new submarine radio codes."

Holmes nodded. "Indeed. And when 'Miss Thorne's' tender persuasions failed to prise the information out of him, when pillow talk with his sweetheart proved insufficient, a more direct means of interrogation was employed."

"I would have preferred the honey to the vinegar," Fraulein Grafenstein admitted. She glanced at the captured torturer. "I ran out of time."

"You did not know that Daniel Tenny was intending to ask for your hand in marriage," I guessed.

She had the grace to flinch. "War requires unpleasant things to be done, to be endured. Sacrifices must be made, even..." She shook her head. "He confessed his affections and intentions during his interrogation, but for all his professed love for me he would not speak about the codes."

"If not for the tragedy of the K-prototype he might never have been found," Holmes observed. "Daniel Tenny would have been listed as a deserter, his name blackened, and him tortured until he revealed what he knew or else died concealing it."

I glared at the bloody-sleeved fellow who had been his torturer, wishing for five minutes alone with the man. "Tenny needs urgent medical aid now."

"He'll get it," Gleading promised. "We will call in everyone now. This investigation will be thorough and official."

"They were preparing to depart," Holmes discerned. He examined the suit-

---

117   The town of Grafenstein lies in the district of Klagenfurt-Land in the Austrian state of Carinthia. All noble and hereditary titles in Austria were abolished by the *Habsburgergesetz* ("Habsburg Law") in 1919, two years after our present narrative, which exiled all persons and confiscated all properties of the Imperial House of Habsburg.

cases of files that Miss Thorne had copied from Pinner's office, and of technical schematics obtained by other nefarious means. "Fraulein Grafenstein knew the game was up as soon as we arrived. The K-prototype sinking was a disaster for our enemies too."

I snarled at the torturer. "Well now they can tell us all that they know."

The fellow said something in German that I assume meant that he would not co-operate.

"We are patriots as much as you," Fraulein Grafenstein assured us. "We will assist you no more than poor Danny-Boy would aid us, whatever the threat."

"Your assistance is not required," Holmes answered the spies pleasantly. "I see you have here radio transmission apparatus and a codebook—a German codebook. You were expecting to depart these shores now that your game was up, taking your ill-gotten gains with you. And that means... a submarine!"

"A U-boat?" Gleading asked sharply. "This close to Portland Harbour?"

"Miss Thorne was ideally placed to know the gaps in patrol routes," Holmes pointed out. "Of course, now we must signal the *unterseboot* to come in for a rendezvous with a stolen fishing smack. Let us see if my German conceals my nation of origin better than Fraulein Grafenstein's English does hers."

The torturer realised what we were going to do and began to kick up a fuss. I was required to smite him upon the nose.

"You must not!" Fraulein Grafenstein pleaded with us. "All we did—all I did—what we did to Danny... it must not be for nothing!"

"Nor shall it be," Holmes promised her. "It will save British lives and further the end of this miserable and futile war!" He reached for the codebooks and the microphone.

Gleading arranged for the spies to be dragged to custody at Portland Base. I do not know what became of them after that.

Three hours later, an unknown vessel was sunk half a nautical mile off Breakwater Fort.

Holmes also submitted a report and recommendations regarding the K-Class of submarines, but whether anyone ever read it we shall never know.

THE END

ABOUT OUR CREATORS

AUTHOR

Sherlock Holmes and Doctor Watson continue to intrude into the writing career of **I.A. WATSON**, arriving two or three times a year to demand additional accounts of their exploits, dispatched by publishers who know the audience for such material. I.A. Watson must thereupon set aside long-running projects such as his Robin Hood series (five volumes now compiled in the omnibus *The Legend of Robin Hood*[118]), his contemporary SF series starting with *The Transdimensional Transport Co.*, his urban fantasy *Vinnie de Soth* books, his high-adventure modern *Bulldog Drummond* volumes, collections of his earlier work as *Attack of the Pulp Story* and *Revenge of the Horror Story*, and standalone novels such as *The Death of Persephone* and *St George and the Dragon*, so as to add to the corpus of Baker Street investigations.

One of the reasons I.A. Watson keeps returning to Holmes is that such stories can cover so many different types of narrative. There is always an investigation, and Holmes and Watson bring their own special flavour to any story, but beyond that there are all kinds of things that might be included, any number of interesting bits of Victorian age to feature, crimes, methods, and motives that change the nature of the case, and plots that can vary the tone from whimsical to grim, from puzzling to visceral. Whatever the situation, adding Holmes and Watson to the scene is always fun for the writer—if not for the officers of Scotland Yard or the malefactor in the case.

For these reasons, I.A. Watson has contributed to each of the twenty-plus *Sherlock Holmes, Consulting Detective* anthologies,[118] to a dozen or so of the *MX Holmes* volumes, and to an eclectic list of other Holmes-related publications, totalling over forty short stories or novellas and the book-length *Holmes and Houdini*.[118] Much of the material has been re-collected in *Sherlock Holmes Mysteries* volumes 1 and 3[118] or in *The Incunabulum of Sherlock Holmes*.[118] Doubtless more will follow.

---

118   Links to purchase these and other Airship 27 titles are available at *airship27hangar. com*

INTERIOR ILLUSTRATIONS

ROB DAVIS - is an award-winning artist with a nearly four decade comic book and illustration career. With comics from Marvel, DC, Malibu, Innovation, Caliber and others Rob has worked on series depicting the crews of *Star Trek*'s original series, *the Next Generation*, *Deep Space Nine*, and other TV series such as *Quantum Leap* and *Pirates of Dark Water*. Characters like Merlin, Robin Hood, Zorro, and Sherlock Holmes have all been subjects of Rob's work. He is presently the Art Director, Designer, and Illustrator for Pulp Revival publisher Airship 27 Productions. He also self-publishes some of his most recent comic book work via his Redbud Studio imprint and is a contributor to Silverline Comics. He is retired from "real work" and lives in Missouri with his wife, two children, their spouses, and their children.

COVER ARTIST

In a previous life, **JOHN WAELTZ** Ob/Gyn, practiced the art of medicine and surgery for forty years. A new life has begun of art and illustration. Howard Pyle and his Brandywine students provide the inspiration and instruction for growth and development.

John lives in Milwaukee, Wisconsin.

THE OTHER WATSON

In 2009 Airship 27 Production launched its series of brand new Sherlock Holmes adventures titled "Sherlock Holmes – Consulting Detective." Among the contributors was a British writer named I.A. Watson. Considered a good omen by the publishers to have Watson on board, that first volume became a huge success; as did the subsequent sequels.

In the past 12 years I.A. Watson's Holmes tales have appeared in dozens of anthologies with various publishers much to the delight of his fans. He is well versed in the original Conan Doyle Canon and his stories are magnificently annotated.

In this new collection aptly called "The Incunabulum of Sherlock Holmes," I.A. Watson delivers six imaginative stories exploring the many facets of the Great Detective and his loyal companion. Each is a rare gem chronicled by a master storyteller. We advise you make yourself comfortable, brew some tea and get ready for a wonderful reading experience as only a Watson can provide. Yes, dear readers, once again, the game is afoot.

THE INCUNABULUM OF SHERLOCK HOLMES

I.A. WATSON

www.ingramcontent.com/pod-product-compliance
Lightning Source LLC
Chambersburg PA
CBHW051121260626
47170CB00005B/1607